Only

And a decision bo
sealed Sigrid's fate. With the
at her heels, the Viking widow had thrown herself
on the mercy of a fierce Saxon warrior. Perhaps it
was madness that had driven her into the arms of
her enemy, but his look had promised shelter
from the carnage surrounding them.

Liefwin's blue eyes were hot, hot as the blue heart of the flame in the hearth.

They burned her, and Sigrid recognized the dangerous force that was in them, the age-old desire of men.

Yet the desire in him sought a response from her that was equal in its searing heat. For one instant it was there. With no thought of who he was or what it meant. It was just there, at the most primitive level a women faces a man.

"No…" The raw sound of her own voice brought her back to her senses. She had never wanted a man in her life. She remembered how much reason they had to hate each other.

And now she had just done the most dangerous, stupid thing imaginable.

* * *

A Moment's Madness
Harlequin Historical #669—August 2003

**Harlequin Historicals is delighted
to welcome new author
HELEN KIRKMAN**

**DON'T MISS THESE OTHER
TITLES AVAILABLE NOW:**

HELEN KIRKMAN

A MOMENT'S MADNESS

HARLEQUIN®

TORONTO • NEW YORK • LONDON
AMSTERDAM • PARIS • SYDNEY • HAMBURG
STOCKHOLM • ATHENS • TOKYO • MILAN • MADRID
PRAGUE • WARSAW • BUDAPEST • AUCKLAND

ISBN 0-373-29269-4

A MOMENT'S MADNESS

Copyright © 2003 by Helen Kirkman

Available from Harlequin Historicals and
HELEN KIRKMAN

A Moment's Madness #669

Please address questions and book requests to:
Harlequin Reader Service
U.S.: 3010 Walden Ave., P.O. Box 1325, Buffalo, NY 14269
Canadian: P.O. Box 609, Fort Erie, Ont. L2A 5X3

To Rosemary, Sarah and Emma:

"inspiration and encouragement"

Chapter One

Essex, England 917 A.D.—Vengeance was a duty

Sigrid fled through the flames of *Ragnarok,* the end of creation, when gods and mortals died.

The world, her world, burned. Death pursued her. Saxon curses rang in her ears. *Dane,* they yelled, *Viking whore. We will have revenge on you.*

The cry of vengeance chilled her to the bone.

Her breath sobbed and her feet slid on the dark shingle path between the buildings. The heavy footfalls kept gaining on her. Was there nowhere to hide in the sacked town?

She allowed one desperate glance over her shoulder and then winced as she ran full tilt into a stone wall.

At least that was what it felt like, but it moved. A skin of flexible metal, tough as the scales of the World Serpent pulled through her hand, almost tearing it.

It was a man clad in a corselet of chain mail, bloodied sword upraised. She screamed. But the sword did not strike. It vibrated between them in the firelit air, like something living. But he held it back.

If she was going to die at the hands of a Saxon warrior, let it be quick.

Her gaze sought his face, hard and stern under the war helm. She saw his eyes, blue English eyes.

They were made of magic.

At least, that was the only way to explain it. Because the insane thing she did next she could only have done if she had been spellbound.

Her pursuers crashed round the corner and slithered to a stop and her body moved of its own accord in a split instant of speed. Her spine straightened and her hands closed round an arm made of solid muscle encased in rings of iron. The words came out of her mouth, without thought, not in her own Danish but in Saxon, so there could be no mistake.

"Go away," she said. "I am his."

The three, in their ripped and filthy tunics, their chests heaving, wavered. Their eyes, still wild with the lust of the chase and heated with ale, looked not at her, but at the mountain of chain mail she was clinging to.

There was silence. Nothing moved.

Sigrid's heart beat as though it would stifle her and her lungs heaved. What had she done?

How could she have gambled her whole life's worth on one instant? How could she have trusted her fate on a momentary impression?

Because that was all she had had: one glimpse of his face in the gathering dark, and there was nothing tangible to tell her that this man was better than any other. He was as Saxon as her pursuers. He was part of an army which had fought all day and had won, and which now had a grudge to settle on the Danish-held town.

She was mad. The chain mail she was clutching at had blood on it. Its wearer was a man and a soldier and trained in the use of brute force; and yet she had seen his face.

But then it happened: something her dead warrior-husband, for all his terrifying power, would never have done for her.

She felt the solid muscle under her hand move and before she knew what had happened, the mail-clad stranger had swung her round behind him, blocking her from the others with his body, and turned the bloodied sword on her pursuers.

The man's voice, deep, English and entirely reasonable, said, "If any man takes a step forward, I shall kill him."

Three sets of eyes narrowed in that age-old assessment of will and strength that every man has for every other. Even Sigrid's own eyes turned to the man who now protected her.

He was tall and well-made. He had body armor, which her pursuers did not, and the cross-guard of his reddened blade flashed gold. There was no chink of weakness in the man beneath the armor, not the remotest consciousness that he might not win. He meant what he said, with a chill finality that brought the sickening realization of just how rash she had been.

If any of the ale-sodden brutes took up the challenge, she would run. He would have to let her go. No one could fight three people, one-handed, with a captive dangling from their left arm.

But her pursuers had seen the terrifying chill that

she saw. They vanished, melting like evil spirits into the shadows. There would doubtless be easier pickings elsewhere.

She would have less than an instant. She twisted, trying to break the grip of the ice warrior's left hand before he realized, before he had time to spare a thought for her. But she did not even have that. The grasp on her wrist tightened.

"Wait," he said, just one word, but it was a command.

There was no one else in sight and she could not break his hold. She was dragged round in front of him.

She took another look at his face and wondered what on earth she had seen there.

It was handsome enough, as far as you could tell under the helmet and the dust, but the eyes—the eyes were frozen to the depths.

Dane. Viking whore. We will have our revenge on you.

"Let me go," she said as steadily as she could.

"Where to?"

She blinked. But it was not really a question, because he did not stop for an answer and the clipped, reasonable voice continued. "This army is completely out of control. It is commanded, if that is what you can call it, by the biggest…fool in the entire kingdom of Wessex. He is not going to do anything to stop what is happening and even if he tried it is far too late."

At least, that was what she thought he said. Her English was good, but he had an accent that was almost incomprehensible. And it was the last thing she expected a Saxon to say.

He shifted his grip, bringing her arm closer under his so that she could feel the quality of his strength.

"Do you not have any kin to protect you?" he demanded.

There was nothing in his eyes but the chill. She made herself look straight into them. "I did," she said. "I had a husband. He is dead."

Her hand went instinctively to her neck where the silver amulet ring hung suspended on a thin leather strap, no longer round the thick, invincible bull neck of her husband.

Her hand shook. The amulet was hidden under the threadbare linen of her chemise, but she could feel every sharp metal outline attached to the ring. There were weapons: two swords, three staffs and Odin's spear. She knew them by heart. They had never left her husband's skin while he lived. Never would, because they were part of him.

Now they were hers. No one else would claim them, because they were afraid. So was she. The thin strips of metal felt like lead weights against her flesh.

Her mind filled with the nightmare visions of eager, triumphant faces bringing her the death news. People she knew, people of the town, falling over themselves to be the first to tell her. That Ragnar was dead. That even the strongest, the most terrifyingly vicious of men might be slain by the death rain of arrowheads.

That was how it had happened. From a distance, because none could abide Ragnar's rage at close quarters. It seemed every man had seen him fall, right at the day's end, driven hard against the forest's edge. Dead.

They had found the amulet among the withering leaves of autumn. But none had reached his corpse. Ragnar was lying somewhere out there, unburied, under the dark shadows of the trees, meat for the ravens. And for his companions in spirit, the wolves.

"He is dead," she said again, and the words were as heavy as the metal round her throat.

She thought, when the Saxon felt her shiver, that there might have been some flicker of reaction in the frozen eyes. Unless it was just a trick of the fading light.

"I see."

It had been a trick of the light.

"Then you are better off with me."

The grip on her arm tightened again and she found she was walking down the hill with him, her feet scarcely touching the ground.

She was utterly lost now, whatever she did. She had trapped herself by her own actions. She would never get away from a man like this, and if she did, then her fate would be exactly the one he had dragged her away from.

She tried one last effort to escape, pulling against his arm, kicking out and twisting her body without warning. She was hauled upright with a faint sigh of exasperation.

It cost him no effort at all and he did not even speak.

She shot him a glance of pure terror. She had used all the strength she had and he had scarcely noticed.

She did not try again.

They walked through the flames of burning buildings. People ran, singly and in small, pathetic groups. Sometimes they screamed. The end of the world. But after *Ragnarok* when the world was destroyed, a new beginning was supposed to come. She could not imagine it following this.

None of the fleeing figures approached them. It was as though they walked through the destruction and yet were not part of it. She began to feel unreal, so that her mind dizzied with it. Her whole life was gone, disintegrating before her eyes and none of it actually touched her.

The only thing that touched her was the man at her side.

She kept walking, but the dizzying feeling of dislocation increased. The dark bulk of the familiar buildings of the town and the glimpses of orange flame lost all meaning, as if they had nothing to do with her at all. The one thing that remained real to her in the gathering dark was the Saxon and his grip on her arm, as strong and inescapable as the grip of midwinter.

She stumbled over something in the street. She did not look at what it was because she did not want to know. She was hauled upright again but this time she could not move. She could not put one foot in front of the other.

He stopped. Perhaps he would let her go. Perhaps he would decide she was not worth the trouble and let her slide into the ditch and die where she lay. She felt the mail-clad arm slide round her waist, pulling her against the solid, metallic mass of his body. She gasped and her head landed on his shoulder. It made her hair fall down, spilling in unruly waves across his chest and his shoulders, and she thought it was over.

But his English voice, close against her hair, said, "It is not far, just by the walls, there is a barn and some storage buildings. That is where we are going," and he started walking again.

She made her feet move. He had not attacked her yet. He would wait until they got to their destination; and there were two words in what he said that revived some stubborn part of her spirit. *The walls.* If where he wanted to take her was right by the wall of the town then surely she would find her chance to escape him, and if she could just gain the shelter of the woods, that was it: freedom.

The flicker of hope became a small flame somewhere deep inside her. She would survive this, whatever it took. She walked. It was easier now, because he could take most of her weight and he hardly seemed to notice it. But the dizziness in her head and the numb feeling of unreality only strengthened. It was like moving in a dream. The light was dimming, no flames in the lower levels of the town, less noise, fewer people, only herself and the mail-clad man.

Nothing else in the world.

She began to drift.

"We are there."

She started.

She could not actually have swooned away. You could not be unconscious and still walk. But she found her head was pillowed on his uncomfortable shoulder and one of her hands had slid halfway round his corselet and was balanced against the buckle of his sword belt.

Panic crashed through her, bringing her senses painfully alive. She jerked away from him and it was allowed, as far as arm's length, but no farther. His heavy hand was clamped round her wrist, holding her with an ease and an understated strength that terrified.

She tried to guess how far it was to the gate.

"The gates are guarded," said her captor, "and the woods are full of the remains of a routed army. I doubt whether the fact that they are fellow Danes will save you."

The sane part of her brain knew he was right. Yet there must be somewhere she could hide, where no one would find her, Danish or English.

There was no other choice.

"Let me go."

He thought, when he looked at her, that she seemed no more substantial than a spirit. Her wrist, caught in his hand, was so slight he could crush it with two fingers.

The woman was a Dane, an invader in his land. One of that terrible, destructive force that murdered and plundered and destroyed all it could find. Her husband, whose death she had thrown in his face, would this day have killed and maimed people he knew, people he had fought with.

The duty of those who were left alive was vengeance for the slain. Anyone would have told him so, except his priest and, for reasons of political expediency, King Edward of Wessex. Perhaps.

He looked down on the white, shadowed face.

So Danish, from her ice-blond hair to her subtle eye makeup to the outlandish dress, a brightly colored sheath of wool over nothing but a thin chemise that left her slender arms exposed to view.

She was an enemy.

She was frightened.

She was nothing at all like his dead wife. He fought down memories of the headlong road to disaster, the road that had allowed no turning from the day he had offered marriage to Elswyth. Elswyth, who had been so beautiful, so haunted by restless energy, so utterly beyond his reach, even to the very last. Elswyth, who had hurried onward, as always, to her fate. The fate she had not deserved.

There had been no redemption for that disaster. Fate would go ever as it must.

Except—it had been wrong. That was all he could think of.

Fate.

This woman had chosen to cast hers in his hands. And he had taken it. He had scared off her pursuers. That had been his choice.

He knew he could not act as they would have done, but now…neither could he let go of the girl's fragile wrist.

He looked at its tiny breakable bones engulfed in his shield hand. He should break them. He should break her neck the way some courageous Viking *hersir* had broken Elswyth's.

He turned over the small hand that lay in his and knew he could not do it.

Far away, in the upper reaches of the town, someone shrieked. It was a sound that held nothing but despair and he was sickened by it, sickened by the senselessness of the battle. And by what had happened after it. At least that was no longer being done by his men. Not now.

The sound came again, piercing them both. He felt her flinch. He dropped the sword that was worth more than a king's ransom in the dirt and both of his hands fastened round hers.

"If you stay with me," he said, "you will be safe. I give you my word."

He stopped. The words, insane words to say to a Danish woman, clawed at his parched throat. But they would not be stopped. He could feel fate clawing at his back. Someone opened a door close by and torch-light struck at them through the gathering dark, making her huge gray eyes luminous.

"Will you stay?"

Sigrid could see the Saxon's face. It dazzled her a little in the unexpected light. That must be what made her believe that she could see in it a pain that matched her own. Her gaze fixed on the stark, masculine lines half concealed by the battle helm.

She saw the eyes.

She forgot the burning town and the Saxon army. She forgot the Vikings hiding out in the woods.

She forgot everything.

There was only herself and this stranger, nothing else in the entire world.

She looked into his eyes and she knew, at some level that defied reason, that whatever answer she gave would decide not only her fate but his.

"Yes."

Chapter Two

The Saxon had put her in a room. *Room* was probably an exaggeration. It was a small storage area at the end of a barn in which half the army appeared to be making its temporary headquarters. They all seemed to belong to her captor.

She watched as a large, bearded man called Ceolfrith removed assorted agricultural implements from her bower. He had a neck as thick as a tree trunk and he had looked at her as though she could not possibly belong to middle earth.

She was sitting on a large wooden chest, doubtless containing someone's looted possessions. They had found her a cloak, but she could not bear to put it on even though she was shaking. She did not know who it might have belonged to.

"Well," said Ceolfrith with yet another look at her, "I will leave you to it." He departed clutching a handful of pitchforks and she was left alone with her fate. The insane one she had chosen with a Saxon warrior.

But her captor, the Saxon warrior, was not looking at her at all. He was not even facing her.

He took off his helmet. A flood of tangled hair streamed down his back, coiling like a hoard of dragon's gold across the baser metal of his chain mail. It was neither blond, nor red yet seemed to hold something of the softness and the fire of both. It was as fair and as bright as flame.

She sat on the chest with her hands folded, one piece of plunder stacked neatly with another, and watched this dazzling display. She waited to see whether he would take off anything else. He did not. The expensive war helm with its gleaming boar images and its comb of twisted wires fell unregarded from his hand.

He turned round.

He had the brilliantly clear, high-colored complexion that went with the hair, and he was handsome, very handsome, in that vivid, boldly drawn way that so suited men. She looked at the strong face, the lithe, well-made body, the brightly glowing hair and the fine skin. Everything spoke of an ardent animation that was not there. The deep blue eyes, which should have held and reflected all that unquenchable life were as cold as ice.

She was quite alone with him.

Apart from half the Saxon army removed by a little distance and a makeshift curtain hung on an ashwood spear across the doorway.

Her heart began to race and she thought that her breath would choke her.

He looked at her as though he could see that, as

though he could mark and count every labored breath, hear the hammering pulse of blood through her veins.

It did not move so much as one thick dark gold eyelash.

Cold heart, she thought, cold heart.

"May I sit down?"

She tried not to jump. So the niceties were to be observed a little longer.

"Of course," she said, playing the game, anything to give herself time. And she politely made room for him on the wooden chest because it was the only thing it was practical to sit on, apart from the floor.

It was better in some ways because he no longer towered over her in his menacing and well-used corselet. On the other hand, it was not such a large box. She wished she had gone closer to the edge, but she could not move now without being obvious and the illusion of civilized politeness was all she had left.

She stared at him.

He was so much younger than she had first thought. He could not be that much older than her. He had a smudge of dirt above his right eyebrow, which he seemed completely unaware of.

"Look," he said, in his strange accent, "I shall have to go now, but—"

"*Go?*" she shrieked in sudden panic.

She tried to collect herself. She did not want the entire barn full of animals beyond the makeshift curtain to hear her.

"Go?" she asked, and resisted an insane urge to clutch at his mail-clad arm again, the way she had when she had first seen him. She felt as though the entire world had been removed from under her feet once more, which was mad. First she was appalled by the thought of him staying and now she was thrown into a panic because he was not. It was hysteria. There was no other explanation for it. She had to get control of herself.

"Oh," she said, because she had no choice, whatever he did. It could have been a question or a statement of acceptance, whichever was the most appropriate, and she tried to close her mind to the Saxon army reposing just beyond her doorway.

"Back to the town," he said. "There are still a few things to sort out."

Sack. Pillage. Of course. How could she forget? He had her stashed away. He might as well go back for more. This was the best part of a battle. Her husband had enjoyed it almost as much as killing.

"Ceolfrith will look after you."

How thoughtful. She tried to imagine escaping through the small window with he of the tree trunk neck and the ham fists watching her.

"He will find you something to eat and whatever you will need for the night. If there is anything else you want, ask him. We probably have it."

At that, she could not resist.

"Of course," she said, turning her head so she could look at the cold blue eyes. "Plunder."

The Saxon just stared back. "I doubt whether much of it was originally Danish."

She had, of course, arrived in the wake of an invading army herself, an army that had invaded England. Her people had first raided this land, then invaded it and then settled. The Englishman, and his like, were actually engaged in reconquering land that had once been theirs.

Her own husband, the monster, had spent his adult life plundering.

There was something in the clear eyes and the dirt-streaked face of the Saxon that made knots of her insides. She could not look away or say another word. But it was he who dropped his gaze. He rose and picked the cloak she would not wear.

"Put that on," he said, "before you die of cold."

He had seen, then, how much she was shaking and when she still did not move, he dropped the cloak round her shoulders. "You might as well wear it. It is one of mine," he said, his voice rich with irony.

She watched him go, with his cold face and his warm, lithe body and his bright hair swinging across his warrior's shoulders, and her voice stopped him at the doorway.

"I do not even know your name."

"It is Liefwin," he said, but he did not ask hers. She would not be a person in his eyes.

"Sigrid," she said to his back, because she would not be consigned in his mind to the rest of the looted goods.

The makeshift curtain swung back into its place and she was left, sitting on someone else's possessions, huddled in a cloak that belonged to a Saxon marauder called Liefwin.

What a splendid irony that was. "Lief" meant *dear* or *beloved*. "Wynn" was *a friend*. Beloved Friend. He ought to have been called something with "wolf" in it, or "stone."

* * *

Ceolfrith, the tree trunk, brought everything she wanted and that which she did not.

She was not, of course, surprised. Promises made in the dark while staring into someone's eyes could only be understood to relate to safety from having your throat cut by some drunken oaf. They did not relate to anything else.

She looked at the extra heap of bedding crowned by a change of clothes that would definitely not suit her. There was no logical reason why it should seem like a betrayal. It was what she had expected from the start. She was Liefwin's piece of plunder and he could do what he liked with her.

She had known that. She would have been a fool to think otherwise. And she was not that much of a fool.

But then Liefwin of the heart-wrenching eyes had had no right to look as though he meant what she had wanted him to mean. Still less did he have the right to look at her in the torchlight as though he could not survive without her help.

It was all nonsense, of course. She had not been able to face what was happening to her and so she had retreated for a moment into some silly dream.

It was just a shame that she had chosen to do it at the moment that would decide her fate.

She got up and began pacing the small confines of the storeroom. Life did not hold real choices for people like her and you never got anything in this world without paying for it. She was alive. And whatever happened could hardly be worse than living with her husband.

She aimed a kick at the pile of bedding with the trousers and the tunic on top and then sat down on her own heap.

The cloak he had cast over her shoulders was incredibly warm. It was heavier and richer than anything she had ever owned. It was a man's cloak, fastened with a brooch at the right shoulder, so usefully designed to leave your sword arm free. The brooch was an intricate design of gold and silver set with an amethyst which must have come from some unimaginably faraway place in the East. There had been another brooch rather like it placed on the tunic.

What must it be like to be so solidly rich, instead of sottishly indulgent one day and destitute the next?

She took the fine cloak off and dropped it on top of the tangled heap that belonged to the Saxon.

She went to bed. She had candles, out of real wax, more sinful luxury. She knew they must be plundered, like everything else, but she was so desperate about the dark that she left them lit. She crawled under the covers, but however much of the bedding she heaped round her she could not get warm.

She lay still and waited.

It was late when Liefwin got back to the barn. He could feel the sickening exhaustion that always followed battle clawing through every muscle. The pain in his chest from the wound had risen to such a pitch that he could hardly breathe.

He had not looked to see what the damage was. There had not been time. Now all he wanted to do was get rid of his armor, free himself from the dragging weight of metal at shoulders and waist. He knew he was so close to the edge of exhaustion that if he could but cast himself on the dirt floor of the barn right now, even he would sleep.

But it was not over yet. Ceolfrith would still be awake. There would still be him to deal with, and the girl.

"Well?"

Liefwin sat down beside the older man's massive bulk, because it was so much easier than standing.

"I got to them first."

"And?"

He thought of the half-dozen men he held captive. He had snatched them from under his commander's nose: the leaders of the Danish-held town.

"They say they had no choice but to join with the shipmen from Denmark and the Danish army. What else could they say?"

Ceolfrith shrugged. "Perhaps it is true. Perhaps they would rather live in peace with King Edward of Wessex as overlord than be stirred up by a raiding army every year. The ones in the town have settled. It is a bit different from plundering expeditions and there are enough English left amongst the people in Essex, and even in East Anglia."

The only word of that which stuck in Liefwin's mind was *peace*. It was like a talisman that shone somewhere far beyond his reach. It was something he had given his heart to years ago, before it had drowned in bitterness.

He shifted his weight and tried to ease the pain in his side and saw Ceolfrith take breath for the next question.

"So what does Oslac-Witlack say to all this?"

Oslac who lacked the wits and the guts and the self-control to command himself, let alone an army.

"He would have killed them."

"And you did not?"

"They are Edward's prisoners, not mine, and not Oslac's."

Liefwin got a look that told him that was not an acceptable answer, but he did not have a better one.

He closed his eyes but that was a mistake, because then he could see the frightened face of the Danish girl, like a delicate white frame for the huge, accusing eyes which could outstare him.

He opened his aching eyelids and tried to focus his attention on the next question.

"So who gets to tell King Edward that although we have defeated the army we have also sacked his potential allies and burned down most of the only fortification between Maldon and Colchester?"

The answer to that, at least, was easy. Liefwin's lip curled. "Oslac-Witlack. Who else? I helped him put together the message describing his triumphs. Once Edward hears that, he will be out of Huntingdon and down here within a matter of days. Besides, this is where he should be now. He could still lose everything we have gained if he does not go on to secure Colchester. It would have been done by now if I had been in command and not Witlack."

"You never know when to give up, do you?"

Liefwin thought that that depended upon your definition of giving up.

But he could see the expression on the other man's face in the light of the torch stuck in the floor behind them.

"Don't panic," he said, supplying the necessary reassurance. "I am not going to start another campaign. I have given the men my word that after this they can go home and I will keep it."

"Oh, *we* can go home, can we? It would be more to the point if you did, instead of sitting there looking like a walking *orc-nea*…"

Orc-nea were the unquiet dead. He could not look that bad, surely…

"…talking about starting another campaign, when you have done more than your share and have not been home for two years…"

The word *home* cut like a knife across exposed flesh. Just the thought of it was impossible to Liefwin. Ceolfrith knew that and to say it now was…to provoke him. He could see the disingenuous expression in Ceolfrith's eyes, which meant he suspected something was wrong and he thought if Liefwin lost his temper it would come out.

Well, it would not. The last thing he was going to do was admit his present weakness and add to Ceolfrith's burdens.

"How can I be a walking *orc-nea* if I am sitting down?" he asked, because he had always been able to talk rings round Ceolfrith. "Besides, if you think this is a slow campaign, take your complaints to Oslac. For Edward to give the command to that… that…just because he owed him a favor—"

Ceolfrith snapped at the bait. "Kings," he snorted, "always owing favors. But then I suppose they cannot help it and favors have to be paid. You cannot be too hard on Edward. We all do things we wish we had not."

Liefwin felt the gasp which rose in his throat. He tried desperately to choke it down. That had not been intentional on Ceolfrith's part. Ceolfrith would not call up the power of such terrible memories deliberately. He had to believe that.

It was Liefwin's own fault. Some chance phrase like that should not be able to tear him apart. He tried breathing through the damage that was hidden under his chain mail, but a small sound escaped him. He thought it was scarcely audible. But Ceolfrith must have heard it because Liefwin felt a hand touch the ripped sleeve of his tunic below where the chain mail ended.

He could not stand sympathy and he did not indulge in memories. Even if now they pressed on him because of what had happened in the town and because of the Danish girl.

Liefwin moved, twisting his body away so that the hand fell off. But he should not have done it so quickly. He did not know how he suppressed the gasp this time and his voice blurted out, "What about the Danish girl?"

"No problems. What would you expect? No one would dare to even look at her if she was yours."

Liefwin could hear the baffled edge of disapproval and he knew the effort it must have taken for Ceolfrith to hold on to his temper. Once they would have enjoyed shouting at each other over something that one of them disapproved of, but not now. The only thing left was the older man's forbearance and there was nothing Liefwin could do about it.

"Of course," said Ceolfrith, delivering the final blow, "she is terrified."

Liefwin got to his feet, far too fast again. He clutched at the wall and he could see Ceolfrith's expression change to one of alarm and anxiety and, of course, guilt. There was far too much guilt. He stood up straight and willed himself not to show the slightest further sign of weakness.

"You are hurt. I knew it. It was when—"

"No," Liefwin lied. He hated lying, but it actually rose quite easily to his tongue. He began undoing his sword belt. "Is there any water?"

"Yes. Hold on, I will help you with the armor."

But Liefwin had to get rid of his companion. Now.

"No. I will do it. Go to sleep." This time the finality in his voice would have told anyone.

He saw Ceolfrith glance away from him, toward the room that held the Danish girl. But there was nothing he could say to his lord.

Liefwin watched until the darkness swallowed his loyal retainer and then he let the jeweled belt fall where it would. He took hold of the corselet, which was when he realized that he could no longer lift his left arm above the level of his chest. Brilliant. Somehow he managed to get out of the mail coat without screaming. The tunic and the shirt underneath were easier because he could tear the seams. He buried them under a pile of junk so Ceolfrith would not see them and stepped into the flickering, smoky light of the torch left burning in the dirt floor.

It was possibly worse than he had expected. The whole of his left side appeared to be black and it had bled, but not much. Well, it would either heal itself or not. That was as fate willed. It held no interest for him.

He took off the rest of his clothes and found the water. It was so cold it stung against his skin, but he welcomed that. It was clean.

He sat down, out of the light, wrapped in his cloak, to think about tomorrow and about how to contain Oslac-Witlack from doing any more damage until Edward got here. And then he realized he was not thinking of that at all.

It was the girl.

In the dark he could see every detail of her fine, heart-shaped face. He heard her voice with its quaint Danish accent. He felt the gentle weight of her body leaning against his in the hell of the sacked town, so slight a thing, no more than the weight of a child.

She had looked like a maiden, with her pale hair spilling round her shoulders and down her back. She had looked so delicate that if you touched her with your battle-soiled, Dane-slaying hands, she would snap in two.

Yet she had outfaced her pursuers and she had taken the step that had plunged them both into something he had never expected.

He moved uncomfortably against the rough mud wall that dug into his back even through the heavy material of his cloak. But he could not free himself of her image. She was so beautiful and her terror had made her so vulnerable. He remembered the way her head had buried itself against his shoulder and the way her slender arm, bare to the elbow, had slid round him like an embrace. He felt her soft warmth infusing his hand through her outrageous Danish dress.

His hard-won breath quickened and he could feel

the stirring in his naked body under the cloak. He shut his eyes, but that only made it worse.

She had looked at him, in the torchlight outside the door, as though she trusted him, and he had lost his head completely and given her his word.

He sat forward and the pain stabbed at him. But he no longer knew whether it was the pain of his body or his mind.

What had he done? And what the hell was he thinking?

He forced himself to stand up.

She was not some willing maiden. She was a woman—a woman whose husband had just been killed by the army he was part of. They were enemies. Nothing she had done this night had been by her choice and she would hate him.

He moved and the pain made him stumble. He must sleep or he would die.

He looked round for where Ceolfrith had left his bedclothes. He stopped. There was only one place they would have been put because he had not explained otherwise. And Ceolfrith had said she was terrified.

He ran the few steps that led down the passage to the storeroom and ripped the curtain aside.

Sigrid did not move, even though her heart hammered and every primitive instinct inside her wanted to flee. There was nowhere to go, and she would keep her dignity.

She lay quite still, feigning sleep. She watched him. He did not make any noise at all, the Saxon marauder. She watched his every move.

She saw the powerful, shadowed bulk wrapped in a loose cloak pause, looking toward where she lay and she kept quite still. She scarce allowed herself a breath.

She saw him cross the room to gather up the pile of bedding she had kicked across the floor. She could see him quite clearly now that he had moved into the circle of light cast by her extravagant candles, whereas she was in shadow. His hair glowed against the dark material of the cloak. It was exactly the same color as the candle flame.

Still no sound.

If there was one thing that had unnerved and disgusted her more than any other it had been her husband falling on her in her sleep. It was low. The smoldering anger of living for six years at the mercy of another such marauder as this burned bright in her heart.

She watched him drop the brooch which had been left on top of the tunic and fail to find it in the murky recesses of the floor. So stealthy. So arrogantly self-focused.

The anger choked her. He would know she was watching him. He would know he would have to fight her every step of the path before the inevitable ending.

''Lost something?'' she inquired sweetly just as he gave up and began to turn away. He started and dropped the bedclothes in a scatter across the floor.

She almost laughed with a triumph that yet held the savage undercurrent of hysteria. Just for that instant she had him. She…she realized what she had turned him back from.

The doorway.

He had not turned toward her. He had turned toward the door. He had been going to leave. Perhaps he already had some other woman whom he preferred, perhaps he had a dozen. But he had not turned toward her, not until she had spoken to him.

He looked round. All huge shadows and glinting eyes and flaming hair.

Her heart shriveled within her. What had she done? Why had she let her temper get the better of her in the one battle she could not win? She must have invoked the wrath of fate this night to have handled things so ill.

"Sigrid?"

He had heard her name, after all. She watched in horror as he straightened up and moved, with nerve-racking slowness, toward her.

She sat up, spine achingly straight, hands buried like fists in the bedclothes.

He sat down on the floor beside her and the cloak slid down across one shoulder. Candle-flame hair scattered across white skin. He did not appear to be wearing anything under the cloak. Well, of course not. He was about to go to bed, possibly hers.

She could not tear her gaze away from the smooth expanse of naked skin exposed by the sliding cloak. The skin that would soon touch her like—

"Have you not slept?"

It was such a mild remark, so incongruous in the face of her terrified thoughts that she could not reply.

"Sigrid?"

There was a little more force to that. She must speak. She must make some answer and then perhaps he would go away. Back to whatever she had interrupted him from with her powerless, ill-placed anger. She opened her mouth to make some stupid, inane reply, something that would pacify him into leaving. But to her horror all that came out was a wordless choking sound, rasping and hideous next to the smooth assurance of his voice.

She jammed her hand against her mouth. She wanted to speak properly. She wanted to make him go away. She wanted to show him she still had some control. But she did not. It was gone. Gone when she looked at his naked skin and the size of him and when she thought that she had put herself in his power because she had believed she could bear it.

She could not. She had lived through too much this day and seen too much. There had been too much death and too much horror. Just as there had been all her life. That was what wanted to escape from her mouth—all the helplessness and the horror. Not words and clever stratagems. There were none left.

She had passed the limits of her strength with her reckless, foolish challenge to him and she could not follow it through.

If she could just stop herself from crying in front of him. If she could prevent him from knowing just how feeble she was. She could scarce breathe. But if she just—

He touched her.

She felt his heavy hand close over her small fist to pull it away from her face. She did try to resist him. She did try for one instant to pit her strength against that warrior's arm. But it was impossible.

She watched her fist drawn away and swallowed

up in his. She looked at the solidity of the naked arm stretched out from beneath the concealing cloak, the way the muscle moved under the white skin covered with fine golden hairs.

She wondered what would happen if she screamed.

Nothing, of course. If the Saxon rabble in the barn down below heard her, they would probably start cheering.

She watched the other arm move.

Her fixed gaze took in bruises, a piece of skin missing and…something dreadfully wrong, surely?

She looked up. The Saxon's head was bent forward in that helpless angle that in any other circumstance would have spelled defeat. She heard a small choke in his breath that might have been the echo of the hideous constriction in her own throat.

There really was something wrong, hideously so. She thought he would stop. But he did not. The hand kept moving, slowly, actually shaking, with an effort that was too awful, too agonizingly stubborn for her to understand. She wanted only to put an end to such hopeless, unnecessary persistence. And, to her terror, she could feel below her anger the dreadful stirring of pity.

She wanted the pity to stop. But it would not. It welled up inside her, like her unshed tears, with a life of its own. It grew until it swallowed up everything else: enmity and hate, anger and the last vestiges of her fear.

She did not understand it. It was wrong. But she felt it, like an extension of her own pain except worse, because at least she was activated by a desire to live whereas the cold eyes of the Saxon had held nothing.

She could not bear it. Anything to stop it.

She moved her free hand and it collided with his and became inextricably entangled with it and then with her other hand and his.

Madness. She looked at the untidy mess of the four interlocked hands and the worst happened. She burst into tears.

She did try to stifle the noise. But even so she just waited for him to give her a clout over the head and tell her to shut up. He did nothing. She thought that was impossible and then she stopped thinking about anything at all except flames and destruction and the long, drawn-out misery of her life.

When she came to herself, she was curled up on her side, in as small an area of the bedding as possible. The Saxon's right hand rested lightly on her tangled hair. She was still holding on to the left hand, attached to the bruised arm, the one that had caused the whole disaster. In fact she was clutching it so hard that the bones in her fingers ached. She managed to relax them, just slightly.

The hand on her head withdrew. But she no longer cared about that or about what he did. She no longer cared about anything. It was as though every emotion it was possible to feel had been used up and there was nothing left.

Whatever was going to happen would happen.

She woke when he moved.

She started. She had not actually been to sleep surely? Not…not with the marauder right beside her and…yes, still clutching at his hand.

She had. He was still there.

The light from the guttering candles wavered as his black shadow leaned over her. She was too exhausted even to panic. She waited for the familiar painful assault and the overpowering smell of stale beer and staler sweat.

His body blocked out the light. His loose hair slid across the side of her neck, making her skin shiver. She felt his hand touch her face. She sensed his warmth, nothing else, just warmth and the touch of skin: clean and solidly masculine, and the hand on her face rather callused.

He was leaning forward. The cloak gaped and through her half-closed eyes she could glimpse the dark secrets of his body, all strong lines and black shadows. So powerful and yet so sleek, so different from her husband. Not one gross mass of male flesh in which bull neck merged into barrel chest into hairy belly; not that, but a fiercely perfect arrangement of bone and tight muscle. So spare and so utterly purposeful. She found all that dark, shadowed perfection frightening. Yet it was so different that it was impossible to look away.

He leaned lower, his face over hers. She did not move. She did not even turn her head or take the breath to cry out.

His mouth found the delicate rise of her cheekbone, just below her lashes. She felt its dark, moist heat, the faint desperation in his breath. It lingered and lingered, until her tired senses swam and there was nothing else in the world except the touch of his lips and the sense of his presence, and she no longer wanted him to go.

Her hand was still entangled with his and she thought she tried to hold on to it, but it slid out of her grasp, leaving a small, cold space.

The next time she woke, it was to reality.

Chapter Three

The cold had seeped through Sigrid's bones. She could not move. Somewhere below her room she could hear the sounds of half the Saxon army waking up ale-sick. She shuddered and it hit her with the force of a storm—where she was and what had happened.

She must, she absolutely must, move before someone came to find her.

She was lying in a ball on her side, her right hand curled up beside her face as though it ought to be holding something. She looked at it and the rest of her memories slid into place. Her mind saw the beautiful, shadowed face of the Saxon, felt the physical warmth of his body, the clasp of his hand around hers, the dark, exhausted touch of his lips. But it was more than that. Her mind was filled with the picture of the bent head and the bruised arm and the feeling of wordless understanding.

Was that what his magic was? Was that what had drawn her to place her fate in his hands? Yet how could it have been? How could she have understood that in one instant in a half-dark street? She did not understand it now. She just felt it and—

In the pit down below came the revolting sound of somebody spewing up last night's ale over somebody else. The complaints of the afflicted led to a fight and she heard bloodcurdling yells and the rending sound of splintering wood. She put her hands over her ears and tried not to whimper with terror and disgust and sheer helplessness. Heaven protect her, that was what life was about, not dreams of supposed magic.

She forced herself to crawl out of the heap of bedding and into yesterday's crumpled clothes. She tried to set them to rights, but she felt dirty, crushed and so tired she could scream.

Someone, yelling louder than the rest, put an end to the fight. She thought it might be Ceolfrith. It was. He arrived at the curtain to her storeroom a few moments later. He brought food. She could not make herself eat it even though she knew she needed it. Because sooner or later she would have to face her captor, in the light of day, no magic and no dreams, just the fact that she now belonged to one of the rabble surrounding her, the rabble which had burned and looted an entire town in a drunken frenzy of destruction.

She had a long time to wait. Her captor, it seemed, was busy elsewhere. By the time Ceolfrith came back again to fetch her she was pacing the small confines of her room.

Ceolfrith was perhaps the same age as her father. She thought he possibly felt pity for her and that was not encouraging. She followed him out of the barn, through the sorry remains of the rabble. They did not

molest her. If her path approached them, they stepped
backward. If they looked at her, Ceolfrith glared. But
behind her, she could hear the hissing run of their
whispers. It was a relief to get out into the open air.

It was cold and it was going to rain. It seemed as
though the memory of summer had died in the flames
overnight and the bleakness of the world matched her
mood.

She was shown into someone's bower, well-made
and furnished and with a fire in the hearth and rushes
on the floor. It was warm. It was…she forgot the
bower. She forgot everything except her captor.

He was standing against a tapestried wall, bathed
in the glow of a polished copper oil lamp. If she had
to find one single word to describe his appearance, it
would be *flawless*.

He turned his glowing, golden head. Just slowly,
as though there was no hurry. It made her so angry,
she could spit.

She felt as though she was about to die on the spot.
She had not eaten, she had scarcely slept, her eyes
felt swollen from last night's crying, her clothes were
dirty and her underdress had rips in it.

In him there was not the slightest sign of a day and
a night spent ravaging.

Her furious eyes took in every detail, from the
heavy woolen tunic that finished in a line of gold
embroidery just above the knee, to the dark gray trousers, to the stylish, intricately made leather shoes. The
tunic was a carefully dyed shade of blue. Whether it
had more embroidery at the wrist was impossible to
tell because the sleeve edges were hidden by arm
rings of twisted gold. The thin leather belt at his waist

had a gilded buckle and strap end decorated in the style of some fabulous beast and set with what looked like garnets.

Well, she thought savagely, that was all as it should be. If you had plundered someone's wealth, you wore it.

She had saved the face for last and it did not disappoint. It was as devoid of any demeaning human passion as she could have wished.

It made it satisfyingly easy to wipe from her mind the frightening memory that last night she had burst into tears over the mere sight of his hands. That now seemed impossible. She could never have imagined that someone like him was either hurt or could have shared the hot and helpless misery of despair. She could forget it. He obviously had.

"Well," she inquired, seizing the initiative before he did, "where would you like to start?" His eyes darkened and she savored the fierce pleasure of having disconcerted him. He had doubtless expected hysterics.

It did not last more than an instant, of course. You did not get to defeat a Viking army by being easily disconcerted. But she had seen that instant of confusion, and he knew she had.

"By deciding your future?" he shot back.

"I did not think there was anything to decide."

He turned away, which was infuriating because she lost the advantage of being able to catch any remotely human expression that might have crossed his face. She glared at the lithe figure outlined against the colored wall, hating its unconscious assurance. They all stood like that, anyone over the rank of conscripted soldier, with their heads held as though the rest of the world was there merely to do their bidding.

She did not know what he was waiting for, but it was some minutes before he spoke again.

Then he said without turning his arrogant head, "You must have some kindred left."

She blinked and then she understood. Her gaze moved from the embroidered tunic to the thick torqued gold at his wrists. He was beautiful and he liked fine things and the easiest ways to obtain fine things were either through plunder or through ransom.

He thought she was worth something to somebody.

He could not have made a greater mistake. She was such a pathetically unloved and unimportant object that the idea almost made her laugh. She must get a grip on herself. Her mouth had actually begun to form the bitter word *no,* when she stopped. He did not know that she was worthless. He knew nothing about her. If he thought she could add to his collection of arm rings, who was she to disappoint him? She took a breath.

"Well," she began, "I do have a cousin who..." He turned round. He would never believe her. She could never fool that clear cold gaze.

"Well?" he prompted in mocking echo, impatience lending a sharp edge to the coolness of his voice.

That did it. Her smoldering anger ignited and brought a courage that was quite reckless.

She smiled, not too sweetly.

"I have a cousin who would pay dearly for my safe return." She let her gaze flick just once over the red gold at his wrists.

She saw his surprise and tried to pull herself upright into as fair an imitation of the unthinking arrogance of his pose as she could manage. She held his gaze. If only she had better clothes, if only the brooches that pinned her tunic were of anything better than iron and copper. But her husband had seldom wasted any of the spoils of war on her.

His gaze did not move an inch.

If she had at least taken the time to comb her hair.

She would never make him believe. No one had ever put the slightest worth on her. Not since the day she had been born and certainly not since she had come here with Ragnar. Ragnar...she did have something of value. Silver. Her hand touched the leather ribbon at her neck, toyed with it, tried to seem casual.

He would be impressed. If he did not steal it off her straight away. But...this was her chance. She would never have another. Now. But her hand on the thin leather, the leather that had been worn by someone else, was strangely reluctant, and her heart beat painfully.

"I am worth much to my family," she lied, and Ragnar's amulet slid out from beneath the neckline of her dress. The charms suspended from the silver ring jangled: two swords, three staffs, Odin's spear.

He watched. Her breath tightened in her throat. His eyes would widen, assess the worth, wonder at the fine craftsmanship of such an exotic foreign trinket. She saw an instant of wonder and then the blue eyes became slits of ice.

"A family heirloom?"

Of course it was an odd treasure for a woman. It

was a man's token, a warrior's token. A Viking's. The Saxon would hate it.

She hated it. Her hand began to shake. She thrust the hideous, evil-looking thing beneath her dress, her mind swirling with helpless fury. She forced breath through her throat, made herself speak.

"The worth of that is nothing to what my cousin would give you."

"Indeed? And just where would he be, this cousin?"

"Skaldford."

She had no very clear idea of where it was. Her horizons extended no further than the memory of her home in Denmark, a nightmare sea journey and the confines of the now ruined town.

"Shealdford?"

"Shh—" Her nervous voice faltered over the peculiar English sounds. *Sh* was a ridiculous noise to make at the best of times and the way he said it... "Skaldford," she snapped, tossing her head with what she fondly imagined was an assumption of arrogance and hoping the wretched place was not in the middle of some Danish army. "You have only to send your messengers there and I am sure it will bring you even as much as you could desire."

He began to walk toward her. Perhaps the assumption of arrogance had been too convincing. She took a step backward and collided with a chair and a table she had not even seen.

"You may sit down," he said, and took the chair on the opposite side of the wooden table.

Placate him. Placate him, for heaven's sake, and he might do what she wanted.

She sat in that unexpected luxury, a chair, just as though she had sat on chairs all her life and not rough benches. She produced another smile. "I could get you my wergild," which was the price her avenging kindred ought to have extracted if he killed her; if she had had any kindred, if he had not been so utterly safe from the vengeance of a mere Dane.

"More..." her voice stopped. He was pouring mead from a silver-chased flask. There were small purple, crescent-shaped marks on the back of his hand. She nearly shrieked.

No. No, it could not have been her. She could not have done such a thing. She could not have been so desperate for his touch last night that she had dug her fingernails into his flesh. Please no.

It must have been her. She could hardly see some Viking *hersir* trying to scratch him to death. How could she have done it? Humiliation crawled through her veins. What if he referred to it? What if he said something about last night that—

"Mead?"

The scratched hand held a cup in her direction. She took it. She remembered how that hand had felt in the other world of last night: like a lifeline against drowning.

She swallowed the entire contents of the cup in one draught. If only he would give her some more. She dangled the cup casually in front of the flask in his hand. He poured some more, but the finely shaped eyebrows climbed.

She did not give the lowest curse. She swallowed more and the sweet liquor burned like fire in her empty stomach.

"And which of my men do you think should be given the glory of a journey to Shealdford?" he inquired in his improbable accent. "I do not think I have any idiots among my retainers."

If she slapped his arrogant face he would probably kill her. She resisted the impulse and her hand curled like a vise round the mead cup. She gritted her teeth.

"Then if it is beyond their small store of valor, let me go and I can promise—"

"*You?* Do not be ridiculous—"

"Well, at least I am not afraid..."

He got to his feet with a force that sent the heavy wooden chair crashing to the ground and made the table rock dangerously.

You should never challenge a warrior's courage. She had watched while her husband killed someone for that.

She looked up into a face that was now brilliant with all the passion she knew should live in that vibrant soul. The blue eyes blazed in a way that made her blood race and her heart beat strangely.

"Do you have any idea where Shealdford now lies?" shouted Liefwin at the huge gray eyes fixed on his. "Somewhere between the last known position of the Danish force of Cambridge and the route King Edward's army is likely to take from Huntingdon."

"But—" she began.

He let his gaze rake from the pathetically small hand clenched round the empty mead cup to the childishly large eyes.

"You will not do such a thing. Do you understand me? I will not allow it," he yelled in a voice that would have deafened a mutinous churl. He kicked the chair out of the way and strode across to the window before he strangled her.

He could not stand the closely confined room with her any longer. He ripped open the shutter and felt the cold wind strike his face like shards of ice, reminding him that the summer was long gone and it was nearly Martinmas and winter. The wind froze his skin but not what was in his heart.

If only he could breathe the pureness of that frigid air deep inside him. But the morass of pain in his chest was too strong and it defeated him.

He told himself it was because of his injury but he knew it was not. It was not physical pain, it was memory. The memory that had stirred in him since he had first seen the Danish girl against a background of flames, and behind the memory lay a shameful blank where feelings should be. He did not have any. He was aware that he ought to, but the only thing that got through was guilt, and now anger.

He had no wish to be responsible for the girl. She was a Dane with bizarre talismans hung round her slender neck. He did not know why he did not either throw her back to the wolves or do what she so obviously thought he was going to do. As for sending some poor churl all the way to Shealdford in the hope of getting some pathetic ransom…

He turned round when she was not expecting it and saw that he had terrified her to the depths of her soul. There was no disguise for it and no help. He thought of Elswyth and how terrified she would have been before she died. The thought still had the power to make his gorge rise but at that moment, sensing the Danish girl's terror of him so strongly he could smell it, he no longer wanted vengeance. He wanted an end to it. There was no other decision that could be made. In fact it had been made last night when he had told her, no *asked* her, to come with him.

"I will take you to Shealdford myself," he said as though somebody else spoke using his cold, uncompromising voice. "I cannot leave until King Edward gets here with the main army, but that will be very soon. Then the men are going home and I am going to Tamworth. I will take you to Shealdford on the way."

You could hardly describe Shealdford as being on the way to Tamworth, but she did not seem to have the slightest grasp of geography.

"Tamworth?"

Perhaps she did. She was looking at him as though she did not believe a word he had said. He discovered that stung even though he could scarcely expect anything else.

"Yes. We are on loan from the lady, King Edward's sister."

"You are from Mercia?"

"Yes." What did she think he was, some lumbering East Saxon or a moron from Wessex?

She poured herself another cup of mead, which he did not think she should. But then maybe that was better for her. He watched her drink the lot and wondered whether she would be ale-sick in the morning.

She put down the cup with her slender little hand and said, "And you are going to take me to Skaldford?"

He tried to swallow the surge of anger.

"Shealdford," he said. The place was not, would

not *remain,* Danish. He took a breath that hurt. "I have said I will do it. You have my word."

"Oh?"

If she had been a man, he would have killed her for the doubt in that single word. He could feel his hand reach instinctively for the seax at his belt.

Now he had petrified her again. He dragged his hand away from the long single-bladed knife and then heard the noise outside, because he was right beside the window. He glanced out. It was not starting already, surely? It was. He could see them in the distance, coming for him. Not just his men, surely, but some of Oslac's West Saxons. That would sit ill with Oslac.

He looked back at the frightened girl. So much left unsaid. So much he did not even know how to say. Such a gulf between them and yet he had made the link that would hold them fast until he took her to Shealdford.

The noise came to him on snatches of cold October wind.

"Look, I shall have to go but—" he paused "—the next two weeks..." he said, starting in the wrong place.

He stopped in the face of the gray eyes.

He wished she had done something with her hair. She looked like a virgin of fifteen, a rather mead-soaked virgin.

"For the next two weeks. I do not—"

"I am to live as your mistress," she said.

No one would dare to even look at her if she was yours. Ceolfrith's words were in his mind and he knew they were true.

"Yes, but—"

"And then when you have finished with me you leave me at Skaldford and go home to your wife…"

Sigrid stopped in the middle of a breath and she was reminded irresistibly again of the man she had been forced to watch her husband murder for insulting him. The look of stunned shock and that terrible whiteness of the victim's face were burned into her memory.

"I do not have a wife."

She had got as far as her feet. But the mead took its revenge, making her light-headed so that her legs would not carry her and she had to clutch at the table for support. She became aware of a roaring noise that was something separate from the dizziness in her head. She thought it came from outside. It dragged her attention from the Saxon's voice, which seemed to be explaining something to her.

"…Sigrid, I do not expect…"

She could not concentrate on anything except the increasing noise from outside. It sounded like yesterday.

"What is happening?"

"It is nothing. It is just—"

It was how a raid started. She could hear yelling and shouting and the drumming of weapons on linden-wood shields, and cutting through it a sound of pure horror: the howling noise of a wolf, but made by a human throat. The noise Ragnar, her husband, had made when he lost his mind.

Her brain went dark.

She became aware that someone had hold of her by the arms.

"Sigrid…"

Ragnar never spoke with an accent like that. Ragnar was dead on the battlefield. Even though she had not seen it, there was no possibility of mistake. Too many people had been only too eager to tell her so and she had the amulet. Ragnar would never be able to touch her again. Yet she shivered and the amulet dug into her skin, crushed between their bodies, hard and sharp.

But she could also feel the warmth and the strength of the hands on her bare arms, controlled strength, not meant to punish, only to hold her. Her blurred vision caught the edge of the red-gold hair and the blue tunic of the Saxon. She was leaning against him. Her hair fell onto his shoulder.

"You are not him," she whispered stupidly into expensive blue cloth.

"What? Sigrid, there is nothing to be afraid of."

Did he not realize? Could he possibly not understand what was out there and the full horror of it? She tried to speak through the hoarseness in her throat and managed to force out that single unspeakable word.

"Berserker," she said.

But the world stayed in its place. His arms were around her and his hands buried themselves in her loose hair. His body felt as it had looked in the candlelight and the shadows: a thing of hard-packed muscle and lithe grace. She could feel its every contour through her dress. She could feel all of its warmth, so at variance with the coldness of his heart.

"Sigrid, it is not—"

"Yes, it is. You do not understand what they are like."

The sound came again, unquenchable in its blood lust, the triumph of savagery over anything human. She raised her head, twisting it to try and see out of the open space of the window.

"You do not know what they are like when they become mad," she said. "They are like wolves. When the fit is on them, neither fire nor iron can hurt them and they will kill anything and nothing can stop them because Odin protects them and…"

"Stop it. Do not. Sigrid, look at me."

His voice was calm. So calm when she was trembling with horror. She felt his hand move round to support her head and turn it irresistibly toward him. She looked at his face. It was not afraid.

"That is not some warrior with the wolf's fury on him. It is just someone drunk on ale trying to pretend he is a wolfcoat. They are my men. They are just…it is just…"

She was looking straight into his eyes and she suddenly realized what it was.

The horror faded, but it left behind it something slightly sick.

She said, "Your men. Yours. They are getting ready for the victory feast."

"Yes." It was said without even the slightest pause and with no explanation, but then there was no need for him to say anything else.

She was clutching at him, her body pressed itself intimately against his. His arms were round her and his hands touched her back and the vulnerable curve of her neck underneath her hair.

Saxon, and outside the rest of them were cheering

and screaming over the deaths of her kind and the destruction of her whole life.

She choked for breath, pulling herself away from his touch. His hands slid from her shoulders, touched the bare skin below where her sleeves ended, making her shiver. She tried to free her arms from his grasp, but the strong, warm fingers closed.

The screaming reached fever pitch. Something thudded against the door.

She stared at his marked hands on her flesh. There was another thud. She flinched, in spite of all her determination not to. The hands tightened.

"Remember what I said."

But all she was conscious of was the screaming, the screaming and the feel of his hands.

Another thud. She could not stand this.

"Why are they here instead of in the town?" Her voice rose in desperation. The inarticulate screaming clarified itself into a word, a single word repeated over and over. *Liefwin.*

The strong hands let her go.

"They want me."

He went. They dragged him through the door, so many hands clutching at him as though he were some godlike hero come back from Valhalla to middle earth. They bore him away, lifted high on their shoulders and she was left, in the bright room with the fire and the lamps and the tapestries. Quite alone.

She thought the noise they made would never stop. She buried her head in her arms, but even that did not block it out. It swelled in sickening waves.

Liefwin.

If only she could not make out what they said, but

she could and that one repeated word scored into her mind. Her hands clenched themselves into fists, tangling in her hair and pulling on it and the small pain was a relief from the greater pain inside.

It was a long time before the shouting began to recede, fading away into the ruin of the town.

She raised her head and her gaze fell on the mead flask. She poured. Her hand was shaking. She drank all that was there.

Liefwin, they shouted in the distance. It drowned out the howls of the mock berserker. *Liefwin,* she thought. And to her shame, what came into her mead-fuddled head was the warmth of his body and the way her head had fit on his shoulder and the way it felt when his arms closed round her.

Her fingers tightened on the cup.

Liefwin was part of the yelling mob that had taken and plundered the town. Liefwin was, if not Saxon, then English. Liefwin was celebrating yesterday's carnage.

Her duty was to think of her dead husband.

Her hand moved to the small white scar at the corner of her eye, which had been her husband's morning gift, just so that she recognized what her place would be in the order of things and what would happen if she stepped outside it.

That was how life always was. She was used to it. You just had to accept it and twist what advantage you could out of it, no time and no thought for anything else. That way, you survived. She was a great survivor.

She swallowed the last small drop of mead in the cup and waited.

He did not come back.

* * *

There was a maid who came in and set the room to rights and menservants who carried in everything, including some locked chests belonging to Liefwin.

She came into the possession of a mirror, a comb, bowls, a pitcher of water, salt for cleaning her teeth, a woman's cloak, material of all sorts including silk ribbon, needles, thread, a pair of tweezers…it went on.

She had a very fine bed with warm covers and bright blue hangings.

She had more mead.

The maid looked at her as though she should have two heads. Sigrid sent her away.

He still did not come back. The victory feast must be going well.

She made a circuit of the room. It was large. It was three-quarters cleaned. There were two beds. The other, still in its original state, had hangings of sea-green. They were faded and somewhat dusty, but the embroidery was worked in real gold thread.

She was not sure who had lived here. It had been neglected, but it was impossible to say whether this was due to bad housekeeping or lack of occupants. Surely, in that case, someone would have stolen the curtains if they had realized it was gold thread. She felt a hysterical laugh rising in the throat. Someone had stolen the curtains. Someone had stolen everything. She was expecting the thief to come back at any moment.

She had drunk too much mead.

She drank some more.

Eventually she went to bed. She kept her shift on.

Chapter Four

When she opened her eyes, it was daylight and she was alone.

But that was impossible.

She sat up and scrabbled at the bedclothes as though there might be some stray English marauder there that she had overlooked.

Nothing.

It was true.

He had not come back. He was lying under the mead bench somewhere in a drunken stupor and they had left him there to rot.

Speaking of mead, she had a crashing headache. She clawed her way across the bed and opened the bright blue curtains.

It must be late, but the fire was in a better state than she would have imagined. It was raining. Sharp drops hissed and spit into the glowing embers through the hole in the roof that let the smoke out. She slid to the floor, her feet stumbling like lumps of lead.

She did not remember leaving her new cloak out by the hearth.

If only there was some mead left.

There was. Perhaps it would settle her headache. She drank.

She noticed the pale green hangings had fallen down on the other bed. How odd. They were such beautiful work in spite of the dust. They were the only relic of the previous owner of the bower and they fascinated her. She wandered across the room in her shift and gathered up a handful of embroidered cloth.

Her hand touched something faintly warm. What was left of her brain seemed to freeze inside her skull. She looked down in the dim light that came from the fire and through the hole in the roof.

It was a shoulder, attached to an arm and a mop of gleaming red-gold hair.

She shrieked.

It moved.

The flood of gold raised itself and someone groaned. Her hand slid across living naked flesh, across a heavy shoulder, down the long, elegant shape of an arm and landed in a tangle of sea-green material.

"It is you."

"Of course it is. Who did you think it was? Beowulf?"

"No, you have only two arms," she said as the other one emerged from the covers.

"What?"

"Beowulf. In the story. Did he not tear off the swamp monster's arm and keep it as a sort of trophy?"

This was not the moment to discuss poetry, not with her heart pounding and her mouth as dry as last year's straw. Why had she swallowed another cup of mead? She tried to think. Liefwin the Saxon had managed to raise himself as far as his elbows. She could not see his face, only the golden sweep of his hair.

"Oh," he said, half groan, half growl deep in the throat. It was followed by a sort of gasp. If his head felt anything like hers, she understood. It would, of course—he had had a lot to celebrate. Her lip curled.

"Ale-sick?"

She looked at the size of his shoulders and the way the muscle in them rippled when he moved. Her heart pounded harder. Moon-mad wantwit. Why had she taunted him with that? Her hand, tangled in the disordered bed hangings clenched itself into a fist so tight it hurt.

"No," said the bright tangled mass of hair and the brutal shoulders. "It is more likely to be frostbite. Did you have to take all of the bedclothes? How many do you need? You could have left me something."

She blinked.

"I did not think—" After one more look at the shoulders, she swallowed. *…that you would expect me to have a second bed made up in case you were too drunk to crawl as far as the first.*

"If this thing is alive," he said, indicating the dusty bed hangings, "I am going to kill you."

She flinched. She could not help it, because that was the way her dead husband had begun many conversations. *I am going to kill you.* And at that moment the Saxon looked up and saw it. Humiliation that he had seen how weak she was, and all the smoldering resentment of the past stung her.

But there was no expression that she could read in the rather bloodshot blue eyes.

"It must be late," he said without the slightest change in his voice, and that was it. Nothing else. No taunts. No display of masculine triumph. Not yet. She let out her pent-up breath.

He sat up.

She thought that he had meant to take the bed curtain with him. But her forgotten fist was still embedded in it and the material pulled with a small tearing sound across the solid expanse of his chest, and she saw what was really wrong with him.

The whole of his left side was an appalling shade between black and purple. There was an area of crushed skin in the middle where something, presumably his chain mail, had bitten through the flesh. She gasped and let go of the bed hanging and he fairly snatched it out of her hand, even though it was too late. She wondered whether or not she was going to be sick and cursed herself again for swallowing mead on an empty belly.

There was one of those dreadful silences during which the only thing that could be heard was her choking breath.

Finally her voice said, "Have you done nothing about it?"

She got a look that would have slain a fire-breathing dragon.

"No. It is unnecessary."

Unnecessary? Well, if he wanted to be dead within the week, that would suit her. Just perfectly.

At least she could not see the damage anymore, only an expanse of pale green cloth. Buried, which was what he should be. What he would be if he did not... "There must be someone skilled in healing who could help you."

The dragon-slaying look intensified, increasing the feeling of rather queasy unsteadiness. A spurt of sudden anger rescued her from it.

"Surely," she snapped, "you could find one. Or if that is beneath you, I am sure your loyal retainer would do it..." He leaned forward. Her voice stopped. His hand, clutching the gold-embroidered cloth, was a white-knuckled fist. It looked as though it would like to have been wrapped around the gilded hilt of his sword. Or perhaps around her neck.

"I do not require anyone's help." Least of all that of a pathetic, insignificant captive. Not said. "I will not have this referred to, particularly not to Ceolfrith. Do you understand me?"

Despite the sickening shortness of her breath, she managed to fix her gaze on the arrogant turn of his head with a look that could have done its own degree of damage.

"I understand you only too well."

His mouth thinned. "It is late," he said with painful restraint. "I must go."

Good. If he wanted to hasten his own end by going out in that state she...she realized what it meant. He was going. He was far too important to stay with a small piece of Danish flotsam like her. She was free. Free until tonight. Her heart leaped.

"Yes, lord," she said, and got to her feet with a speed that did nothing for her headache. She began to gather his clothes from where they had been drying near the fire.

"Sigrid, leave that."

She clutched at the tunic. Surely he had not changed his mind already? She shook out the heavy folds and began straightening the material as fast as she could. Could he see how unsteady her hands were?

"Will you leave that and come here?"

She stood with her back to him, her fingers twisted in the rich cloth of his tunic, unable to make herself move.

"Please."

The last word choked, as well it might. She did not believe it could have been spoken by the same person. Well, it was either him or Beowulf. She looked round and found he had moved and was, she fancied, regretting it. It was hard to tell for sure, because the large hand she had scratched the night before hid his face. The way he had wanted the dusty bed curtain to hide his body.

But it was words from another story that came into her mind. The one about a man who was quite alone and kept his thought-hoard to himself and his heart bound fast, just as a noble warrior should.

She knew by heart every song and every poem there was to know. They were so much better than real life.

The one about the solitary man was English, very appropriate. The lord Liefwin seemed to have got it badly.

There had been something odd about that small choking sound that had been forced out of him. She knew it.

"All right," she said.

No response.

Always assuming that he had a heart to bind.

She took another look at the drooping head and moved first to the table, where she found the other cup and poured. Fair was fair. If she could start the day on the mead, so could he. She turned round with the cup in her hand.

He was leaning back. He had his eyes shut.

It made a lot of difference if you could not see that frozen look. It left only the golden warmth of his hair and his skin. He was braced against the wall, his large, naked body half-smothered in the faded abundance of the bed hangings. It made him look rather exotic and not quite real: a fit subject for a saga.

He opened his eyes.

Perhaps a saga with trolls in it, made from stone.

She proffered the cup and got a rather narrow look. Surely he could not tell she had been on the mead herself?

"Sit down."

She wondered whether she could get him to choke again on the word *please,* but he was taking the cup out of her hand and his fingers touched hers, not the stuff of legend at all, a man's hand. She sat down rather abruptly.

She sat on the very edge of his bed and she did not say another word. But she was burningly aware of his closeness and of the fact that he was clothed in nothing but gold bracelets and a rather thin piece of cloth. Even though all she could see were the tops of his shoulders, his arms and a glimpse of one shapely foot.

She waited.

* * *

Liefwin swallowed the mead in one go. It did take the edge off physical pain, but it did nothing to help him deal with the girl.

She was wearing her fragile maiden look again, all flowing hair and delicate arms, delicate everything else. His gaze took in all of it from the slender shoulders to the bare ankles, every smooth and softly rounded part of her that could be glimpsed or imagined through her shift.

She seemed utterly unaware that she was still exactly as she must have been when she first got out of bed. She had gathered up his things for him and fetched him mead and now she sat so passively next to him while he was wrapped only in some motheaten rag.

She seemed to have no consciousness of that, and yet he could make her afraid of him. He was beginning to think that someone else had done the same before him. But despite that, only two minutes ago she had been trying to tell him what to do.

She was incomprehensible.

There was no particular reason why he should bother about what she thought. No reason why he should have to bear with her vagaries and the things she said, the painful memories she seemed to cause just by existing. He had not asked to be encumbered with some stray Danish piece.

Except it was too late. He was trapped by his own word. He had to see it through, like everything else. Only a coward backed down from what he had set his hand to.

She sat so quietly and so still. But he was used to

assessing people and he could sense the nervousness that lay hidden in her. He seemed to do nothing but snarl at her like some bad-tempered warg.

"Sigrid," he said, trying to pronounce its Danish syllables properly.

She looked up and the great gray eyes held his gaze. But he could see in their depths that she really was afraid of him, even though he had given his word she would be safe. It stirred something unpleasant in the dead hollow inside him, and he realized he disliked seeing the fear in her eyes quite intensely.

"Sigrid," he said with sudden strength, "I know we agreed for the next two weeks to the pretence that you are my mistress, but that is as far as other people are concerned. In these four walls there is only us. I do not expect you to have to wait on me or…"

He stopped. She was looking at him with her little mouth open, and the gray eyes were so large he could have tripped over and fallen into them. Had he been bellowing at her again? He took a breath, which hurt, and began again more slowly. Perhaps her English was not as good as he had thought.

"It is as I said yesterday. There are no expectations. We need hardly see each other. I will be out. You have a maid to look after everything. I have servants. I…" His voice trailed off. Nothing seemed to be getting through. She was looking at him just as though he really were some warg. He moved and the pain in his ribs hit with the force of a Norseman's ax. But behind it was the other pain and he was staring again into the abyss.

How could she do this to him?

He should have had more than four hours sleep in

the two nights after a battle. That was all that was wrong with him. He leaned back against the solid hardness of the wall, trying to take the pressure off his damaged ribs.

The pain would become quite bearable if he just breathed properly.

He became aware that someone was pressing the mead cup into his hand again. It was full. The cool honey liquid splashed onto his fingers. The girl's small hand withdrew.

"You did not believe me..." He stopped. He had not meant to say that. It was unnecessary. It did not matter what she thought. But he could not stop himself.

Her eyes became opaque.

"About what? Oh, of course I did. It was just that—"

He stared at her and the cozening words died on her lips.

"Do not lie to me about such things." Just the force in his voice was enough to make the rapid color come and go in her face. He could not soften it, and he had to fight for the control that had always come so easily to him.

"Sigrid," he managed, more evenly, but it was too late. The surprise and the apprehension in her face had already hardened into defiance, and she no longer took the trouble to disguise the animosity that lay beneath.

"Why? What should I believe?"

He held on to the shreds of his temper with an effort.

"I have given you my word." She seemed to have

no concept of what that meant. "I have said that while you are with me you are safe."

"Oh, I see. Everything else might have been taken from me, but I am to have my…safety?"

But the memories in his mind made him proof against that sort of scorn.

"It is more than some had." The coldness in his voice now covered everything. "I must go. Now."

He paused, waiting for the wench to move, but she did not. Why should she? It was nothing more than a conceit of his to keep thinking she was a maiden who could be shocked.

He made his way past her, letting the obnoxious rag fall to the floor. He did hear an agitated rustling noise behind him, but he was still too angry to look back. He had spent far too long arguing already.

He slid the gold rings off his arms and poured water, one-handed.

He washed. Everything. Including his hair in case there really had been something alive in that moth-eaten curtain. He did not give so much as an empty curse what she thought.

He found his clothes.

He could feel by now the sickening light-headedness that came from lack of sleep and the damage to his left side, and the emptiness of his life, the futility of all that he was trying to do, hit him as it had not done for two years. But there was no choice but to go on.

He managed the trousers, the leather *windingas* around his legs, even the shoes. But he could feel how slow and awkward his movements were becoming.

He picked up the shirt and the tunic which had to be pulled on over his head.

There was another rustling noise from his bed as though the Danish girl had moved again.

Well, she would doubtless enjoy the weak-kneed fool he would make of himself over this bit if nothing else.

He closed his eyes.

It was done and he had neither fainted nor thrown up the remains of last night's ale. He looked round and reached out for his sword belt, carefully because the scabbard was damaged, but it slid from his clumsy fingers to the floor. He could not move. He wondered what he would do if the pain in his side became more than it was possible to control.

The rush-strewn floor seemed an unlikely distance below his feet and his sight began to distort.

Perhaps he was going to disgrace himself in front of the wench after all. He could not. He knew that his pride would not allow it. He gritted his teeth and leaned forward with his good hand outstretched. The floor got no closer.

There was another agitated rustling sound and then the slender, bare arm of the Danish girl swam into his blurred vision. She was going to pick the sword up for him.

"Don't!"

He could see the pattern-welded blade splitting that small hand in two. He dropped to the floor and his right hand snatched hers out of the air before it could touch the sword. But he was off balance and he landed in a jarring thud on his knees and his left elbow. The floor and the naked arm and the sword disappeared for one searing instant.

He fought the blackness out of his mind. Pain always receded in the end if you kept your head. He concentrated with the discipline born of practice.

The girl's unscathed hand lay softly in his.

"What did you think I was going to do?" said her lightly accented voice from the other edge of the cosmos. "Try and cleave you in half with the blade?"

It was not a thought that had occurred to him. If his prisoner had been some Viking *hersir* it would have been obvious and yet there was no reason why her heart should not hold the same desire for vengeance. But the small hand had somehow entwined itself with his even as she spoke and it stayed there.

He was not used to seeing the face of his enemy in the face of a woman. There was a small pause during which he was aware of nothing but the pain and the feel of her hand.

He clawed himself upright. It took the weight off his left arm, but that did not seem to help much and he could feel the faint beginnings of sweat under his newly washed hair. He shoved the heavy mass out of his face and looked up.

She was sitting next to him on the floor in her indecent shift. He expected to find the same mockery in her eyes that had scorched through her words. But the eyes were as opaque as when she had been lying to him.

She kept his hand.

His gaze dropped to the sword.

"The scabbard is broken." At least his voice sounded in reasonable shape. He reached slowly across to show her where the wood had cracked open and the leather covering scarcely held it together. He had to use his left hand because she did not let go of his right.

The leather split when he moved it and the bright blade spilled out onto the floor. He heard the faint hiss of her indrawn breath.

He caught the gold-embossed hilt and it slid obediently enough into his fingers, but it felt strange in his left hand. Swords were alive just as much as people were. This one was old, yet as sleek and deadly as the lightning it was named for.

"It is a snake-blade," she said. "One that will never break."

Her voice told him she knew how old it was and what it was worth and he wondered at that.

But then she would know, if her husband was a warrior.

"Its name is *liyt ræsc.*"

"Lightning." She frowned and then repeated it, somehow getting her Danish tongue round the final *sh* sound this time. *"Liyt ræsc."*

"Yes."

He stared at the pattern-welded steel, tempered and hardened beyond the skill of any smith now living. The separate twisted bands of metal visible in the blade were overlain with the runes of power, one from each aett: *Ur,* the strength that must be controlled; *Eolhx,* protection, the sword symbol, the mysterious other self; and *Tir,* the just victory.

His hand tightened on the hilt. They had been placed there long before the sword was his. He should have had *Hægl,* the sudden destroyer.

Shivers touched Liefwin's spine and he made himself look away and toward the cross carved on the ornate chest in his corner of the bower. He let that sign fill his vision. That was the new Way. That was what should be thought of.

He became aware, again, of the faint warmth of the girl's slender fingers around his. He glanced at her face, but she was not looking at him. The fine eyes still watched the sword as though it was some uncontrollable animal that would strike. He noticed for the first time that there was a jagged notch in the blade from the carnage of the battle for the town and that that was the focus for her eyes.

There was a pause and then he gathered up the jeweled belt and the broken scabbard and moved to stand up. He wanted to use his right hand to steady himself, but it remained in her hand and he was helpless to break that grip.

He managed it but the light-headedness made him stagger. She had risen with him and her thin, bare arm moved seemingly without thought around his body to stop him falling. He did not understand why she did that.

It was as though they were battle opponents in the strange Viking convention of the hazelled field. Inside the ring of hazel branches you fought to the death; outside it, honor permitted no act of aggression. It was as though by unspoken consent, his wounds and her tears lay on neutral ground.

She was so close to him, touching him in much the same way she had when he had half carried her through the streets of the burning town. He could not take his eyes from the bare skin of her arms and neck, the gentle rise of her collarbone and the softness of her figure, half visible, half guessed beneath the thin shift.

Her nearness and her half-clothed state brought warmth to his body like a flood. Stronger than fatigue or pain it beat in waves he could not control, until he was aware of nothing but the desire to do what she would most hate him for.

She was staring at him and her eyes were wide and dark.

He pulled himself away. Heaven knew why. He had no honor left. He knew it, if others did not.

But he still could not harm her.

Perhaps she was his atonement.

He picked up his cloak. Oslac and the six prisoners and an argumentative and ale-sick army made up of men from two separate provinces, that was what he had to deal with.

He threw the cloak round his shoulders and turned to the door, remembering at the last minute to pick up the gold arm rings with which to impress Oslac.

The girl watched him in silence.

There was also, of course, the remains of the helpless Danish population and the liberated English desiring revenge.

Chapter Five

Sigrid staggered back to the bed and fell on it. She dived under the warm covers, trying to bury herself, pulling them high round her naked shoulders as though she could hide what had already been seen and assessed to the last detail. She shivered. How could she not have thought until that last breathless moment that she had been walking round half-naked in front of the Englishman? She covered her aching head with her hands. How humiliatingly stupid.

Except that he did not actually want her. Not unless she threw her arms round him while she was wearing nothing but her shift. And perhaps not even then. All he saw when he looked at her was a ransom in waiting. She was lucky it was so, and if things turned out differently it was likely to be her fault for flaunting herself.

What a fool she was. Why should she care for the fact that he had been hurt by some now defeated and probably dead Danish warrior? She should be glad.

She came up for air and fixed her gaze on the bright blue bed hangings. Perhaps it was because the Englishman met it with a determination that would not have disgraced the monster-slaying Beowulf. But courage did not make him any less her enemy. It just made him more dangerous.

It was her lawful husband she should be thinking about. Ragnar. Ragnar the Wolfcoat. Ragnar the Dead. It did not seem possible that a terrifying force like Ragnar could be gone. She tried to imagine that formidable shape lying slain beside the trees. So close to the sanctuary of concealment and unable to reach it.

And no one had been able to reach his body. No one had been able to bury him. She would much rather he had been properly buried. Otherwise a tortured spirit like his might not rest.

Nothing left of him but the amulet. She drew it out. It felt warm against her hand, as though it had life. The metal was heated by the warmth of her own body, of course, and yet the strange shapes still seemed alive, still seemed wholly Ragnar's.

She tucked the ring away, out of sight under her shift and her hands clenched. She could feel the shock of her husband's death still there, deep inside her, but she could not make herself grieve, not after what he had done.

Wolfcoat.

She shuddered.

Her fingers twisted in the bedclothes and her tired, frightened mind turned to the way the strong body of the English marauder had been there between her and her thoughts of the berserker and how unexpectedly gentle his arms had been.

She sat up. That was madness. There was no help for her there and neither should she wish it.

What would happen when it was time to go and collect her make-believe ransom? She did not care to imagine the depth of the fury in that winter-cold heart.

Liefwin was .prepared to put up with her on the promise of money. It was what he wanted. His very last thought as he had left the bower had been for the gold arm rings.

One thing was clear. She could not sit still and wait for disaster to strike. She had to escape before it did.

All she needed was money and an armed escort of about thirty. Easy.

She started when there was a noise at the door. Not her captor come back. Please.

But it was only the maid, carrying a jar and a pitcher and what smelled like fresh bread.

"What is this, lady? Not up yet? How tired you look. Did you not get much sleep?"

Sigrid clutched the bedclothes round her. The insinuation in the words and the antagonism beneath were so blatant it occurred to her to wonder whether this was the bed companion that kept the lord Liefwin away from his Danish captive. She was so comely. Sigrid glared at the shapely hips and the breasts that were far larger than hers. Trollop.

The maid smiled. Sigrid smiled back with equal sincerity.

"Of course," said the wench, setting down a pitcher of fresh water. "I did not get much sleep myself…" So it was true. *That* and the English marauder. "The victory feast, you know. I was there, as cup bearer…oh, and I suppose my lord Liefwin told you about the prisoners? They say he will have them killed. A public execution…oh, lady, should I not be saying that to you? Perhaps you knew them?''

''Prisoners?'' she asked, and her throat was so dry she could hardly get the word out.

''The leading men of the town, so they said. But they were a sorry-looking lot to me. The execution…''

''They cannot kill those men.''

''Can they not?'' The taunting voice suddenly changed into bitterness. ''What mercy do the Danes ever show? Lady?'' The wooden bowls Liefwin had used for washing clashed in the girl's hands.

''But they did not want to…it was not…he could not…''

The maid turned round and looked at her, and the words died on Sigrid's lips.

''Anything else, lady? Would you like me to help you dress?'' The bitter eyes of the Saxon girl took in Sigrid's thin shift and the rumpled mess of the bed. It was impossible to tell from the wreck of the sea-green curtains across the room that Liefwin had slept elsewhere.

''No, I want nothing.'' Sigrid watched the girl leave.

I want nothing from any of you Saxons, she thought. But it was not entirely true. Her hands touched the parcel of clean white linen. Bread. The scent of it. It made her belly churn. She touched it. Still warm. And made of fine wheat flour, not rough barley and grits from the quern stone. Cheese, fresh and white. A jug of ale. But she suddenly did not care for the ale. She wanted food and an end to drowning her sorrows and wallowing in the consequences. She ate. Everything. And then she heated water over the fire pit to wash.

Sigrid dipped her hands into the warm water in the fine bronze bowl. There was soap. Two lots of it. She reached for the first with dripping hands. The scent of lovage, clean, astringent, released by the dampness of her fingers, the scent that…Liefwin. That scent had clung to the Saxon's newly washed skin and his damp hair.

Liefwin. Her mind seemed to expand and blossom with the one glimpse she had had of him, washing himself. Before she had been able to force herself to look away. She thought her memory would hold forever the power of that smooth sinuous line that stretched from strongly made shoulder to hip, to taut buttock, to thigh and tightly curved calf muscle, narrow ankle and lithe foot.

It was so stupid of her to think of that. It was irrelevant if he was beautiful. It was nothing to her if he did not seem to belong to the same kind as Ragnar. He was still a predator, as all men were. He was the kind of man who arranged public executions.

Her hand tightened and the soap slid out of her grasp, landing in the rushes on the floor, buried in murk.

She bent her head, but what came into her mind now was not Liefwin of the scented skin but her husband. Her husband and the prisoners.

It was not her fault. She took off her shift. A wife was not responsible for her husband's crimes.

She buried her face in soothing water and then her whole head. She had her own disasters to cope with.

You had to look out for yourself in this life. No one else would.

She came up gasping. She picked up the soap made with honey and sweet marjoram that was obviously meant for her and began to wash her body.

Six captives she hardly knew were not her problem. She was a captive herself and she had nothing. She began to dry herself, but the cloth shook in her hand. It was not true. Women always had one thing. And the way he had looked at her just before he left...

It was how the world worked.

She could not do it, not after she had just escaped from one form of slavery.

But she had nothing else left to bargain with. She could not let six men be hanged for her husband's fault.

She prepared herself to grovel.

He did not come back until it was well dark, but she was still sitting with rapt attention by the well-stoked hearth. She had ale warming by the fireside. She had flavored it with agronomy and precious caraway seeds.

She heard him coming and she leaped up to cast dried lavender heads on the glowing fire. Their scent filled the warm room while the rain beat and hissed outside.

She heard the door latch. She saw it open. She stood up.

She had spent most of the day making herself a new underdress from the loot—no time to pleat it, but the material was very fine. It had short sleeves despite the autumn weather, because he seemed so fascinated by her arms. She had brushed and cleaned her tunic. She had compromised with her hair by leaving it uncovered but coiling it softly up behind her head.

She wished she had the English maid's generous bosom. She smiled. It was not returned.

He moved forward into the light. She swallowed. She had forgotten in the space of a few hours just how formidable he was, how utterly frozen his eyes were. How could she ever have thought she could bend that to her own will?

He might as well have still been wearing his glittering chain mail and helm. Invulnerability walked with him.

He undid the amethyst brooch that held his wet cloak and, sliding it from his heavy shoulders, swung it round to spread it to dry before the fire.

She should be doing that for him instead of standing stock-still like a wantwit.

"L-lord," she stammered, and her voice sounded not husky and seductive but as rusty as though she had not used it for a week. "Let me."

"No need."

But she managed to catch some of the swirling folds in her hands. He shrugged slightly and let it go.

"It is late," he said. "I thought you might have been asleep."

Was it a reproach? Perhaps he wanted solitude. Perhaps he was tired because of the wound. Perhaps he had already rutted his fill on the English maid. Perhaps the last thing he wanted was to be bothered with her. She stole a glance over her shoulder as she arranged swathes of cold, wet wool out to dry. It was impossible to tell anything from that face. She fiddled uselessly with the cloak. He said nothing. She turned round.

Stone face.

This whole thing was hopeless. She did not know why she had started.

He moved away, and because she was watching him with every fiber of her attention, she saw it: the slight, carefully disguised awkwardness, and she had it, the one chink in the close-wrought battle armor.

"Sit down," she said in the steady nonconfrontational tone she had used when it had been necessary to deal with Ragnar. "I have mulled ale. I will pour you some." She did not pause for any response but moved as smoothly as her words. She was used, after all, to dealing with wolves.

He sat in the chair she had placed at the perfect distance from the hearth and she held out the steaming cup. He took it, but the eyes that met hers held not the heat of brute force to be soothed but a cool intelligence as sharp as a sword. She was aware of a small flutter of alarm in her stomach. She quashed it and dredged up another smile, daring to add the faintest challenge this time.

"So," she said, "if I ask you how you are faring, will I get my head bitten off the way I did this morning?"

He did not smile. He never seemed to do anything so human, but there was a small change in the quality of the gaze that held hers and she knew that was, perhaps, as close as it got. That minute change in the cold eyes made little shivers run across her skin and she trembled as she had not done with her fear when he came into the room.

"Was I really that bad?"

"Worse," she returned with a strange courage. The change in the eyes deepened in response and she felt as though the ground had disappeared beneath her feet and she had plunged into something she would never be able to control. It terrified her. But it was also exhilarating.

"Well?" demanded her now reckless voice.

"It is—"

"—nothing?" she supplied.

"Nothing anyone can do anything about," he amended, and the brilliance, the…whatever it was in his eyes made her tingle and she sat down beside him rather abruptly.

"Can you not tell me what happened to you?"

If there was one thing she knew from living off and on with a warrior, it was that they liked nothing more than talking, nay endlessly boasting, about fighting. But she did not get the complacency she expected. She got a look of surprise and something sharp behind the brilliance that almost made the alarm flutter again.

"I do not exactly remember. My attention was elsewhere at the time."

But she had become something of an unwilling expert on the craft of battle.

She watched the faint movement of the muscle in his throat as he drank some of the ale.

"I would say someone hit you with a shield boss, more than once." A shield could, of course, be just as much an offensive weapon as an ax or a sword.

She got the surprise again and this time, perhaps, the acknowledgment she expected.

Was this the moment?

If only he would guzzle down the ale as Ragnar would have done instead of holding the silver-chased cup between his hands. He hardly seemed to want it. He put the cup down.

Now.

She reached out and her hand settled prettily over his where it lay on the table. His flesh was warmed from the heat of the room.

Would he remember how they had touched just so that morning? How he had moved like lightning to protect her from the sword's bite? That was in her mind now. It had been inexplicable, instinct perhaps, the way he had saved her from harm. Nothing more. No reason for her to feel suddenly unclean. She focused her memory on the notched blade of *liyt ræsc*.

"It was a splendid victory," she lied, trying to find the right tone with just the correct mix of natural distress and reluctant admiration; not too much bitterness, some acknowledgment of his superiority.

No response. No vaunting tale of his own achievements. The blue eyes simply narrowed. Why would he not say something, anything?

She leaned forward. She had left the neck of her dress loose under the brightly colored tunic. Surely he must notice.

He did. She was sure he did.

"I know how much I owe to you."

Nothing, not one word. She began again, trying to keep the desperation out of her voice.

"You…you have every right to wish your revenge on me, on all of us. But you chose only to show generosity." She could not quite force her tongue

round the word *mercy*. "For what reason, I know not.
I know only that you must have some reason for it in
your heart that..." And it came, the reaction she had
wanted, just when she had given up hope. It came
and the cold eyes were suddenly luminous with feeling, the loosely clasped hand under hers tightened.

She had him.

She did not understand why, but she surely had
him.

"You have shown so much mercy—" she could
say it now, the words swam from her mouth "—that
I would not ask more but..." She allowed a pause,
entirely contrived.

He reacted.

"Sigrid, what is it?" There was sharpness in his
tone. But the eyes still held light. He bent his lovely
head with the rain-darkened gold hair and the finely
colored complexion toward her, and because she had
knowledge of him, her ears caught the faint indrawn
breath that betokened vulnerability. She tightened her
hand over his in counterfeit of the true coin of her
instinct to pity his hurts that morning.

"Lord," she murmured. He frowned. But whatever
it was still lived in the depths of his eyes, and that
was what she would go for. Except that something in
her own chest seemed to constrict with a pain just
like his. She closed her mind to it. She must not fail
now.

"Lord—" she began again.

"You can use my name."

"Liefwin," she purred. *Dear friend. Her enemy.*
"I have no right to ask you for more than you have
given, but I heard of the...of the men of the town

who are your…your prisoners…'' The hand moved under hers. She closed her fingers on it with the strength of her desperateness.

"I would beg your mercy for them even though you have the right to kill them. I know there is nothing to offer in compensation, no *wergild,* and as for me, I am yours already and I would be so with all I have if…'' She slid her hand suggestively across the back of his, and then up his arm, across the heavy gold bracelets and the fine wool of his tunic. It was like sliding her hand across one of those stone pillars wrought by the giants in earlier time.

Her mind again filled with the one searing glimpse she had had of his naked body, all tough muscle and sinuous lines, as hard and uncompromising as his heart. Her chest tightened further.

She dropped her other hand to his knee, below the table. Her fingers found the smooth material of his trousers, the thick muscle beneath. Her hand curved round the hard mass of his leg. Her heart was beating like August thunder. His thigh was so solid, bigger and thicker than she had expected. It filled her hand and made her palm burn like fire.

Her hand shook. She made herself push it higher. Something sharp and unknown stabbed through her insides so that she thought she must be fit to swoon. It was fear. It was that or it was the strange exhilaration she had felt when she had sought to seduce him with words and she had seen the reaction in his eyes.

Her fingers tangled with the embroidered hem of his tunic. She could sense the dark, secret warmth of his body underneath the fine material. That warmth,

the heavy masculinity of his body…it set her senses
alight and yet it filled her with terror.

It was too much, too unknown, too dangerous.

She looked up and saw his face.

She should not have done that. She should not have
looked at his eyes. She could not move and she could
not draw back.

Her throat locked up so that she had to force the
words past her lips.

"Such gratitude as would be mine to show
would—"

The stone-hard arm flicked out of her grasp in one
small, controlled movement that sent her hand spinning harmlessly backward through the air. It was so
effortless, so utterly unexpected, she scarce understood what had happened.

He stood up.

No overturned chair this time, no shouted words,
but the entire world had changed.

Two steps to cross the room with no sign of the
weakness she had thought to exploit, only the raw
strength that she had seen from the first, that she had
felt under her hand.

He leaned against the wall, in the black shadows.
She could not see his face, only the poised, arrogant
lines of his body.

"If you are going to take up whoring you would
do better to save it for Oslac. He is in command here,
not me. I lead only the men of the *éored* of Mercia."
How that must rankle. She glared full at him.

"I am sure Oslac would give your charms all the
appreciation they deserve," he said, and his gaze on
her body was as cold as ice, "but you are just as

unlikely to get the payment you want. Assuming I understand you properly.''

He did. His scorn cut. It was unfair. The whole thing was unfair. She had suffered enough through being married to an abomination. She had not asked for this. She had not asked to have her home destroyed and her life. She had not asked to be captured. To have to abase herself by pleading with some mood-proud English thane who thought everything and everyone was beneath him.

She was not a whore.

She ground her teeth. If his precious sword had been within her grasp now, she would have used it.

''I am asking you to show mercy to those who are in your power.'' It came out like some vile accusation and it was treated as such.

''Why should I? Do you realize what they have done? Do you know where I have been this last hour? Watching my cousin Alfwin struggle with death. He has scarce seventeen winters. He is unlikely to see any more and it will be up to me to tell his fifteen-year-old wife that she has no husband and the child she is expecting will have no father.

''Do you know how many more men are dead and how many more will never be whole again? Do you know how many more women will be grieving like Alfwin's wife? Like you?''

''I...but I did not ask for—'' It made no difference. She might as well not have spoken. He moved in the shadows and the bright, cold eyes raked her.

''Did I or did any of us ask to have our country invaded, our homes robbed and destroyed, our families killed or taken as slaves?''

"Well, you have had your revenge," she spat, focusing her thoughts on the burning hell of the town. "Now I suppose you wish to complete it on a group of poor captives who can no longer defend themselves." Why had she ever thought...

"No."

"I suppose you think vengeance is...what?"

"I said no. Even though it is what I should do."

"I...but then..." She stopped, utterly confounded. *Why?* If his cousin died, that alone would be enough to cry out for vengeance, let alone everything else he had said.

It could not be for her persuading. He could hardly be expecting any return of her pretended affections after this. He was not even looking at her, but at something else across the room. Yet there was nothing there except the carved chest. Perhaps he was looking at nothing at all because, when he spoke again, his voice held nothing.

"I am not going to kill six people for doing something they were forced to do."

"Forced?" Her voice came out as a sort of squeak. He knew.

He knew what had happened. Someone in his position would know, doubtless. She should have realized, would have, if she had thought about it. But he could not know that...she wanted to ask, to make him speak. The blue gaze flicked over her and then away again. No, she did not.

"If you lived in that town, you must know, surely. Those men had no wish to oppose King Edward. One of them, for heaven's sake, is English. Yesterday's battle took place because the Danish army of East

Anglia and the shipmen wanted it. It was their rep-
resentatives who *persuaded* the men of your town,
was it not?''

She would not betray herself if she could only stay
silent, stay still. But her hand went to the amulet at
her neck. Her luck he did not see. He was not even
looking. It was the other corner of the room which
fascinated him.

''One of those sent to persuade was a wolfcoat, a
berserker. It was a Dane who caused the first deaths
here.''

She bowed her head, forced herself to stillness. Her
fingers were clenched tight round a long thin shard
of metal shrouded in thin linen. Odin's spear. Berserkers belonged to Odin.

She forced her hand away, as though the Englishman could see what she did, guess the significance of
what she held hidden. She straightened her fingers.
She must try to appear as though nothing…he had
not finished.

''The agreement to join the battle,'' he said, ''was
made across the body of the man the berserker killed
outright and the screams of the one he left half-
alive.''

Her head was forced up. She had not understood
quite that much. Sickness choked inside her.

She must not let him see it. She swallowed bitterness. But his eyes watched her with the look that
could measure the wellspring of her breath.

It had not been her fault. What had happened had
not been something she had had any control over. She
had to cling to that thought, because if she let even

one suspicion of weakness, one harsh searing trace of guilt enter her mind, his English eyes would see it.

She held her head very high, very still. But she wondered whether he did see it. There was a small flicker in the depths of those watchful eyes and she thought nothing could deceive that careful assessment of what people truly were.

"I did not know," she said, "but even if I had—" The words *it could have made no difference* were cut off as something frighteningly dangerous flared in the piercing eyes.

"It is not my way," he said. "I would not care to complete that man's handiwork."

Contempt dripped from the cold preciseness of his English voice.

"But they said you were going to have them killed." Her gaze never left that elegant, jeweled figure.

"No, not so. That was only Oslac's drunken boast and they are not his to kill. It was not something I said. Who told you I did?"

There was no reason why she should protect the English maid from that chilling wrath.

"Who was it?"

"It was just something I overheard. I must have misunderstood," then, "so they are safe?"

"Perhaps. I have told you, I am not in command here. You might still need to use your charms on Oslac. Or perhaps you should save them for King Edward since I took possession of the prisoners in his name."

She could not even respond to the gibe, not with the screams of the maimed man ringing in her ears.

"Edward would kill them."

"Not if he has any sense."

"What do you mean?"

"I mean that if Oslac can be prevented from sacking and burning everything in sight, the entire countryside is set to rise with Edward when he gets here. I think a magnanimous royal gesture from him is going to have far more effect than six heads."

If that were true...if such a thing were possible. The poised, arrogant figure and the cold voice of the Englishman seemed to mock her.

"He would not do it."

"My money is on it." The irony in his voice was unmistakable and the thought occurred to her that for someone who was here on loan he had been rather high-handed in taking prisoners off his commander.

"Edward's goal is the same as his father's, a peace that lasts."

The irony was quite gone from his voice. She thought of the English King Edward's father, Alfred of Wessex, the one called "the Great," the one who had stopped the advance of her people. She could not see his eyes for shadows.

"Unlike Oslac," said Liefwin the Mercian, "Edward is a king." He used the word *dryhten,* which could also mean war leader. "He will do what is best."

The handsome face swam out of the dimness and the irony was back in full force. "Understanding and forethought are to be preferred in every case. That should be the duty of kings. And thanes. I thought you knew Beowulf off by heart."

He picked up the still-damp cloak. She watched

him, so perfect, so seemingly untouchable, as he crossed to the door.

He paused. ''Were you expecting me to behave like some Danish berserker? I would not sully my hands so. Such people do not deserve to walk on middle earth and they would not if I found them or any of their like.''

She turned her head away, in case he saw, in case he could read what was inside it. Surely it would not be beyond those cold blue eyes to do so. She heard the door shut.

Such people do not deserve to walk on middle earth.

They would not if I found them or any of their like.

He knew there were so many things she had not told him.

What would he do, Liefwin the Mercian? What vengeance would he not feel bound to take if he found out? If he suspected for one moment that the berserker was, had been, her husband?

Chapter Six

The next day, she made herself go outside.

Raw, cold air pinched her face and her fingers, and she had to hold her skirts high out of the mud. It was going to rain.

She made sure she had her back to the ruin of the town and then she looked up.

She expected the brawling rabble of three days ago, but it was…orderly. Men moved between the straggle of buildings with an air of purpose. They called to each other in Liefwin's accent. Someone laughed.

It seemed impossible after so much destruction and so much hell. She lifted her gaze higher, across to the shadows of the distant woods where Ragnar had died.

Was that dark fastness still crawling with the fugitives who had managed to gain its shelter? She did not know.

How would she ever get away? And she had to, as soon as possible, before…her name. Among the men's foreign voices, someone had called her name. Liefwin. But it was not. It was Ceolfrith, the loyal henchman. He looked almost furtive.

''In here.'' She was hauled into a small dim room with nothing but benches and a bed. Her eyes widened and then she saw that the bed was already occupied.

''Do not worry. Alfwin cannot hear us, poor lad.''

''Alfwin? The lord's cousin?''

Watching my cousin struggle with death. The bitter words seemed to strike at her out of the air, driving her feet forward, toward the bed.

She looked down and stifled a scream. It was what Liefwin would look like if he were dead. Behind her, something moved. A dense, hulking shadow tilted crazily down the wall, uncanny, death-dark. It fell across the ash-pale face before her and she felt the small hairs rise on the back of her neck, the way they did when only one person was near.

The amulet round her neck dragged like lead, as though it would force her head down, as though it had the power, as though it still held the life force of its owner.

But that was impossible. Its owner was gone from this world forever. The dead were dead. They could no longer harm anyone. Except *draugar.* They were never dead. They were shadows that—

''What is it?''

She blinked and found the familiar bulk of Ceolfrith standing beside her. The grotesque shadow he had cast across the bed solidified into something quite ordinary. The arrangement of light and shade on the pale face of the warrior lying in front of her changed and she saw how young he was, the strong structure of the man's features stretching the rounded flesh of the boy. He was not so very like Liefwin after all, just the bright hair and the wide cheekbones, perhaps. It was…it was a much more open face than Liefwin's.

The muscles in her neck unclamped.

"Will he live?"

"If you had asked me that yesterday I would have said not, but now, maybe. It is Liefwin I want to know about, not Alfwin. Perhaps you could tell me what is wrong with him."

"Me? Why should I know…" She stopped. She was supposed to be the lord Liefwin's trull and bed companion. "Why do you not talk to him yourself?" she snapped.

"For pity's sake, woman, if I could talk to Liefwin, would I be asking you?"

Of course not. Who would ask the opinion of a Danish bed warmer? He was as bad as his master. Except…except he was worried, miserably so.

She clenched her teeth. What was this? A conspiracy to make her feel sorry for Saxon marauders? Mercian marauders? She would not. She did not. There was a faint groan from the bed. Ceolfrith's gaze flicked toward it.

"Looks so like Liefwin. Like Liefwin used to look before…"

Before *what?*

"Do you know how old Liefwin was when his father was killed?"

No, and I do not care. "Killed?" But she knew the answer before it came.

"By Viking raiders."

She glared at him.

"Not six winters. It was me that was like a father to him even though he had enough kin. He was a good lad, for all he was too strong and too clever by half.''

She could imagine too clever by half, but her mind balked at the thought of Liefwin as a five-year-old running around with muddied knees. And no father.

''We used to have some terrible arguments,'' said Ceolfrith, with what she could only describe as wistfulness. ''I was hard on him, but you have to be when someone is going to be in charge of people and is as strong as he is.'' For strong substitute *arrogant* and *coldhearted*. ''Perhaps it was too much. But I wanted to teach him to think.'' Ceolfrith kicked some non-existent debris under the bed. ''I succeeded.''

Understanding and forethought are to be preferred in every case.

You would have done better to teach him to feel. Her lip curled.

''And now he repays you by not bothering to speak to you?''

''It is not the lad's fault.''

But she had lost patience with such sentiment. She did not see who else's fault it could be. It was hardly likely to be Ceolfrith the misty-eyed retainer's.

''It is nothing extraordinary,'' she snapped. ''Six broken ribs, I would say. Perhaps he should not have been so busy sacking the town.''

''*What?*''

''Bruising,'' she relented. ''It must be, or he would be in a worse state than his cousin by now, surely. It pains him and sometimes he seems to find it hard to breathe. But,'' she added at the sight of Ceolfrith's face, ''he is not coughing up blood and he certainly doesn't seem to think it is something anyone needs to be concerned about.'' Particularly not someone who brought him up. ''I do not know why he has to make such a mystery about it.''

''I do—''

''Ceolfrith, have you seen…''

They both started. They must have been too deep in their own thoughts to hear the door.

''Oh, I am sorry,'' said the newcomer, coming to a crashing halt in the doorway. ''I did not realize…''

He was a large young man with bright red hair and freckles, clad in a byrnie. He obviously knew she was his lord's foreign bed warmer because he looked at her with that avid curiosity that made her skin crawl.

''Later, Cerdic,'' said Ceolfrith, ''just—''

But she did not stop to hear the rest of it. She did not want to hear anything else Ceolfrith had to say and she had nothing to say to him.

The carrot-headed youth grinned at her with gap teeth. She picked up her skirts and surged past him, out into the cold daylight. The folds of her cloak brushed across his chain mail. But she did not deviate from her path by a hairbreadth and he jumped back with what might have been another apology, but she did not stop to hear.

She had to get away from the turmoil of her thoughts.

She crashed past two more idiots in chain mail. They stared after her like the gap-toothed redhead. She surged round the corner, out of their sight, anywhere she could be on her own and not plagued by Mercians.

She would bar the door of the bower and bury herself in eternal darkness if she had the slightest hope that it could keep a man like Liefwin out. If it would give her peace. If—

She heard his voice, unmistakable this time. He was shouting. The way he had shouted at her when she had suggested he might let her go to Skaldford to collect a nonexistent ransom.

A shudder took her as she remembered the force of that. Her shoulders sank closer against the cold damp bulk of the wall behind her. The wind whipped at her cloak, shadows tugged at its flailing edges and she realized the desperate urgency of her steps had taken her in entirely the wrong direction.

"Colchester could have been taken," yelled the scourge of the Essex Danes. "I could have done it."

She imagined how his face would look, just as she had seen it, with the fires that lay beneath that frozen surface shockingly visible.

"The fortress could have been ours by now, just like this town."

The voice had an utter, blood-freezing confidence. Memory took her further back, to the moment of bottomless panic when every defender of this town had realized they were lost. The moment had had a hideous inevitability of its own. After the first shock of disbelief had come the growing, numbing awareness of just how unstoppable, how terrifyingly competent the assault had been.

She thought she knew, now, where that competence had come from.

"Nonsense," said another voice, attempting to counter, drawing out the shape of the word in the heavy-toned speech of Wessex. "Nonsense," it said again. It spoke louder, blustering to cover the unease, and she knew without even seeing the speaker that he had been favored with his own glimpse of the fires beneath.

"We needed time after the battle..." Anger gave the voice a sharper edge, volatile and full of aggression, the kind of anger that sprang quickly and willfully, and so was all the more dangerous.

"Time for what?" Liefwin's voice in answer sank back into ice, black ice that had its own danger. The sort that made knots out of her insides, the sort to be avoided at all costs. But her feet drew her closer toward the open window, the open door round the side of the building. Because she could no longer make out Liefwin's words, only the ice.

"...wholly wrong..." Her shoe caught a small stone. "...lose people's support..." She held still but the stone wavered, skittered into a ditch with a tiny smacking noise. "...not just raiding parties. Something outside the walls of this town that..." Her heart thudded. If only she could hear. *What* outside the walls? What raiding parties? Where? And if there were, how would she ever get through them, ever get away to where she might be safe?

The Wessex man protested, muffled, indistinct, mumbling against Liefwin's cracking ice.

She eased farther forward.

"Dead," said Liefwin, "all of them. So that you would now know mercy existed." Her hands tightened on the roughness of timber. Her skin crawled.

"I will not just stand aside and do nothing." She jumped. His voice was suddenly so close, beside the door. She heard the heaviness of booted feet, fast, angry. She clutched at her windblown cloak, twisted.

''My men will find these raiders, these Vikings, these Danes. They will never escape.'' The chill of the words cut through the thickness of the wall between them, inside her skin. She sprang for the concealment of the next building. But she had left it too late. She heard the footsteps in the open air. She had nowhere to go.

She turned round.

''What the—'' It was not Liefwin. ''By all the saints…''

Small brown eyes sunk in too much flesh, a scraggly beard, nondescript hair, massive flesh. Not particularly tall, just massive. Gold. Laughter. He saw her and he laughed, the man from Wessex.

''What a little prize.'' His hand moved. She actually saw it move but it was not *his* hand that caught her, just above the elbow, in a jangle of heavy gold.

''Sigrid. Here? How…how opportune.''

She looked up. At Liefwin's eyes. They held hers and they sought something out of her eyes. She did not know what. All she knew, all she read, was that the anger was still in him, too, and behind it a terrible frustration. It was quite different from the other man's anger. It was controlled, by some ruthless exertion of willpower. But that was not the only difference. It was different because Liefwin was different. Everything, but everything inside him was directed to the purpose his mind chose to give it.

''Let me take you back.''

Of course. The prisoner had stepped out of her cage, had gone out of her allotted sphere, was wandering around the enemy camp as though she had a will of her own.

The pressure of his grip on her arm increased, not exactly punishing, just inexorable, drawing her away, toward the sunlight pooling round the door, toward him. Her feet moved.

''Saint Birinus! That is never your—''

She missed the rest, because Liefwin spoke, in his ice voice, and her feet were moving down the path they should have taken, toward the bower. She did not know the exact words that were said because she could not bear to hear herself described as she was, in that flat Saxon drawl. Not even in Mercian. Particularly not in Mercian. Not from his lips.

But he was drawing her away and there was no room in her mind to think of it. The only thing she could think of was the touch of his hand on her arm. She could feel each separate finger through her clothes.

She spared one glance for the other man nearly hidden by the deep-blue bulwark that was Liefwin's shoulder.

He was standing in the mud staring after her. She felt as though she could sense his gaze through her shoulder blades all the way back to the bower.

''Who was that?''

Liefwin shut the door. The bolt clicked home.

''Do you want to know?''

Yes. No. She did not know. She just had to say something. The scourge of the Essex Danes, close up, standing over her while she sat at the little table inside four close walls was too much.

''Why not?''

''What were you doing outside?''

Talking to your loyal retainer because you will not,

said her mind. *Introducing myself to your dying cousin.* Not a single word would come out.

"Sigrid?"

She knocked over the mead flask by accident.

"I wanted air. I did not realize it was forbidden to step outside the door." She tried to keep her voice firm, but she was already on her feet, mopping up the mead by reflex. Ragnar would have flattened her by now. Mead was expensive.

She could not get it mopped up fast enough. It dribbled over the edge of the table. The cloth was soaked. It smelled sweet, pungent. Too sweet, too pungent. Too much. It was not her mead. It was not her expense. It was not even the Mercian's. It was plunder. Sack and ruin, now endlessly going on somewhere outside the town until the scourge of the Danes stopped it.

She flung the soaking cloth at the wall and the scourge of the Danes caught it before it could strike the bright tapestry, quite absentmindedly, by working out where it would land and how fast it would fall and in which direction. He was not even trying. She sat down again.

"You do not have to tell me who that man was," she said. "I do not want to know. I do not see how it can possibly matter." She sounded childish. She was so furious with herself for letting weakness show. Her hands were not steady.

The mead cloth hissed in the fire pit, a shadow moved, collected itself into the savage shape of the Mercian beside her.

"That was Oslac. Commander of this army. Vaguely related, in a way that no one but he can remember, to the High King Edward of Wessex. He is an idiot.''

She blinked. Oslac. Oslac who wanted the six prisoners Liefwin held. Oslac who stood back and allowed looting and rape and pillage after the battle. Mead fumes rose out of the flames. Flames. Flames all round her.

''I remember now,'' she said. ''I remember you said that to me when I thought we were all going to die in the fires of the world's end. You said it was because of an idiot.''

''Yes.'' There was a breath of hesitation and then skin, mead-damp, warm beyond compare, touched hers. As though it had a will of its own, like compulsion.

But once it touched, it settled. No half measures, just assurance, so full of purpose, always.

''I have never heard anyone speak like you.'' She thought of Ragnar the Wolfcoat and what would have happened if one of his men, someone like Harek perhaps, had spoken openly just so. Or even if someone as invincible as Ragnar had spoken so of some jarl or king. But thoughts of retribution did not seem to affect Liefwin of the clear, steady eyes.

''Are you not...wary.'' She had enough sense to substitute another word for *afraid*. ''Even a little wary of what power that man, that Oslac, has if he is in command?''

''No.''

Her eyes sought his face. Such coolness.

''Are you not wary, not *afraid* of anything?'' The face did not change, but it was odd how eyes so bright blue could go quite dark in an instant. Black.

"Not anymore. Except—"

"How enviable."

"Nay, do not envy me that, Sigrid. It is no boon."

"It seems so to me." Shivers crossed her spine. "There is so much in the world eager to do harm and now there are wolves howling outside the walls—" She cut herself short. She did not want him to know she had been slinking outside his door, standing there, deliberately listening to all that he said to his commander.

"Wolves?"

Her gaze turned away, fixed on the flames in the hearth. But their warmth could not reach her and she shuddered because Ragnar was in her mind, would not leave it. She had not meant to think of him, only of the unknown raiding party. But Ragnar would not go. His memory hung between them like a death shade, visible only to her.

"People can be wolves." The words seemed to force themselves past the dryness of her lips.

"Human wolves? Why do you say that? What do you mean?" His voice was sharp and the hand touching hers seemed to vibrate with a sudden tenseness, but she could not look at him, only at the heart of the hearth whose warmth could not reach her. "Berserkers?"

Her hand clenched. At least it would have done, but his stopped it, quite deliberately, so that his fingers interlaced with hers and she could not move. It could have been a response to the betraying sign of her fear or it could have been the physical counterpart of the sharpness in his voice.

This time she did not dare look up. She hardly

dared breathe. She tried to fight the tightness out of her body, because he would feel it through the helpless bond of her hand.

"You are afraid, are you not? You were afraid before, when they came to get me for the victory feast and someone howled like the wolf-mad. You were terrified."

She bit her lip. The urge to blurt it out. To tell him exactly why she was afraid and exactly what her particular wolf-mad husband had done was almost overpowering. But she could not. He had made it so clear to her what he thought of the things her husband had done. He hated it. He was fast on the path of vengeance. That hatred, that stone-hard contempt would fall on her.

He had every reason.

So she suppressed it all and her voice said only, "It is because I have seen what they can do. We all have. The whole town has." The whole town had landed in destruction because of it. There could be no doubt in her mind now about that.

She could say it. Common knowledge. It was all she could say, and the only warmth left in the coldness was the Mercian's hand touching hers.

She thought he would speak, question her further— she even heard him draw breath. But he did not. His hand, incredibly and beyond the limits of imagination, closed gently for one instant around hers. She thought she would never forget that touch as long as she lived, never be able to survive without it. But it slid away. His hand hovered for an instant above her skin, so close she could sense its touch in her mind.

So infinitely far beyond her reach.

She wanted to clutch at it. But she could not. Because of who he was. And then the hand withdrew and she was left with nothing.

Her breath scratched in her throat.

"Do sorrows never end?" The words burst out. Like an accusation, with all the force of despair, not just for the hopelessness of her situation now, but the despair that had crawled with deadly strength beneath the surface of her life, ever since she had grown old enough to understand what life was.

Her shoulders hunched and she glanced up, because she expected some reaction to that. It was there, in the wide darkness of his eyes. But it was not the bitter cold of his anger. It was something else, something she recognized by instinct. It was a raw, mirror image of her own despair.

Then it was gone, suppressed so quickly she might only have imagined it. Because there was nothing she could see now but the relentless shield of his will.

But she knew she had judged aright. Because judgments like that arose not from knowledge, not from skill, but from recognition.

"There is no end, is there?" she said out of the dragging weight of her life.

"I do not know."

She recognized the weariness in his words, saw how the whole fierce unsparing power of his mind was summoned up to push that aside.

"All that is given to us is to do what we can with the strength we have."

"And if we have no power to do so?"

Her gaze was caught in his, just as her mind was caught by that resolve.

"We all have power over our own deeds."

It was terrible, the way he said that, the look in his eyes.

"I do not know," she said, "that that is true. There are others who have their part in shaping out lives. No one is isolated, whatever choices we make."

"Yet our choices are still our own."

His eyes, those eyes that saw and thought too much, pinned her, as though he could see inside her head, right through to the deepest parts inside, to where Ragnar's death shade lurked and the shades of all those other deaths her husband had caused.

"I cannot see an end to this. Not for me." He did not say anything else.

She did not reply. Because there was nothing she could say.

He held her gaze a moment longer and then he stood up. His cloak swirled. Gold flashed. He went outside and she watched him go. Watched until he was long beyond her sight. Watched the space where his body had been. Watched the very air that he had breathed.

She buried her head in her hands. She was so tired. But there was no rest. And no other choice but one.

She had to get away.

Chapter Seven

Hᴏᴡ?

The four walls of her prison would suffocate her. Sigrid's feet paced the room in ever-decreasing circles. Everything jumbled in her head: the burning horror of the town, Liefwin, the pallid face of Alfwin the child warrior and the death shadow over it, Ragnar. Ragnar and the screaming man. Ragnar forcing compliance on a whole town for the blood lust he craved. Ceolfrith's worried face. Liefwin. Liefwin's touch.

Liefwin who never stopped thinking. Liefwin whose father had been killed by Vikings. Liefwin who was on the path of vengeance. Liefwin who never, never rested.

Liefwin with the cold heart and the warm, warm body.

She tried not to remember yesterday in this room. How it had felt when she had laid her hand on that solid knee and touched that muscular arm hung with gold. It had been pretence. She did not want Liefwin in that way. She did not want any man. They were vile.

Pain and sorrow had no ending. It was beyond anyone's deeds or anyone's choice to change that, whatever he said. She remembered the weariness in his voice that had underlain the unceasing determination he so fiercely believed in.

She thought of his wounds.

Her hands balled into fists. She did not feel sorry for him.

Her choice was made. Anything else entertained in her mind was madness.

She had to get away. Now.

But she had nothing. Nothing except what she could loot in her turn. The silver-chased cups and the silver-backed mirror were worth most. If she could only pilfer just one of her captor's arm rings she could make her way to the ends of the earth. Back to Denmark if she wanted to.

Back to a family who did not want her.

She dropped to her knees beside the two chests in the corner that held the Mercian's possessions. Locked, and far too heavy for her to carry.

She ran her hand over the nearest, so beautifully carved, a cross in the middle. Her hand traced its outline. Liefwin was English, that was naturally what he believed in. If only she knew more about it than what she had picked up from her Saxon neighbors. The new Way held such comforting thoughts.

Thoughts. She must think. If she was going to survive, she needed food and more clothes than she had and anything she could get her hands on that was portable and salable. The moon was waxing. Tomorrow night there might be enough light to make her way, and still enough shadows to hide in. Surely one person could evade whatever evil lay beyond the walls.

The storm that had been gathering out of the cloudy, windblown sky hit. She could hear what sounded like hail drum against the roof. If only it were possible to steal a horse. She would look at how they were kept.

She came to the conclusion that it would be easier to subdue the whole of Britain single-handedly than to steal anything off Liefwin.

She had made two forays, one after dark in a freezing rain that should have kept all of Liefwin's churls and hearth companions where they belonged, beside the hearth.

It had not.

She was watched. Guarded. She might not actually be kept in fetters, but it came to the same thing. She could not move without some Saxon oaf breathing down her neck.

Liefwin the clutch-fisted was not going to let one pile of ransom money, however paltry, escape him.

When he came back, she was sewing, not fine clothes for seducing the unseducible, but thick, solid clothes for surviving autumn in the rain. Hail. She could hear it.

The door shut with a bang.

His thick cloak was black from the rain. Water streamed off his rain-darkened hair. That was surely not a small lump of white ice on his shoulder. It was a hailstone. It fell off and began to melt on the floor.

''Lord?''

She did not know what to expect after all that they

had said. Coldness, perhaps, to match the traces of hail that still clung to his cloak.

Their choices, such as they were, had been made long ago. Their feet trod paths that were quite different. Quite set.

"You are soaking. You must be…" frozen.

There might be anger left over from yesterday's disastrous attempt at seduction. There might be anger left over from finding her running loose round the camp while he was discussing with his commander the next step in King Edward's campaign of conquest. Reconquest. There might be suspicion.

There might be…there might be the terrible destructive weariness that seemed to dog not just her footsteps but his. On their quite separate paths—

"Liefwin?"

She had used his name. What on earth had she used his name for?

He looked at her. His face was white, dead white, no trace of its habitual color. It looked like his cousin's face. The chill prickling of dread stroked the back of her neck. The light from the oil lamp threw his shadow across the tapestried wall. Dark, moving. She got to her feet and her sewing fell to the floor.

"You look as though you have seen a ghost," he said.

"No!"

He frowned, because it was far too vehement a reply and she wondered whether that would be enough to call down his wrath on her head. But he said nothing else. He moved into the light of the fire. His strong fingers reached up to unpin the amethyst brooch at his shoulder.

He was not very handy at it. The solid fingers fumbled with an awkwardness that was painful to watch. Would he never manage it?

She was not about to offer her assistance after last night's stupidity over seduction.

She picked up her sewing and shook bits of dried meadowsweet and woodruff off it.

She looked up just as the momentous task of undoing the brooch pin was accomplished. He swung the sodden cloak off his shoulders.

He was still soaking.

The tunic and trousers clung to every last muscle of his body. The bone needle stabbed into her finger through two thicknesses of cloth. She swore. In Danish. At least he would not understand it. She clutched at her finger underneath the cloth and he glanced across at her but made no comment.

Then, "I should get changed."

It might help. Puddles of melted hail were forming round his feet. The stylish shoes were probably ruined. He took a step forward. You could see the shadows of the muscle in his thighs through the soaking tunic which clung to the soaking trousers which clung to his soaking flesh. The ruined shoes stumbled.

She dropped her sewing for the second time.

"The blue tunic and the gray trousers are dry and there is some mulled ale on the hearth. I..." Mulled ale flavored with herbs and spices, the weapon of failed seduction. Yesterday suddenly thrummed between them like ringing harp strings. She got a look colder than the hail that beat against the roof and found its way hissing into the flames of the fire. She snatched up the fresh tunic and trousers.

"Dried by the maid, not me. I am sure you can accept them without the slightest danger," she said thrusting the clothes in his direction.

He took the other end of the tunic. A droplet of water fell off the end of his streaming hair onto the back of her hand. So cold. It stabbed her flesh like cutting ice. She jumped. Her hand slid down the tunic until it touched him. She let out another Danish oath. Nobody could be that cold and still be alive.

"For pity's sake," she snapped in English, "come over to the fire and take your clothes off."

It was a second before the realization of what she had said hit her. Her jaw dropped. How could she have…

But he laughed.

It had the force of a small miracle. She had never imagined him capable of such a reaction. Neither perhaps had he, because the laughter faded under her stunned gaze into a breathtaking smile that yet held behind it the uncertainty of something long unused, or perhaps long forgotten. The oath, this time, was only in her head, but it lost none of its force for all that.

If he possessed such a smile, why did he never use it?

It vanished even as she looked at it, but a little of it lingered, perhaps, in his eyes.

"It is all right," he said. "You do not have to tell me you did not mean that as it sounded. But all the same, I think it is an even better approach than last night."

Her face flamed. But he did not seem angry as she had expected and the softness lingered surprisingly in his eyes. She wondered whether he was just too exhausted and perhaps too ill to bother with fury. She remembered the glimpse she had had, or imagined, of the savage power of his weariness that morning.

She thought he looked ill. She thought he looked like Alfwin. She shivered and pushed the thought of black shadows aside. And of despair. If he wanted to call a temporary truce she could do with it.

Perhaps it really was not possible to face sorrows without end. She was simply too tired.

Too tired to deal with anything more complex than wet clothes.

So she concentrated on things as they were and, making a derisive noise to show that she was not afraid of him, she inquired, "Are you going to die of cold while you stand there flattering yourself?"

But he was an impossible man to put down, and the remains of the unexpected smile kindled again, making her face burn hotter. She let go of his clothes and turned away to look for some hot water, putting as much space as she could between them. But the warmth seemed to seep down from her face and her neck deep inside her.

She found the cloths, a jug of steaming water and a bronze bowl. She risked the smallest of glances in his direction before bringing them across.

The sword belt was slung over the back of the chair. He was peeling off the wet tunic. He did not know she was looking at him. She saw with no disguise the painfulness of his movements. She could not understand why so much had to be hidden. Why he did not at least trust in Ceolfrith. Even if they had had one of their fondly remembered arguments, surely it could be forgiven in one who loved him with the unstinting love of a father.

So cold.

"Cloths," she said, before his hand could move to the trousers, "and hot water."

"It is all right. I can get it."

"I have already done it."

He half turned. She did not react by so much as the movement of a muscle to the hideous mess that was his left side. She tried to gauge, without appearing to look at him, whether it was better or worse. Ceolfrith would never believe that this was the only glimpse of Liefwin the coldhearted that she was likely to get.

She held out the cloths.

While you could hardly say it looked better, it did look clean. Perhaps it was the length of time he seemed to spend out in the rain, but the area of crushed skin in the middle of the bruising did not look elf-shot.

She handed over the water jug and the bronze bowl and her gaze was caught not by the hideous bruising but by the creamy skin and the light covering of golden hair across the undamaged part of his chest, the way the compact muscles moved.

She looked away and became very busy with the mulled ale. The strange warmth seemed to have spread right through her body, radiating outward from the pit of her stomach to the tips of her fingers.

She gave him a long time to get dressed while she concentrated on getting the strange and tingling feeling of warmth under control. When she turned, he was dressed again, although his tunic was unbelted and his feet were bare. He was dragging a comb through his tangled hair with a ruthlessness that made her wonder how many teeth it would have left by the end of the process.

"Here, drink this." She held out the heated cup. He stepped across to take it. His whole body was shaking. No one should be that cold. No one should drive themselves into such a state. She understood that much if nothing else. Right or wrong, friend or enemy no longer seemed to matter. On a practical level it was something she could deal with.

He swallowed the ale with a satisfying speed and she refilled the cup. Perhaps he was not shivering quite so much.

"Drink the rest of that and sit down. No, not there—" and when he gave her a startled look "—closer to the fire." She did not say *lord* and she did not say *please*. She just looked at him.

He stared back.

"Anything else?" he inquired with a certain understated challenge. She took it up instantly.

"Yes. Turn the chair round a bit so the heat can dry your hair."

She caught up the heavy, wet swath as he moved and fanned it out over the back of the chair.

"What are you doing?" There was no amusement, now, only sharpness.

"Being more practical than you," she retorted so that there could be no possible misunderstanding that she was trying to seduce him again. She was no longer afraid of him. Not right now. In fact she felt rather light-headed and daring.

She slid down beside the chair and touched his naked foot. It moved just as she had expected and she caught it deftly and held it fast between her two hands so that he could not free it without either treading on her or kicking out at her. She did not think he would do either, not unless he really lost his temper.

She was right, but his voice when he next spoke told her that it had been a rather dangerous ploy after all.

"Sigrid, just what do you think you are about?"

She took a breath and then she plunged on with it.

"I am not thinking at all. I do not want to." She could not explain it, not even to herself. It must just be that a person could only take so much of disaster and loss and uncertainty and sheer…aloneness before they had to seek something else. Or at least pretend to themselves that there was something.

"You said right at the beginning," she persisted, "that in these four walls there was only us, nothing else, and we could do as we wanted. I am doing what I want."

She knew it did not make sense. Perhaps it was just cowardice on her part. She could not face what had happened and what her future held, and just for to-night, she wanted to shove it away somewhere unseen where it could not torment her. She tried glancing up at the face above her, but it was impossible to read. The smile was no longer there, although she did not think there was antagonism.

She took a breath and added carefully, "But it is as you said, there are no expectations."

There was complete silence.

Perhaps she would have things her way. She would soon know. Her hands moved experimentally across his flesh. Nothing. Her touch firmed, moving from the strong arch of his foot to the thickly padded heel.

But if the frozen foot did not pull itself out of her grasp, neither did it relax.

If it was not precisely a victory, at least the truce seemed destined to last. Her fingers moved with greater gentleness along the more delicate bones in the top of the foot and then down toward the toes. His flesh chilled her fingers.

"If you want to get chilblains," she said on the chance that there might be a remnant of the amusement still left in the frigid depths of his mind, "just carry on as you are doing."

"I am sure I already have them. What do you think I do? Come home to this every night?"

The remnants of amusement were still there. She hid a smile. *I am sure you could,* she thought. *If you were moved to allow it, I am sure all the English trollops would be falling over themselves.*

Her hands moved faster and with more confidence and for no reason at all the foot suddenly relaxed. She looked up. He sat with his head thrown back and his eyes half-closed.

The closed eyes and the pale face. For an instant she lost the safe warmth of the room.

"Do you believe there are such things as *draugar?*" she blurted out.

The blue eyes opened, startled.

Why on earth had she voiced that, and so abruptly?

"As what?"

She did not know the English word for them.

"The undead. They walk. *Draugar* seek vengeance. They are usually round burial grounds but…"

If they had been killed on a battlefield and not properly buried, who knew what they might do or where they might roam.

"Oh. Something like *orc-neas?* No." There it was, just like that, complete confidence. She was aware of a twinge of envy at such single-mindedness.

"Why on earth would you be thinking of such things?"

Because of you. You and your cousin. Because your cousin is on what might be his deathbed, and because you behave in a way that is likely to drive you there and I do not know why. Because of shadows. Because I am still afraid of my dead husband.

Draugar seek vengeance.

"No reason."

"No reason?"

His hand landed on her shoulder. It was still half-frozen. She could feel its coldness seeping through her dress, but it was alive and he was no longer shaking and there was, perhaps, just the faintest tinge of color in his face.

The hand, despite its coldness, felt... "What do you think happens to the dead?" she asked, because more of his single-minded conviction was what she craved.

There was no hesitation at all in the answer.

"They are dead and their souls rest in a place marred by no sadness until they are called on the Last Day."

A place marred by no sadness.

"Do you really believe that?"

"I have to."

She was touching him and this time she felt a faint

shiver. But then his hand moved from her shoulder to touch the nape of her neck in a gesture of such unforced tenderness as she would not have believed him capable of.

The hand felt blissful. She might as well admit it to herself. Blissful. He was so close and so large and so unafraid of the things that frightened her. She was even favored with a faint return of the devastating smile.

"If you had had as many sermons from Eathelward the priest as I have, you would not dare believe otherwise."

He did not really know why she had asked, but he had said what she most longed to hear, and it was inexpressibly comforting to have his smile and his touch.

She picked up the other foot and began to massage the life-giving flow of his blood back into it. The foot was such a pleasing shape, big and solid, but so well formed, so free of marks. But then he would always have had the best shoes of the best leather made just for him. The arch held a particular fascination. It did not look as though it could hold up anything so large and heavy as him but it did, without the slightest ill effect. It was like magic. She traced her thumb across it. He did not move.

She glanced up again, carefully, so as not to dislodge the thawing hand which he had forgotten to move from the hollow where her neck met her shoulder.

The eyes were really shut this time. She was not sure whether he actually slept, or whether he just floated in that dreamlike state between sleeping and waking.

His body was totally relaxed and she thought he might, after all, have drifted over the edge into sleep. His skin had taken on a golden glow that might have been largely a reflection of the firelight but which was nevertheless reassuring. Little strands of his hair were beginning to dry, lifting away from the heavy mass in a nebulous cloud.

The foot in her hand became slowly heavier. It was an unconscious movement, something he could not help, and it brought a small savage thrill inside her, as though that slight, involuntary movement was a chink she had made in the armor of his cold indifference. His flesh pressed against her fingers, quite warm now, and intimately alive. Hers. She held it, wrapped close in her hands, as long as she wanted, until its heaviness made her arms ache.

She let it go at last, very gently, so as not to disturb him. His hand still rested on her shoulder. Outside, the wind howled its will and the rain beat against the walls.

It was so warm beside the fire and he was so warm.

She reached up and plucked the empty ale cup out of his hand. No reaction. He really did sleep.

His hand slid across her shoulder when she moved, like a caress. It was not by his will. It was quite unconscious, yet it had the power to make her shiver, not with cold but with a feeling that arose from the power of the unknown warmth simmering deep inside her.

She caught the hand just as it reached the very edge of her shoulder. Warm. Warm, now right through. She pressed it gently against her and the warmth seemed to melt her entire body into a feeling of yearning that was like pain.

Her breath caught and she held the hand tighter. He did not move. He did not know what she did. She slid the hand round to touch her bare skin, above the neckline of her underdress. She felt the shape of the solid fingers against her skin, the flat palm, the thick firm rise of flesh at the base of his thumb. It made the yearning need well up inside her until she thought she would die of it.

She twisted her neck, pressed her face against his hand. Her lips parted, sought that firm, solid mound below his thumb, touched him. She felt him stir.

She looked up in terror. If he woke, if he woke and found her like this, if she had to face those bright, fierce Saxon eyes…but he did not wake. His head moved against the chair, not conscious, not full of whatever bitter spirit it was that drove him so hard.

She watched his face and it held her like a spell. That was the spell you could surrender to. That was his magic and she wanted him like this, just for this moment. All the dangerous force, all the unknown English thoughts of his mind buried, only the uncomplicated warmth left and the strength. The strength that had first saved her from her attackers.

She wanted his comfort.

The east wind hit the wall of the bower with a viciousness that threatened to flatten it.

She wondered if it was ever possible to feel peace. If it was possible for her, if it was possible for someone like him, if it was possible for anyone.

She shivered and her fingers clutched at his again. He did not wake and his hand stayed in hers.

She was alone in the world and she had nothing. She moved closer toward him. Her body touched the solid shape of his leg. He slept. There was no one else here, only the two of them.

She buried her head in the folds of the loose tunic that covered the swelling hardness of his thigh, just above the bent knee. They had each other and the world outside could rage in bitterness. She curled her arms around the solid curving shape of his calf muscle as though she was a small child and clung to it.

Chapter Eight

It was the cracking of a log in the hearth which woke her.

She started in alarm and felt the same movement in the person she was leaning against. She blinked and tried to cudgel some coherent thought out of her sleep-fogged brain. What was she doing? Why was she...she looked up and saw the face of the Mercian. She gasped.

She saw his eyes widen and for an instant saw the same bewilderment that she felt, the same confusion, like waking from a dream. He was leaning back in the chair, his tunic disordered and open at the neck, his hand resting on her bare skin. She was curled up on the floor beside him. Her weight pressed against him and her arms were wrapped round his lower leg, like a little girl no taller than someone's knee.

Her eyes met his and there was no coldness. The blue eyes were hot, hot as the blue heart of the flame in the hearth. They burned her and she recognized the dangerous force that was in them, the age-old desire of men.

Yet the desire in him sought a response from her that was equal in its searing heat. For one instant it was there. With no thought of the danger or the consequences, of who he was or what it meant. It was just there, at the most primitive level a woman faces a man.

His hand, the hand she had placed on her own bare skin, moved across her flesh in the very caress she had tried to make counterfeit of. The heat scorched her. Her gaze dropped from his face to his hand. She watched the slow sureness of its movement. She watched her own flesh press against his and the heat inside threatened to consume her.

"No..." The raw, desperate sound of her own voice brought her back to her senses. She looked at his hand. She thought of his strength. She remembered how much reason they had to hate each other. She did not want him, not really, not like this. What she had done before had been by her will, under her control. She could not face what he really was. What he might do.

She lunged to her feet, scrambling away from him, blindly, colliding with the edge of the table with a force that brought another gasp. She clutched at the rough, solid wood and it bit into her hands. But the pain was a relief.

It brought sanity.

She had just done the most dangerous, stupid thing imaginable. She had never wanted a man in her life. It was vile, what men did. Something you had to endure and she was so lucky that Liefwin the Mercian had not wanted her.

He had not, did not.

Please say he did not.

He would know it was a mistake. Just the shock of waking so suddenly, like coming out of a dream. It disordered your senses, nothing more. But she did not dare to look at him.

Until she heard the door latch. That made her move.

"What are you doing?"

"Going out."

"Out?"

He shut the door again, closing out a frigid blast of rain-laden air.

"I thought you might prefer it."

He turned his head and looked at her, not with the anger she expected, but with a kind of weary patience that made her feel like a child again. He just stood, perfectly dressed, belted tunic, fresh cloak, new boots, and waited.

She watched him and knew it had all been of her imagining. Everything. Thoughts of warmth and comfort as much as thoughts of terrifying lust. It had all arisen from her weak, idiotic behavior. He must think she was simply moon-mad. Please let him think she was mad.

She tried to get her thoughts into order, to say something sensible, not what rose out of her sick imaginings. She tried to speak to him as she had before, as though the truce between them still lasted. As though that moment of hideous revelation had not happened to her.

"You should not be going now," she said. "Not this late, in the middle of a storm. You are ill. You will kill yourself if you carry on like this."

"Hardly. I have a few things to sort out with Ceol-frith, that is all. I will be back later."

So coldly said. Only she who was the shaking, bab-bling, lame-witted fool.

"It...it is not necessary for you to go because I..." She stopped and yet there was nothing in his eyes now to frighten her, just the habitual coldness and with it a weariness even he could not disguise.

She had fallen asleep without intending it, just like him. He had known she had been sitting beside him and it was quite a natural accident that she should have leaned against him. He did not know what she had done or what she had thought while he was asleep. He need never know. And as for that moment of confusion when they woke, it had been nothing but her own foolish fears.

He seemed to set no significance on it, not now. So surely she had enough confidence to retire behind her bed curtains with him in the room.

After all, he was there at some time each night, while she slept, and he had not slaked himself on her yet.

"It cannot be necessary," she said again, trying to turn the emphasis away from the danger of what did or did not lie between them in this room toward the world outside. "You are ill. Ceolfrith will under-stand."

He turned right round. He leaned with his back against the door, his heavy, cloaked figure totally blocking it.

"Ceolfrith will understand, will he? What will he understand? What you have told him, perhaps?"

And she realized what the intolerable confusion in

her mind had betrayed her into saying. *No*. The denial
sprang ready formed to her lips, just as it always had
when she had done something to displease Ragnar.
Self-defense. It was how you dealt with those who
were stronger than you were. You lied and cajoled
and cheated.

"Yes," said her voice.

It did make the blue eyes flicker. He had obviously
expected the denial just as she had. What on middle
earth had made her tell the truth? She waited for the
uncontrolled storm of wrath.

"Perhaps you could explain that?" asked the one
who had been taught to think but not to feel. His voice
was very calm.

She set her shoulders back. She found that she had
the courage to meet his eyes squarely. She did not
flinch, and it was actually a relief to be able to say
exactly what you thought, on equal terms and hang
the consequences.

"Because he was so worried about you and I could
not stand to see it. No one should have to be that
worried about you just because you do not happen to
want to speak to them, especially not someone like
Ceolfrith, after all he has done for you."

"Is that what he said?"

There was no change in the voice. *Think. Think, do
not feel.*

"Of course not. He cares about you too much."

"Yes. I know he does. That is why I did not tell
him."

The words shocked. The shock should have been
hers, but it was not. It was Liefwin the Invincible's.
The mask slipped for an instant and she saw it.

He had not meant to say that. She, the useless piece of Danish ransom in waiting, had made him say it.

"Perhaps you could explain that?" she asked in turn, with a calm just as dangerous as his.

"It was in the battle for the town."

Something inside her flinched, even at the mention of that. But she listened and she watched him. She could not help it.

"It happened near the end. Ceolfrith was…battle weary. All the men were. They have been here too long. Have fought for too long. They should have been back at their homes before now."

She stared at his perfect English face. There was no mention of himself in that brief statement that said so much and implied so much more. No mention of his having been at war with her people for too long. No discernible trace of longing for his home. Just the opposite. Liefwin seemed to think of himself in some quite different category from the rest of his fellow men.

I cannot see an end to this. Not for me.

The words rang in her head. She had thought it was despair. Perhaps it was not. Perhaps she was wrong. Perhaps there was nothing more in the heart of her enemy but implacability. But she could not leave well enough alone.

"What," she insisted, as though this would give her some clue to the frozen wastes of his mind, "happened with Ceolfrith?"

"Weariness can make people reckless. Ceolfrith got himself into some trouble. I got him out. That was when it happened. The wound."

He spoke not as though he had rescued someone

he cared about from mortal peril, but as though he was explaining Ceolfrith's behavior as one of the foibles of some species of being other than his own.

"But…" Her mouth opened and shut. There was no clue there at all. There was nothing.

"But—" she began again.

"I could not see the point in telling him."

"You could not see the *point?* The man is worried sick about you. I have told you. He cares about you. That is the point…" Her words gave out under a silence that could have frozen the North Sea.

More fool Ceolfrith, she thought, more fool him.

What was it she had thought the first time she had set eyes on all the cold perfection of Liefwin standing in the torchlight? A face you could break yourself on.

Just as well that she would never be such a fool. Just as well she would never wish to care for him.

Just as well he was her enemy.

"The fault," she said, with a finality that was completely reckless, "is not with Ceolfrith. It is with you. Your coldness and your arrogance."

He did not react. Not in any way she could see. Well, she would make him react. She would make him see that it was his own fault.

"When I spoke to Ceolfrith, he told me no more than two sentences about your childhood. That was all I needed. The rest was obvious. It should be more than obvious to you. If you cannot recognize loyalty when it is staring you in the face, what sort of a *dryhten,*" she spit his own English word back at him, "are you?"

That made his perfect mouth twist. But his eyes did not flinch from hers.

"Ceolfrith knows exactly what sort." And if he tells you that, thought Liefwin, I will probably kill him.

The wind nearly tore the cloak off Liefwin's back, the slanting rain stung his face, half blinding him. He shouldered his way through it, like knocking aside a living opponent.

But it was not to the lighted communal building where Ceolfrith would be that he turned first. It was to the quiet room that held Alfwin. He would be asleep, doubtless, and everyone said he was not going to die, but still...

It was only the servant who slept, curled up in the warmth of the fire, not Alfwin. He sat down beside the bed.

"Alfwin? Why are you not asleep?"

"Is there any ale left?"

He looked at the tightly-drawn face. So it was that bad. He poured ale.

"You do not have to lift me. I can—"

"Don't be stupid."

But it was harder than he had expected, harder than it should have been, surely. He did not think that he gave anything away, but he could see another protest forming on Alfwin's lips. He forestalled it in the most direct manner to hand.

"Swallow," he advised, "before you drown. No, not that fast, or you will...choke," he added as a quantity of ale landed on his sleeve.

"S-sorry."

"I could get them to bring you some poppy—"

"No. I am all right. Liefwin."

''What?'' He settled Alfwin's weight back against the bolster and tried not to let relief show.

''You really are hurt, are you not?''

''What?'' The hellcat Danish wench. It had to be. Who else had she been talking to and about what?

He should not feel surprised. She had made it abundantly clear tonight what she really thought of him. So there was no reason why it should feel like the bitterest kind of betrayal when she lied to him, or if she broke his confidence, or when she tried to pretend she really wanted to share his bed. She had more than enough reason to hate him. He thought she did.

''Do not be angry. It was just that I overheard Ceolfrith talking to that Danish girl you took.''

Liefwin's hand tightened on the empty ale cup until the carved pattern cut into his flesh.

''I know why you did not tell Ceolfrith about your wound. You are always so—''

There was nothing worse than praise that was not deserved. Liefwin's voice cut across the word *generous* with the sharpness of a sword.

''It is easier for me if people do not know, that is all. Particularly people like Oslac, for example,'' he added more lightly. ''So you can just keep your ale-dribbling mouth shut.''

That brought a creditable attempt at a grin and then, ''But it is not anything serious is it? I mean…''

Yet another reason for keeping such things to yourself. People did not like their leader to have too many problems. It made them nervous.

''It is just annoying, not serious at all.'' And it was not. He could not understand why this time he should find it so difficult to carry on and do what had to be done.

It was the Danish girl.

It had no explanation and no reason, but ever since he had plucked her out of the disaster of the town, the entire landscape of his world had changed, and yet she had not done anything. Except seen through him, to every weakness he had.

She knew what he was and she had said so. She had told him what everyone else was too afraid to say. She was able to say it because they were enemies. Utterly and inescapably. His past and hers forced that.

And yet sometimes it seemed possible to believe it was not so. She was so beautiful, his reluctant prize for ransom. She fired his senses. Even when she argued with him. Even when, oh, sometimes they did not argue, even when they should. They were enemies and yet sometimes that truth had no meaning for them. They forgot, inside the four walls of that stranger's bower, who they were. Just as he had said they should that first morning, without understanding what it might mean.

That was how it had started tonight. She had had no fear of him and no enmity. She had made him laugh, which he had not done for two years. She had offered comfort.

And she had sought comfort from him.

Which only went to show that she knew nothing at all.

He shifted his weight against the wall.

"Liefwin."

"Yes?"

"That Danish girl…"

The ale cup spun out of the tenseness of his hand and he spent a considerable time trying to pick it up off the floor. Perhaps he really had broken his ribs.

"She is a piece of skirt that would heat any man's blood is she not? We can all see why you would have taken her to warm your bed."

He straightened up. You did not smash your fist into the face of your sick cousin. It was not done. He put the ale cup down on the bench. He did not use any force at all, but something had already put the alarm into Alfwin's eyes. He tried to move slowly and make his voice quite even.

"I will not have her spoken of in that way. I thought I had made that clear. She is under my protection until I take her to her kindred at Shealdford."

"I am sorry. I did not mean to offend you."

"You have offended her. She has no one. She has lost everything she ever had and she has met it bravely. You ought to respect that."

He was aware, even as he said it, that he could sound like nothing more than a hypocrite, but he could not have let it go.

"I am sorry. I did not think. Are you really going to take her all the way to Shealdford?"

"Yes." *It is on the way to Tamworth, did you not know?*

"But it would be dangerous, surely. Is there a big ransom?"

"She says so." It was always possible to end a conversation dead if you used a certain tone of voice.

"Why do you not try sleeping?" he added.

"All right."

Liefwin gritted his teeth and tried moving his arm off the bed so that he could lean back again, but there was something stuck in his ale-soaked sleeve. It was Alfwin's fingers. He stopped.

He was not sure that Alfwin even knew. The taut face had taken on the flushed look of fever.

"Liefwin, when the king gets here…"

Never admit you are afraid, that you are terrified that you might die, that you might never see your home and your family again. Not if you are on the path to glory.

"It will all work out. Nothing will stop Edward this time. He will win and you will go home and they will be making up songs in your honor. Now shut up and go to sleep."

He did not allow anything but firmness and reassurance to touch his voice. He could feel Alfwin begin to relax.

"You do not have to stay. I know you must have things to do."

It was quite a creditable attempt at sounding offhand.

"A dozen things probably. But I thought I might finish your ale first while you are too feeble to prevent me."

"Ha. I shall know how to take my revenge later."

"Try it."

"Just wait," sneered Alfwin.

It was the way they used to speak, a long time ago, before everyone began to be so careful of him. He had that strange consciousness again that the world had shifted.

But the world of a long time ago was gone forever.

He did not bother with the ale. He left his damp sleeve where it was and watched Alfwin fade into unquiet sleep.

But Alfwin's image kept vanishing under another, a small, white face with wide smoky eyes, eyes that spoke…all sorts of things to him.

He was a hypocrite.

He did want to get the captive girl into his bed. That was all his desire, in every muscle and every pulsing drop of blood in his body. And when she had seen that, even though for one moment he had thought otherwise, she had recoiled from him in horror.

Chapter Nine

It was the gleam of gold that caught her eye.

Sigrid blinked. The unknown thing glittered in the cool morning light, half-smothered in the rumpled folds of Liefwin's empty bed. She slid across the room, fingers outstretched. But her hand stopped just short as she reached where he had slept.

Her gaze ran over the bed. The rumpled covers still held the faint remembrance of the shape of her captor's body. Her stomach clenched. She remembered touching him when he slept. She remembered the gentleness of his breathing. Her whole body ached with the memory of his warmth.

How still and quiet, how strong and tender he felt when he slept.

She clenched her fists. Stupid. She had been stupid over that and the Mercian despised her for it. She leaned forward.

The glittering object was lodged in the small space where the mattress met the wall, as though it had fallen there and been overlooked. An arm ring? Her breath quickened. The arm rings were impossible wealth. Even Ragnar at the height of his luck had only boasted silver.

No. It was oblong. She lifted it out. It was made of such filigree work as she had never seen. She turned it over. Its front was covered in finely wrought patterns, and winding through the riotous intricacy was the sinuous shape of some fabulous beast, a dragon, perhaps. Its smooth lines, the mind-numbing complexity around it were utterly and unmistakably English. Its eyes were made of garnets.

The oblong fell open in her hand. A book.

A scattering of ink marks like the traces left by birds' feet unraveled under her eyes. Latin script. She had not even known it existed before she came to this land.

She turned one thick, creamy parchment leaf.

It had pictures, colored, in the margins and at the top of the page. She looked further. There was an arm, green, muscular and detached: a monster's arm. Small splashes of bright red cascaded down the margin. It ended not in a conventional hand, but in a dragon's claw: the claw of Grendel. It could be nothing else.

Her eyes were damp.

She remembered leaning over this bed, just as she did now, and touching a warm, white shoulder. She remembered making jokes in her desperation about Beowulf the monster slayer who tore off Grendel's arm. She remembered sitting on the very edge of the bed, shaking inside with terror, and then realizing there was no need to.

Something wet dropped on the page.

What did she think she was about? Suppose the ink smudged? She turned the book over and shook it, and the coldness of the gleaming metal was hard against her palm.

You did not cry over things just because they were beautiful, or because they belonged to people who were. You calculated precisely how much they were worth and you took your chances. Chances did not come twice.

She crossed to the door, grabbing her cloak on the way. She had nothing ready. It would be raining and cold and impossible to walk because of the mud.

But she would not need anything else with this kind of wealth.

She opened the door. Sunlight and a crisp, drying wind touched her face. It was warmer. She stepped outside.

She had no food, no coins, not even a knife for protection. *The woods are full of the remains of a routed army.*

Could she really get away now, in broad daylight? Just like this? Her feet felt as heavy as quern stones. She could not think straight.

There was no one in sight. Except…Ceolfrith, across the yard. She ducked into the shelter of the nearest doorway and held her breath.

He would go past, surely.

He was getting closer.

She stepped back into the room, clutching the loot under her cloak. *Thief.* The word scorched in her mind.

Ceolfrith vanished—

"Hello."

She nearly fainted.

"Sorry. Did I startle you?"

The voice came from behind her. She turned and her gaze fell on bright hair, a pale boy's face with eye-catching cheekbones, a tense body lost in the dimness of a bed.

''Are you all right, lady? Were you looking for Ceolfrith?'' asked the lord Liefwin's wounded cousin.

''No! No, it is all right. I am all right. I just…''

''Oh.'' The pleasant, confused face cleared. The blue gaze focused past her. ''You came with Liefwin.''

She spun round. The book shot out of her hands.

He was standing in the doorway, the sun glinting on hair longer and richer than Alfwin's, lighting a face stronger and finer and more challenging.

The book slithered halfway across to his feet.

It landed garnet-side up.

She could no longer see his expression because her gaze had fixed itself on the book.

''Keen on reading?''

''Oh, yes,'' she said through a dry throat, and then as though it was nothing at all to be found wandering at will in possession of more than her ransom, ''it is Beowulf.''

''With the three arms. Of course. Your favorite.''

She remembered the naked brutal shoulders rising out of the bedcovers. He would kill her.

''Three arms?'' piped up the invalid, somewhere in the dimness behind her. ''I do not remember that bit. I thought Beowulf had only two arms but the hand-grip of…twenty men was it? Anyway, if that is your copy of it, would you take pity on a man dying of boredom and read to him?''

''Perhaps the lady might oblige.''

"Oh, would you? Could I have the monster fight? The one where they are all asleep in the hall and Grendel the Swamp-monster comes stalking up from the marshes...you know the one—"

"Oh, the lady knows exactly."

He was using his polite thane's voice, but underneath, if you knew how to listen, it had the bite of a steel blade.

She crouched down to pick up the book at his feet. Her gaze took in the mud-splashed shoes and the solid muscle of his legs in the tight, dark gray trousers. She looked up from the heavy folds of his cloak, the jeweled waist, the wide expanse of his chest. The stone face.

Somehow she got to her feet.

"Well?"

The book fell open in her hand. The black claw marks danced beneath her eyes, sharp as knife cuts.

"I do not think that is it," said Alfwin helpfully. "It must be farther back, surely."

She looked from the golden book to the gold rings at Liefwin's wrists and it was not just fear that gripped her, but shame, hot and clammy. Not so much because she had tried to steal. A captive was entitled to seize whatever means she could to escape, surely. But because she did not know how to read. And she had lied about it.

The gold bracelets moved and a handgrip that had the strength of twenty men and could probably slay monsters snatched the book out of her grasp.

She looked up at his face and saw that he had realized. Not just that she was trying to steal his book. No doubt of that existed. But he knew that she was so ignorant and so low that her only possible use of a book lay in the richness of its cover.

He turned away from her and looked at his cousin. He would say that—

"I will read you the monster fight, you pathetic nuisance. Just because Sigrid speaks English so well, you cannot expect her to toil her way through the copying of some obscure monk from Mercia. But—" the handgrip caught her arm, above the elbow "—I am sure she would like to stay and listen. Do sit down," said the perfect thane.

She sat, out of necessity, jammed on the wall bench, far too close to Liefwin, in the inadequate space left between him and the bed. She could not look at him.

Alfwin grinned at her, utterly oblivious to the possibility that there might be anything wrong.

She moved her own lips into the same odd shape.

She could feel the solid mass of Liefwin's thigh pressed against hers. She could feel the desperation growing deep inside her. She wanted to pull away, but she could not move without falling over onto the bed.

"This will be really good," whispered Alfwin. Sigrid forced a smile at the face, so like and so unlike Liefwin's.

Liefwin.

He was reading out loud from the incomprehensible marks. About Grendel, the shadow walker.

She looked round. She could not help it. Because the words were like something out of the otherworld, like the music of the harp made out of speech. Hopelessness and painful envy stabbed through her.

To read such words. To know how to do it. To do it as though it was nothing. With so much ease and unconscious assurance.

Stories were rare pleasures that relied on people's memories and on being able to weasel your way into the audience around somebody else's hearth to listen. Yet this one had been captured, stuck onto a piece of parchment, so that it could be revived whenever you felt like it. The power of that made her head spin.

He turned a page. She watched reflected firelight dance on the gold book and the gold arm ring and the thick gold hair that almost, but not quite, hid his face. She watched his firelit profile and the movement of his lips and the faint flutter of his lashes as his eyes scanned to the top of the new page. Effortless.

Beowulf, the hero strong in thought, sprang off the page, took shape through Liefwin's voice, through Liefwin's clever mind.

She could not tear her gaze away from his face, even though he was angry with her and he might sense she was staring at him and look up. But he did not raise his head. He kept on reading. He might have been as oblivious as Alfwin. Yet he was not. She knew that he was just as aware of her every movement, her every breath, as she was of his. But he gave no sign. He did not need to. They both knew it. It was always like that. It held them like a bond of iron.

Was that why she had rushed out so blindly with the book, in a panic? Because she was afraid that if she delayed, if she so much as saw him again she would lose her resolve?

She could not bear the thought. She looked away.

But she could still feel the warmth of his thigh against hers.

She tried to fix her attention on Alfwin. The boy's eyelids drooped. She could see how much the strained body had relaxed just from Liefwin's presence and the sound of his voice. She knew what it was to have Liefwin's full attention, what an irresistible spell that could weave.

She thought Alfwin drifted into sleep, just the way she had yesterday. She could see the peace in his face. He was so young, and it seemed a criminal thing to squander a life like that on fighting. She was sick of the thought of it. It had been the background of her life for so long. She was sick of misery and loss and death. It never ended. Never.

The voice stopped, jerking her out of her thoughts, back into what was real. Her head snapped round. There was no such thing as magic and no peace.

She was trapped by a man she had tried to steal a fortune from.

"He is asleep."

Her heart thundered. But she was hanged if she would let him see she was afraid.

"So," she said, just as she had on that first morning, "what now?"

"Not here. Get up."

"You do not read at all, do you?"

She was, for the moment, untouched and unpunished, but her feet paced the bower and her head pounded with all the helpless fury of the trapped. But Liefwin the Mercian thane just stood, leaning against the doorjamb, the golden book dangling from his jeweled fingers.

"No," she snapped, "I do not read. I am incapable of it. I am sorry if I embarrassed you in front of your cousin."

"Do not be ridiculous."

Ridiculous? Perhaps it was. Why should she imagine that a rich lord would be embarrassed by the failings of something he happened to have picked up in the street?

The book was twirled absentmindedly in his fingers, as though he did not really care whether he dropped it in the rushes. It was only worth more than she was, after all.

"Lots of people do not read," stated the thane. "It is nothing to be—"

"—*ashamed of?* Is that what you were going to say?"

"I did not mean—"

"No," she yelled. "You probably did not. You do not have a clue, do you, with your fine wealth and your fine thane's honor and your perfect life…" That last actually hurt. She knew how to read the small expressions in his eyes where before she had thought there was nothing. But it was suppressed without much apparent effort. Blank eyes watched her frantic steps. He did not move.

"Do you realize," she spat, "what I have come from? Do you have any idea how some people have to live? Like the animals stabled at the other end of the longhouse. There is not much difference."

She stopped beside the open window.

"My father," she said to the clear blue English

sky, "had a small farm, on poor land, and too many children. We grew up, those of us who lived, with a will to survive. That is all I was ever taught, not reading, not what to do with fine things. Just all the ugly, despicable things you have to do to live when you have nothing."

She could not see the blue sky now. She was back in the smoke-filled dimness of the longhouse, choking on the winter stink of the cow and the pigs in the pen at the far end. Her younger sisters were clamoring at her skirts, howling. Her mother was screaming at them with all the fury of hopelessness.

"Just surviving. That was all it was—endless meals out of next-to-nothing, grubbing out the kitchen garden, gutting stinking fish, spinning coarse wool until your eyes could not see, standing at the loom until you thought your back would break, and it was never enough. Someone always needed something else."

She swallowed furiously. She did not know whether the fine figure by the door was even listening to her. There was no reason why he should. She had attempted to steal something of unimaginable value from him and now she was railing at him with all the miserable, disgusting details of her life.

But she could not stop it. She had to make him know what she was.

She swallowed tears and said, with all the force of twenty-two years of bitterness, "I wanted to get out of it. I knew there had to be something else to this life, somewhere. If I could just get to it. I thought if I tried hard enough, I would find it. That is how stupid I was.

"In the evenings," she said into the answering silence, ''when I was supposed to be asleep I used to listen to them telling stories, about heroes and treasure and magic places and I knew there was another world somewhere.''

She stopped. Because the next bit was the disaster.

''And?''

Just one word, impossible to gauge the slightest feeling from it.

''I left. I left my home and went looking for my new world.

''It was exactly this time of the year, with another winter coming on.'' She could feel the shiver over her skin that had nothing to do with physical coldness, but she would not stop. He should know. She would make him know.

''It was a day just like any other and then... strangers came. I saw them first. Nigh on twenty horsemen. Warriors, with spears of ashwood and mail coats and flying hair.

''No one ever came to our village because there was nothing there. People thought they would kill us even for the little we had. But they were not interested in that. They were on their way home. They were already loaded up with—'' her voice faltered ''—with wealth.''

''Do you not mean with English plunder?''

His voice was as cold and as full of danger as it had been the first morning after her capture. Her hands gripped at the rough wood of the window frame.

''Yes,'' she said, and she heard him move. It was like dicing with death, but the need to face him with the truth was greater. ''Yes, I do mean that and I did not care.'' Not then. ''Do you want to know what I did?''

The faint rustle of his clothing again, then, ''Not really.''

You could be frozen alive under bitterness like that, strong as her own. Her breath seemed to be out of time with the thick pulsing of her heart. She wondered whether she would choke.

''I married one of them. I was near sixteen and quite ready for it. I gave myself to him freely. No, not freely, for a silver bracelet and a bag of coins my father took. He was the strongest and the tallest and he wanted me. He was not exactly handsome, perhaps, but I did not care. I…I wanted somebody to love and he was a real prize.

''I thought he must be very brave because they were all afraid of him, even the stoutest of them.''

How could she have been so stupid? How could she not have known why?

''I escaped. Just as I wanted. He carried me away with him and we came here and we lived on the plunder until it ran out. But that was all right. Because there was always more to be had. From your people.''

She would see his face. She would see his reaction to that. She spun round, fast. But she could never be as quick as a warrior. She was anticipated. The Mercian thane was no longer looking at her. She saw only his back, and the cloak still swirling from the force of his movement.

But the position of his bent arms, surely…he had to shield his face from her with his hands.

Never had he done such a thing before her. Always

the control of his expression and his voice had been enough, more impenetrable than a mask.

So there it was: a small piece of vengeance over her enemy. She had meant to taunt him with the devastation that had been wrought on his country, to remind him that the destruction of the town was only a small victory after all. She had meant to show him what she was, a Viking. She had wanted to fling that in his superior, cold, emotionless English face. To show him she hated him. To show him how much reason he had to hate her.

This was to have been her triumph. This was to be vengeance.

She felt sick.

Chapter Ten

The sickness in Sigrid's tight throat choked her at last. The sound was raw, ugly. It made the Mercian look up, so that his face was uncovered, his eyes without any protection at all.

She had not done that.

She could not have done that with her pathetic story and her taunts. It was impossible. The naked eyes held an expression that was insupportable.

The choking took all her breath. It burned her throat and clenched her stomach in agony, doubling her up over the window frame.

Something dragged her away from the window and dropped her on the bed. She struggled up through a haze of nausea, but something had hold of her and she could not get away. She would be sick again. She thought she would faint. There were tears on her face. She could feel their cold wetness. Her teeth clashed against something metallic.

"Take a mouthful and then spit it out."

"No..." But that only let liquid spill into her mouth.

"Spit it out into the bowl. Now. Spit, or you will choke yourself."

She spat.

"Do not…" A cloth, dampened, scraped roughly against her mouth. She shut it.

"Now swallow." The edge of the cup again. Mead. Strong. Life-giving. "That will do. I do not want it all returned over my tunic."

She tried to stop her hand clawing after the silver-chased cup held tantalizingly just beyond her reach.

"Slowly."

She nodded. She drank. The mead seeped through her veins like balm over a sword wound.

There was none left.

Her head dropped forward like a stone.

There was smooth wool under the side of her face, blue, clean, the tunic she was not allowed to be sick over.

His hand was on her head. It was not steady. She knew what she had done and there was no way out of this. There never would be.

"Why do you not just kill me?"

She felt the force of her words jolt through his body.

"So I should take my vengeance? Is that what you wish?"

His hand slid downward, knocking the headdress off her hair, coming to rest against the side of her neck, large, hardened with fighting, so unsteady.

"Is that what you want of me? To dispatch you to join your husband, the hero?"

The heavy hand curled with terrifying gentleness round the naked skin of her neck.

"Such things are not always given to us, are they?" The voice was harsh and shot through with the same unsteadiness she felt in his body. It was more terrible than the thought of his physical strength. She had never seen that careful control broken. She did not know what lay beneath.

"Is that what you are wishing for, Sigrid, when you are with me?"

No. That was not what she wished when she was with him.

It was the truth and she told it. Because there was nothing else left.

"No," she whispered against the fine folds of the blue tunic. "That is not what I wish and neither is it what my husband would wish. He…he is with the gods of war, as he was in his life. He had no wish for a wife. It was just a mistake."

"How can you know that? A man can scarce choose when he must fight."

She thought there was some choice involved in making a career out of harrying, out of the perverse pleasure of feeding the monster that lived within.

Her body trembled like the Mercian's. The memories in her mind were too hideous to contemplate. Her hand moved to the scar at the corner of her eye and she felt it all again, the pain and the anger and the helplessness, and the hideous fear that she would not be able to see properly again.

The heavy warrior's hand against her neck moved, quite softly to cover hers. She stiffened, wanting to hide what was so obvious.

There was no reason why something that someone else had done to her years ago should humiliate her.

But it did. The muscles in her arm tensed in resistance against the Mercian's hand, but it was no use against his kind of strength. He probably did not even notice. She would only humiliate herself further by resisting.

Her hand was engulfed beyond hope of retrieval.

"That was your husband?"

There was no point in denying it, not with him.

"Yes." Then into the silence, "It was nothing. He was not even angry."

"*Nothing?* He could have blinded you."

She could feel every rigid muscle in his hand. She raised her head from against his shoulder. The final confession lay on her tongue.

"My husband was a…" She looked up and the word *berserker* died against the raging fury in his eyes. She could not speak it. Not to those eyes. She could not explain any more and she could not expose Ragnar's madness to the Mercian's contempt.

"You do not understand," she said.

Silence. Nothing but silence and the bitterness in her throat and the formless, pulsing beat of his anger.

It was the end. She would not cringe from it.

"There is nothing left that is worth saying about my life. I stole that book from you and I was going to sell it for the weight of the gold and for the gems. That is all your book was to me and all it could be. Nothing can change that…ahh—"

She had not even sensed that he would move. The same speed, the same irresistible power as Ragnar. It was men who had the final strength in this world and sooner or later, they would use it.

"Sit up."

She thudded back against the pillows and her

breath gathered into a scream. But he was gone, away from her and across the room in two strides.

"Sit up."

He had turned even before she had realized what he was about. He had the book in his hand. She clawed herself upright.

"Here. Hold that." And it was in her hands, hard-edged gold and smooth gems.

He balanced himself on the edge of the bed beside her, full-length, muscular legs stretched out, trapping her so that she could not move.

"Well, go on. First page."

"But—"

"Do it."

Her hand found the page. She looked at his eyes and they burned. He had not touched her but he was going to humiliate her with the book and the words and everything a peasant like her was incapable of.

She had rather he had hit her like Ragnar.

"Look at the page."

"What is the point?" Her voice was a crawling whisper. Her gaze lighted on the glossy page and the bright colors and the demented birds' feet.

"What is on that page is a means of recording someone's thoughts, setting down ideas, making us think. It is that that will keep us out of cow byres, not my sword, not your husband's battle-ax. That is the point."

She blinked.

"But you know that already. You knew it when you listened to people telling stories. I do not care what you say or what you were going to do. It was in your face, just now in Alfwin's bower."

"No. It is not for me. I am not...it is too late. Nothing can change now."

"I do not believe that."

She was no longer looking at the page but at his eyes. He had such eyes, such strength of will. He could make you believe that anything was possible, anything at all. Her heart thudded.

"I cannot."

He leaned across to grasp the book. Their bodies touched. His hands covered hers, so large that she could not even see her fingers. He smelled of the clean herb-scented soap. The gold arm rings were hard against her wrists.

"I cannot," she said again. "I do not know how. I do not know what to do."

"It is easy."

It was to him, everything was. But she was lost, out of her depth. Her gaze seemed to be fastened to the gold arm ring and the embroidered sleeve and she could not even look at the page.

"What is the first word?"

"I do not know."

"Yes, you do. Think in English. What is the first word any poet says to grab your attention? He strides down the length of the hall after the meal, through the people and the dogs and the spilled beer and the bones. He takes the harp, glares at the drunks sprawling at the far end of the mead bench, strikes the strings as hard as he can and bellows..."

"*Hwæt,*" she said.

"Yes."

He spelled it.

"See? Each letter is a sound. Look at the second

letter. That starts the next word and the next letter is
e, we, and that is *g-a-r,* spear.''

She made herself look at the page. It was true. It
was odd but—

''So what is the next word? I will double your ransom if you do not get that. That is *d* and *n.* You have
already had *e* and *a.*''

She stared at it. It was impossible.

It… ''Oh! It is *d*—'' She choked. Her ransom and
the plunder and…but he was smiling. She did not
know how she knew that because she could not see
his face.

''You can say it. I am not going to strike your head
off with my sword.''

He really was smiling. It was in his voice.

''*Dena,*'' she said, ''Danes,'' and she was still alive
for saying it.

'''Lo, we have learned of the glory of the Spear-
Danes in days gone by, of the kings of that people,
how the princes performed deeds of bravery,''' he
said, and there was all the irony of the world in his
voice. But the smile still ran through it like a silver
thread. It was obvious to her ears.

Her eyes followed the tantalizing marks on the
page, no longer random scratchings, but forever trans-
formed into ranks of separate sounds. Words. The
parchment rustled, the very colors in the margins
seemed brighter. It was like magic. She was suddenly
aware of the warmth of his hands round hers.

She looked up.

The magic was not in the words. It was in him. It
always had been. She had known it from the start.
Heat surged through her body accompanied by an

overwhelming awareness of him, of the touch of his hardened palm, the shape of his body, his face, the sharp line of his jaw dusted with dark gold stubble, the fierce gleam of his eyes. The remainder of the smile was still there, but there was so much else. His eyes held secrets, secrets she would never fathom.

"Well? Is it still impossible?"

"Yes," she said. "No…" But she did not know what she said or what question she was replying to. Her heart beat and her breath caught and her eyes were fixed on his. He was all masculine force and he was dangerous. All men were. They…if only he would not look at her so. If only he was not so close. If he would let go of her hands. If only he would take the disastrous book away and leave her.

Why did he have to make her think she could do things she could not, like read and have opinions that mattered?

He leaned toward her and the book disappeared, but it did not help because he still had hold of her hands, as though he wanted to, as though it was something important.

He drew one of the hands quite slowly toward him. They lay together on the bed. The heat in her body burned. The callused flesh of his palm slid softly across her skin, his fingers tangled with hers, moved round them in a caress, so light, so careful, as if she were fragile, as if she could draw back at any time.

He placed her hand across his heart. She could feel its fast, harsh beat through the fine wool of his tunic and fear crashed through her, taking her breath.

It was not fear, it was excitement.

His hand tightened, imprisoning hers against that harsh tumult.

No. It was fear. It twisted inside her so that she wanted to pull away, to tell him to stop. But then she would lose him. And she wanted him. Horribly. She did not move. She felt his heart thunder, pulsing the blood through his strong body. The hot eyes, the face, fine skin, strong male bones, dark gold stubble, blurred her vision.

It would happen. She knew what would happen now because she had not moved away from him. She wanted to stop it. She did not want such a thing from him.

She did not want him to show her that he was just as vile as Ragnar.

Her hand stiffened under his. She felt him move, shifting his weight in the confined space of the bed. She could pull away from him now, while he…she heard the faintest gasp as he came down too hard on his bent arm. She felt the sudden stillness in him. Gold hair hid his face. He did not make another sound. But she knew.

She reached out and touched the disordered hair, smoothed it back from his face with all the gentleness that she had. She was such a fool. She saw his eyes. She saw the suppressed pain she had expected, but she was not prepared for the passion.

He did not have passion. He was as cold as ice, like something blighted by hoarfrost. He did not have feelings like other people. He was not subject to the desperation and the formless longings that tortured her.

"Sigrid."

His voice was rough, as harsh and uncontrolled as the breath in his chest.

He was not as she expected. Nothing was as she expected. Her heart leaped as hard and as painfully, surely, as his. Her hands were still tangled in his hair. They touched his face, grazed the roughness of his chin, the smooth skin flushed with heat along the top of his cheekbone.

She did not know who moved, how their bodies came to cleave together, full-length. The touching made her gasp and her breath was lost as his mouth came down on hers.

But it was so smooth. His kiss was so smooth, smoothness and heat and…pleasure. Beneath the urgency and the desire in him and the frantic beat of his heart lay a molten core of pleasure. The pleasure grew. It surrounded her, like the magic that lived in the air when she had first seen him, like the closeness that she had felt when she had fallen into sleep touching his body, like the rare excitement of his smile. All that, all those things that she longed for, were still there in his kiss. You had only to believe in it.

She closed her mind against the sick, terrifying memory of Ragnar and let him kiss her.

And it was so different.

Not something that was over in two minutes and left your mouth bleeding. He did not hurt her. But the kiss held its own force. There was no hesitation and it seemed to expect something from her that she did not know how to give.

Her hand slid down his neck, twisting in the folds of his tunic and his arms closed round her, imprisoning her, dragging her closer against him. Her arm was crushed against the hardness of his chest. She could feel the frightening force of his heart. It terrified her, the blind, grasping impulse that drove men in their lust.

Yet despite her fear, the excitement was still there, as though there was something yet to be discovered that she did not know, as though this was a way to reach the secrets that lived inside him.

She gave a choked gasp as his arms tightened against her ribs, taking her breath. It made her mouth open under his and she felt his tongue enter her, hot, demanding. But the pressure around her ribs relaxed. He was so warm.

She craved that. She wanted his touch. She wanted to hold him as he held her.

Her other arm inched its way around the heavy thickness of his body, trying to avoid where she thought the bruises were. Her hand caught in the leather belt at his waist. It was such an inept and tentative movement compared to his. But it made him shiver and some small sound caught in his throat.

It was such a shock.

Ragnar had never even noticed what she did, or cared that after the first time she had not even tried. It had made no difference to what he wanted.

She had not expected to make the Mercian react so.

Unexpectedness. That was what made her mouth cleave to his and her lips burn and her hands tighten on him with all the desperation that he had used on her. Except she had no force compared to him. Her hands were lost against the thick muscle of his shoulder, the hard turn of his waist.

His body moved against her and her hand fell off the leather belt, sliding downward across the taut swell of his buttock. She had not meant…she felt the taut globe of male muscle tighten under the touch of her hand. His loins pressed against her so that she could feel his jutting hardness.

His hand skimmed her breast, enclosing its shape, his fingers finding the tightened bead of her nipple though the fabric of her dress. Her body rolled in a response that was deep and uncontrolled. His fingers circled that sensitive peak, arousing shivers of sensation across her skin, even through the barrier of her clothes. It made her body arch toward him, wild, shaking, blind to all but the craving for his touch.

The craving was so strong she could not stop it. But somewhere at the back of her mind she knew it would only end in horror.

His touch hardened, meeting the insane, betraying thrust of her body toward him. His hand closed over the vulnerable flesh of her breast and then slid down across her body, her waist, the curve of her hip, tangling in the long rumpled fall of her skirts, dragging the dress and the undergown out of the way, finding the naked skin of her thigh beneath.

It was like a jolt of lightning through her flesh, sensing his touch like that. She tried to pull away from the feel of his hand. It was more intimate than she could bear.

But she could not move.

Her leg was trapped under the weight of his thigh. His body covered hers. He was so large, so heavy. So heavy like her husband, holding her down. With that casual strength that could overcome her without even trying. The strength that she had only ever made one attempt to resist.

Cold fear clutched at her. It obliterated the Mercian's warmth, the smooth power of his lips, the soft, teasing touch of his tangled hair. It left only the strength.

She was trapped. The hard body over hers, the strong hands. She could not breathe. She could not bear what would happen next. Never again. Memories blacked out everything in her mind. Panic flooded her.

She pulled herself away, with all the force that she had. But it was impossible in the confined space of the bed. She could not get away from him. Her body thrashed. She thought he tried to catch her hands. He spoke. But she evaded him, twisting free of his grip. She thought he shouted at her. But she would not stop, not if he killed her. She struck out and her flailing arm hit something and then nothing and then there was silence.

Her first coherent thought was that he had gone. That disgust of her had somehow exceeded anger and he had left her. It was the only possible explanation of why she was still alive and still whole. She lowered her hands from around her head and opened her eyes.

He was sitting on the end of the bed watching her. She saw first the spine-chilling expression in the bright blue eyes and then the blood. A thin trail at the corner of his mouth.

She had hit him. Not all the new saints that now lived in heaven would preserve her. She had injured him and he would kill her.

She shot backward, her spine jarring against the

wall and something flickered in the overbright eyes. It was fathomless anger.

He moved and she screamed. Except nothing came out of her mouth but some thin, formless sound that was lost under the sudden hammering on the door of the bower and the loud Saxon voices shouting his name.

"Liefwin."

"Lord."

"You are needed."

He glanced at the door.

Leave, she thought, her spine pressed into the wall, her mind blank with shock. *Go. Just go.* But he looked back at her. Her breath caught.

"Lord, you must," shouted the voices, "It is Oslac. We cannot stop him."

He wiped the blood off his face. He got to his feet, in one fluid movement that belied wounds or the cloying fingers of emotion. His hand had already gathered up sword and cloak.

"I am here."

Less than two long strides took him to the door, but there he turned. Blank, freezing eyes held hers.

"You will wait for me. Here. Is that understood?"

But it was not really a question so she did not reply. The door closed after him.

"There is nothing wrong with me."

Sigrid sat on the chair by the freshly banked fire and glared at the English maid. The last thing she wanted was a witness to the wreckage.

"Lady, the lord Liefwin sent me to you because you were not well. Indeed you do not look it."

The lord *Liefwin.* The words froze her. Why would the Mercian have done such a thing? He would be too angry and…had he told this preening wench what a fool Sigrid had made of herself? Were they laughing, Liefwin and the buxom serving maid? Boasting of how he would punish her?

She set her chin. She hoped the wench could not tell she had just been bawling her eyes out.

"I do not require anything. You may go."

"Did you argue?"

Sigrid glared. "I do not…"

The woman's gaze traveled from Sigrid to the disorder of Liefwin's bed, plain to see in the midday sunlight.

"Shall I straighten that?"

"Leave it! Leave me."

"Very well, lady. No need to look so. I am sure if you do not want him in your bed, there are others who would."

Sigrid would kill the saucy wench. She would…but there was something else in the woman's English eyes that she could not fathom. The idea came to her that it was blame.

But Liefwin was the one with the power, with everything, including, there could be no doubt, a supply of women who were willing and better at bed sports than she was.

"I have no doubt there are plenty of others." Sigrid smiled into the pretty face to show she did not care.

The girl shrugged. "He is a…generous man."

Sigrid ignored the lewder meaning of the words.

"He can be as generous as he likes. He has all the plunder of the town. It must dazzle you all."

She got a shrug. "It is not just that. He is kind. I thought you might be kind. You never told him it was me who said he was going to kill the prisoners."

Sigrid blinked. That seemed a lifetime ago.

"So I thought you would see. Not many men are kind."

"*Kind* has nothing to do with—"

"Does it not? Do not say he is not a generous bed friend to you because you are Danish. He has no thought for anyone or anything but you and—" a sweeping gesture around the luxuriously fitted room "—nothing was too much for you."

"He does not...none of it is for me. It is all his. He—"

"He? He no longer cares for the treasures of this world. It was all for you and none of us dared to say a word that might offend you."

"But I am Danish. An enemy. A thing for ransom. What else could I be to him but that?" *And I cannot please men.*

The woman shrugged. "As you wish, lady. Doubtless you are right. Such things cannot be changed."

"No," said Sigrid. But she felt like a traitor.

She sat quite alone in the middle of the Mercian's looted treasures and buried her head in her hands. She wanted to weep for pain and confusion and loneliness, but the tears would no longer come.

It was all for you....

It was impossible. The woman was mad. Or jealous. Because she thought that Sigrid had stolen the source of so much sought-after *generosity.*

Memories of what had happened between Liefwin and her spiked though her mind like knife blades, painful and without mercy. But what stayed with her most clearly was his kiss and the smooth caress of his hands.

She had wanted her generous bed friend and his hot, pliant mouth and his knowing touch then. She had actually wanted the pleasure of it. And she had wanted to…oh, she could not explain it. She had wanted to be close to him, to mean something to him. She had wanted him to want her.

And he had. He had looked at her in such a way, as though she was as beautiful and desirable as Freya. Then he had touched her and the excitement had sprung between them, and she had been dazzled by him. No. By the fact that she had thought he needed her.

She had wanted to give him what men so desired. More than that. She had wanted to know and understand what it was. And he had made magic of what was hideous. At the start. But then everything had changed.

No. It had not. *She* had changed, not Liefwin. Liefwin had wanted what was the natural conclusion and she had not.

She had.

Until she remembered what it would be like. She did not know how anyone could bear what men did to women.

She got up and her foot caught against something hard. The book. She snatched it up off the floor. It was covered in rushes. It might be damaged. She brushed them off, careful of the garnet eyes of the *wyrm.*

It looked all right. She opened the first page.

Hwæt we Gar-Dena…

It sprang off the parchment at her. She could read it. Not the rest. Just the first four words he had taught her. But the rest was there, on the page, ready to be changed into meaning. Magic. Unspoiled and unspoilable by anything.

He is kind.

He was. She had never given him a chance. He had been nothing but kind to her since he had chosen to pull her out of the carnage of the town. Even though he was Mercian.

Liefwin. Beloved Friend. He had been a better friend to her than anyone she had ever known. Though every death in the unwanted, ill-fated battle lay between them. He had believed in her in spite of that.

There was more worth in that than there was in vengeance.

She had been blind. She had taken everything, his wealth, his protection and his kindness. She had taken his kiss and encouraged his hands and his body in its loving and then she had turned on him like a hell-fiend.

He had not taken his revenge on her, even though it would have been so easy for him to do. Forbearance had been stronger and she had made no return for it.

She put down the book.

She would not cry again.

She crossed the room and poured water for herself. Its coldness stung her swollen eyelids, fresh, cleansing. She buried her whole face in it, gasping. Her disordered hair fell over her shoulder. She wet the hair, tore her clothes off, covered herself in pure coldness until her skin tingled and shivered with it.

She used the honey soap and rinsed her hair in elderflower water.

She scrubbed her body dry, as hard as she could. Then, wrapped in her clothes and her cloak, she huddled beside the fire, fanning out the long, wet strands of her hair to dry. She would have the time to set the pleats in her new underdress. If she hurried…

She did not admit what she was doing until she was standing in her new dress, dusting a thin line of finely powdered charcoal round her eyes.

She looked at her reflection in the bronze mirror. Her hair shone and was softly scented. Her eyes were subtly shadowed. Her dress was beautiful, of the costliest materials anyone could have. A high born English lady could not have had better. Its style was still Danish, but that was only the more flattering.

She began to tremble.

He would never forgive her.

Not for what she had done. It was not a thing a man would forgive a woman, not even if she really was as beautiful and seductive as Freya.

Seduction.

She was mad. As if he would let her begin that trick again. She had tried before over the prisoners and it had not worked. He had not even wanted her and then today, when he had, she had been first inept and then like a hellcat.

She sat down.

If she told him, if she explained…

How could she possibly explain it? And why

should he listen? She was foreign, part of an alien force in his country that he hated.

Yet even though he knew that, even after all she had said to him, he had given her the gift of the book.

She cast dried lavender heads on the bright fire. The scent filled the warm room that held all she could want.

He would come back and she would tell him.

She sat on, long after it was plain he would not come.

The fire died down and the cold came creeping in with the dark.

If you do not want him in your bed, there are others who would.

She did not go to her empty bed until dawn.

He did not come but it made no difference. Because there was nothing, in truth, that she could have told him.

She woke to the sound of someone else in the room.

She scrambled up, dragging the bed curtains aside before the noise could stop. The morning light was bright.

"Liefwin?"

But it was not him. The maid, carrying a pitcher of water, stared at her. The other bed was empty, undisturbed.

"I doubt you will see him before noon today, lady. There was a feast last night, in the town. You can imagine what that was like with Oslac's army. Drinking and...wenching.

"He stayed."

Chapter Eleven

"Liefwin. Wake up."

Ceolfrith's voice, calling him out of the cloying, fetid darkness. It sounded as rough as a blacksmith's file, which meant that Ceolfrith was anxious. So that Liefwin thought for a moment that he must have been caught up in the horror of the Dream. This time terrifyingly unremembered. But it was not so.

He forced his eyes open. Every muscle in his body ached. He managed to get as far as his good elbow.

"Hard night?"

Ceolfrith's gaze drifted across to the pale shape of a female leg somewhere beyond him in the murk.

"Oh, very funny."

He was frozen. He should have taken a place closer to the fire, but he had not wanted to get within spitting distance of Oslac.

Ceolfrith's interested gaze roamed farther across the hall and the prostrate bodies and the remains of the feast.

"Had a busy evening, I see."

Liefwin fixed his eyes on the disingenuous face.

"Chance would have been a fine thing. Even if I had wished it, I would never have got past the guard dog."

"Guard dog?" The bland expression slipped slightly.

"The guard dog." Liefwin glanced down from his uncomfortable bed on the mead bench. "It was on the floor somewhere. Unless you have sent it away. Your nephew Cerdic?"

"Oh. Cerdic. Good keen lad. You have said so yourself in the past. Always eager to be useful."

"I did not know the half of it. I could not breathe without that idiotic freckled face looming out of the air and asking whether I was *all right*. Tell me, just why should your nephew Cerdic think I needed a nursemaid like some sick girl-child? And who else did you tell?" he snapped before Ceolfrith could recover.

Ceolfrith's hairy jaw jutted further into the gloom. "You mean who else knows that you are ill and will not do anything to help yourself? No one except you, me, Alfwin and Cerdic. And the *bedda*...why are you looking like that? You *are* sick. It is the wound. I knew it. It is my fault—"

"Do not be so stupid. It is just too much ale. Do not..." Liefwin tried to turn his mind from what he had done to the *bedda*. Tried to close his eyes against her terrified face. Tried to move. But Ceolfrith was already hauling on him.

"Leave it." That he did not yell was an achievement, but his voice came out like cracking ice and the convulsive movement away from the pain was beyond his control.

He was dimly conscious of the large, clumsy hands releasing him and then Ceolfrith's voice saying with lethal formality, ''I am sorry, lord.''

There was a deadly silence during which Liefwin tried to breathe through the stabbing pain and wipe out all memories of what had happened yesterday. He forced himself to fix his whole concentration on what was happening now, on what had to be got through before he could see the girl again.

If she would see him.

Ceolfrith's feet were shuffling in the nameless debris. Liefwin gripped the edge of the bench.

No one should have to be that worried about you just because you do not happen to want to speak to them.

The voice, in his mind, sounded real.

The *bedda,* Sigrid, knew every weakness he had. They seemed to be as obvious to her as clouds in a February sky.

Impossible to turn his thoughts from her. He tried to steady his breath enough to say something coherent.

''I do not—'' But Ceolfrith was already speaking. It was just as well. Because he had no words at all.

''I came to tell you the patrol got back this morning.''

Liefwin looked up.

''And?'' But Ceolfrith's face told him. He swore.

''They did their best. There is a lot of ground to cover and we do not have enough men. The village was alight when they got there. Our men gave chase, but it was too close to Colchester and they would have had the remains of the Danish army on them, not just a Danish raiding party.''

"It was…like last time?"

"Aye. They were in time to save some of the villagers, four of the women and a young lad and some children. But the rest were hacked to pieces so you could hardly tell what they were, and one man with his throat ripped out.''

"Then it is the same raider is it not? The berserker. The one who terrified this town into fighting against us.'' Liefwin's jaw tightened. "This will not go on.''

Ceolfrith shrugged. "There is not much more we can do until Colchester is taken. It…it has been a long campaign and it is hard for some of them to face something like this. If only we had more men.''

"More men? We have a whole army. Just look at it.'' Liefwin made one savage gesture toward the sprawled bodies in the murk.

"But no one can do anything about that except the king.''

"I will not wait for King Edward.'' Liefwin surged to his feet, forcing movement through his stiffened muscles.

It was so clear.

"I will go out with the patrol myself. Tomorrow. I will take only those who wish to come.''

"*You?* You are mad. You are in no state. You cannot—''

"What I cannot do is expect my men to do something I am not prepared to do myself.'' That was unanswerable. He started walking toward the door as though there was nothing wrong, but Ceolfrith was suddenly standing in his way. He banged into a barrel chest which did not move.

"Your men," said Ceolfrith, "owe you their loyalty and their lives. They have a duty to you. You have been a better lord to them than any man has a right to expect."

Liefwin stepped back, from the unexpected words as much as from Ceolfrith attempting to bar his way. The emptiness of such words was unbearable.

"I will go." His voice had turned into ice again.

"Then I will go with you."

"No. It is not necessary. I do not—"

"You think I will let you down again, like last time—"

"Do not say that! Do not ever say such a thing. Do you hear me?"

"I think I...understand."

Liefwin had no recollection of shoving Ceolfrith into the wall. He let go.

Ceolfrith sagged at the knees. There were small choking sounds which made Liefwin wince. "I am sorry," he said with as much lethal formality as Ceolfrith had used before.

"Ha! I taught you that hold. Left hand was a bit weak." The choking sounds turned into a snort of derision.

It was so typical of Ceolfrith that Liefwin laughed. But it came out as a strange sound, forced and out of place. Ceolfrith stared.

"You are in a mess, are you not?"

Liefwin had got to the point where the possibility of saying no did not exist anymore.

Because it was no longer only himself who was involved. He cleared his mouth. "I need your help."

The words seemed strange and rusty from lack of use. He could not remember saying such a thing since he was five years old and fatherless. He could not think of an adequate reason why Ceolfrith should help him. He did not know whether friendship could survive.

"I need you to look after Sigrid," he said, before Ceolfrith could even think of drawing back. "There is no one I can trust like you. I need to make sure that she is safe, and that she does not...run away from me."

"You think she might?"

It was not a time for face-saving lies.

"Yes. She nearly did yesterday. She...she has more reason now."

"Oh?"

But some things were not possible to answer.

"She has no idea," he said rapidly. "Yesterday she tried to walk out with nothing but her cloak and the Beowulf book. Someone would have killed her for less than half the gold on that. She...I cannot have anything happen to her."

The words, which had been falling over themselves off his tongue, dried up. He could not say another thing. But surely Ceolfrith would understand.

"All right."

It was done. If Ceolfrith gave his word to something, it was carried out. Only one thing left. Liefwin took a breath that shot pain through the cramped muscles of his chest.

"I promised her I would get her back to her kin.

She offered me a ransom. You will not take it. She is to have all of my share of the plunder from this campaign and the book.''

"*All* of it?''

"It is fitting,'' said Liefwin in the voice that did not permit argument. "Will you see it is done?''

"Aye, but—''

"I am giving you that farm you have always wanted back home, the one with the oak wood—''

"You are what?''

"One of us has to be able to go home to something, otherwise all that we have done here has no purpose.'' He stopped. He could not explain further, but Ceolfrith would know. Surely Ceolfrith would know what he could not say. He turned away.

"Wait,'' shouted Ceolfrith's voice through the gloom. "You are talking as though you will not come back.''

"Oh, I will come back,'' said Liefwin. "You know my luck. I always win.'' But even as he said it, his skin shivered and he wondered whether *wyrd* had turned at last. He could smell death in the reeking air of the hall.

It made no difference whether he was *fæg*, doomed to death, or not. He would not shirk what had to be done.

"I shall find the berserker, and I shall kill him.''

He was suddenly aware that she was there. Standing in the shadows beside the door of Alfwin's bower. Right behind him. Liefwin hardly needed to turn his head to know it was her.

He had come to see how Alfwin fared. He had not

expected to land himself in a deadly argument with an invalid. Sigrid must have been just in time to hear the final damning words from Alfwin's lips.

"You do not care. You are as cold as frostbitten stone."

She could only have heard the end of the disastrous argument, but Alfwin's hurt, furious, unsteady voice had hardly spared his Danish foes. Of course, Alfwin had every right. You had only to look at the tortured body, the shaking head resolutely turned toward the wall.

Only a stone heart would be unmoved by that.

When Alfwin's voice had stopped for lack of breath, and the sleeping draught Liefwin had shoved down his throat had its effect, she came forward out of the shadows to help him rearrange the pathetic mess of his cousin on the pillows.

She must have been too afraid, before, to make her presence known. Alfwin had not seen her. Yet she had chosen to stay, despite Alfwin's bitter unrestrained curses on Danishness, and now she was helping him.

She did not ask about what had caused the argument. She neither spoke nor looked at him.

When everything was done that could be done, she followed him back, like an obedient servant who had no choice, to their bower.

Her bower.

He shut the door and faced her.

The light from the open window showed that she had slept about as much as he had. Her face was ash pale. She was wearing her old, patched dress, the one she had worn the first time he had seen her, even

though she had new ones, out of the goods he had
given her.

He saw her eyes clearly. They were as bitter and
defiant as when she had first confronted him in this
chamber.

He watched her across the full distance of the room
and it was as though they were complete strangers.
As though everything that had happened since he had
found her in the town, every word they had said,
every touch, every argument, every small step toward
understanding had been wiped out by what he had
done yesterday.

Those eyes, every tense line of her body told him
that she wanted him gone. But she was so beautiful
to him that he knew he was quite capable of doing
what he had done to her yesterday again. Even with
that bitter look of accusation in her eyes.

The knowledge of that was intolerable. If anything
was needed to make his decision right, it was his reaction just to the sight of her.

She raised one small hand to push the ice-blond
hair out of her face. Her wrist was scarcely thicker
than a child's.

He could not have used his own strength against
that. The thought was not to be borne.

He would not do so again. She had to know that.

"I have arranged for my servant to collect my
things. The room is yours, of course, and everything
you need. I—"

"You are moving out?"

There was none of the relief he had expected. She
finished the question on a sort of gasp and her face
lost the last of its color, as though he had turned round

and punched her in the stomach. He did not understand it and he could feel the guilt increasing by the second.

"But you told me that...you said you would stay with me..." Her voice trailed off and just for an instant the defiance crumbled and the eyes held the haunted look that twisted something inside him.

He could not bear knowing that he had put that look back into her eyes.

"You gave me your word—"

"My *word*? My word is worthless. It is already broken." The shame of saying that made his gorge rise, but she just looked at him and shook her head.

"No. It was not so." Then before he could speak, "You should have let me go—"

"No!" His voice cut across hers instantly. "That is one thing I will not permit." Despite all his resolutions not to upset her further, the words came out with the deadly force he had used on Ceolfrith in the mead hall, with the coldness that had taken him in the appalling and unexpected confrontation with Alfwin. He could not seem to escape it this day.

At least Ceolfrith and Alfwin knew what was happening outside these four walls. Sigrid did not. He had not meant to speak in such a way to her above anyone, not after the way he had used her.

He had to tell her before she did something else as stupid as yesterday morning's attempted flight.

He had the sensation it would mean stepping further into disaster, into something he could not control. But it was not possible to draw back. The stakes were too high. She had to know, even if it was not what she wished to hear, even if it only increased the gulf between them.

He forced his voice into something like calmness.

''Will you sit? I must speak with you.''

She did not move.

He took a chair at the table himself, largely because it was a matter of necessity. If only he had slept. Then his head might be clearer. Then he might find the right words to say, the words that might distress her less.

There was no way to get through what must be said, what he wanted her to understand, without touching on the world outside. The world that she had deliberately shut out. It had not escaped him that the shutters across the window that faced the town were always barred.

He had recognized why she had done that and he had respected it. He had made everyone else respect it. He had not allowed anyone to plague her with what was going on outside, to say anything to her that might add to either her fears or her grief.

He had succeeded in that too well. She had very little idea of what was happening beyond these four walls. So little that yesterday she had been prepared to plunge herself, heedless, into a danger she did not understand. A danger that would have killed her.

That much he now had to make her understand. For her own sake.

Yet he felt incredibly reluctant. She never spoke, or asked of anything directly related to what happened outside. Except of the prisoners.

That brought him right back to the start.

"I have to talk to you about last night and what happened at the feast and what—"

"No! No. It is not necessary."

Her eyes held a kind of helpless fury, as though he was trying to humiliate her in some way. He would not willingly do such a thing. He did not want to speak of this, of any of it. But there were so few choices left.

"Sigrid, I would not talk of such things to you if it were not necessary—"

"It is not necessary. You do not have to say anything."

"I do—"

"I know already."

"You know? About the prisoners?" He could not understand her anger. Yes, he could. In her eyes he would be as much to blame as Oslac. But she must listen. For her sake.

"The prisoners are only part of the picture. You must—"

"What have the prisoners got to do with anything?" She was looking at him as if his wits were begging. "I thought you went to the feast last night and...I thought..."

"You thought what? What did you think I had gone there for? The whoring?"

He stopped.

"That was what you thought."

Her mouth opened and shut. But there was no point in her saying anything. Her eyes, her face, her stumbling words had told him exactly how he figured in her mind.

She thought because he had not got his satisfaction with her he had taken it elsewhere.

It was an obvious conclusion. The fact that she was more important to him than anything in the world was only something in his mind. The fact that yesterday's disastrous attempt at closeness had meant so much to him, so much that he had fooled himself it could transcend all the differences between them…that had been nothing more than his own self-indulgence. He had wanted her so much that he had been able to make himself believe that she had wanted him. It was his own desperation that had made him blind.

But she had not desired him. She had thought she had no choice but to humor his lust. So she had tried. But in the end she had not been able to.

He had promised her she would be safe and he had—

"I am sorry," she said in a small voice that made him want to smash something.

"No. What else should you think? That is how I behave, is it not? I regret what happened," he added before she could say whatever else she was trying to get out. "I would not have it happen again and I will see that it does not. It was the last thing I wished."

"Yes. Of course. I realize that. It does not matter." Her voice was stiff and she was not looking at him but at something on the floor.

"Sigrid," he said, and just the sound of her name seemed to burn his throat, "there are some things I must say to you before I go."

"Must you?"

There was a small light in her voice at that, surely?

"About the prisoners. About what is happening."

"Oh."

He was mistaken. The voice was as blank and life-less as the averted head.

"Will you not at least sit down?"

She sat, as though doing his bidding.

"Lord," she said, which was the one word from her that he had begun to hate.

His hands clenched themselves into fists. He straightened them out in case she saw them. He tried again.

"This does not have to go on much longer. Not for us. For you," he corrected himself, but her eyes seemed to darken with every word, as if he took the life out of them.

He tried desperately to explain it so that she might be reassured about some things, at least. "It can only be about three days, four at the most before King Edward arrives with the rest of the army and—"

"And then you will go home, to Tamworth."

He paused, distracted by what seemed irrelevant.

"I do not…live at Tamworth. I am not going—" he could not even pronounce the word *home* "—to where I live. Sigrid, I will see you get back to your family…"

Her eyes slid away from his. She did not believe him. She no longer believed a word he said.

"I will do it. I will keep my word on this. Ceolfrith knows it and if I am not here he will—"

"If you are not here? Why would you not be here?"

And he saw that everything he had said had only served to put the fear into her eyes again. More fear than would seem possible. It was not what he had expected. Every word he spoke seemed fated to make things worse.

"Sigrid, you will not be in danger. But you must understand how things are for your own sake. When Edward gets here it will be like putting a torch to a hay barn. If he goes about this the right way, the whole countryside is going to rise with him. There will be no stopping it. You must have guessed something of that. Your whole town knew it. They would have accepted Edward as overlord with no bloodshed if they had not been persuaded otherwise by the shipmen and the army from East Anglia."

He paused. Her pale face was turned away from him again and he felt a terrible pity for her. But it was no longer possible to hide things from her.

"You know what happened, what persuaded the town to fight. The berserker and…"

She gasped. She tried to stop it but the whole of her slight frame shuddered. He remembered how terrified she was of the very idea of a berserker. That must be forever linked in her mind with the cause of the battle that had made her lose everything. He should never have said the word.

"It is all right," he said. His hand reached out instinctively to touch her arm and then stopped. His touch would no longer be reassurance to her. If it ever had been.

"What I am trying to say is that Edward's advance is so certain it should give him enough assurance to forget what is past."

"Spare the prisoners, you mean?"

He watched the bent head.. "Yes. Oslac is a fool. Last night they were all…ale-glad and looking for amusement. Oslac-Witlack thought the prisoners in fetters might provide it. I dissuaded him.''

She did look up then, but the eyes were strained and suddenly seemed full of secrets he could not fathom.

''That was why you went to the hall? That was what you did? Saved the prisoners?''

''Yes.''

It was what she had wanted. What she had begged him for and what, some unimaginably long time ago, she had been prepared to humiliate herself for by seducing him. He had given her what she wished, but it seemed to bring them no closer. There was only distance between them, dark and unbridgable, and the strange secrets in her eyes.

''Then,'' she began, with the chilling formality Ceolfrith had used on him, ''I owe you my grat—''

''No,'' he said, and the combined forces of the past and the present and the future seemed to force him back into that state of black ice. ''It was something that had to be done, a matter of strategy.''

''Yes, of course. Strategy. A…a magnanimous royal gesture, was that not what you called it?''

''Something like that.'' He could remember in every detail how they had sat at this same table and she had tried to beguile him with her bare arms and her untied dress. He remembered the touch of her hands on his body and the burning reaction it brought in his loins. Even though her touch had been counterfeit, he had still wanted it. He wanted it now, despite everything.

He could feel the heat in his body and the frustrated desire for her that would ignite like flame if he so much as touched her. So that he would be lost to everything except the need to take her.

But that would kill him. Because his mind would be unable to bear the knowledge that he had forced himself on her when she did not want him.

The only thing left that he could do for her was to make her safe and stop her from running headlong to her death.

"Edward will spare the prisoners rather than take vengeance," he began, as though every word was some carefully weighed piece of gold, "if he is assured of his position."

He could see the alarm gathering again in her eyes and he was almost glad of it if it would make her understand the danger she had so nearly put herself in yesterday. But he still pitched his voice with caution.

"We have been plagued by a raiding party—" She flinched immediately at his words, making him pause. Her eyes were wide, fixed on his. They were full of the fear he expected, the fear he did not want to put there. But there was no surprise.

It was as though she knew already.

Of course, it was not impossible for her to know. People gossiped. It was the world's way. Someone might have spoken despite what he had said. He plunged on. "They are shipmen it is thought, raiders and opportunists." She did know. It was in her eyes, even though she tried to disguise the knowledge from him.

She knew it and she had been quite prepared to risk the dangers of that with her stolen and lethally valuable hoard of gold, just to get away from him.

She knew more than he had looked for, but she could not know the worst: that one of the war band was a berserker, *the* berserker. He hesitated about telling her, he who never hesitated over any decision. And then she made a small sound as though she wanted to say something but could not. Her thin hands bunched themselves into fists.

"Sigrid?"

If she would just say it, whatever it was. But the unknown words were suppressed into silence, and the gulf of separation was wide between them, beyond any power to bridge.

"It is something I must deal with." The truth stabbed through the tautness of the air between them, bitter as iron-tipped arrows. "And it must be soon. You may think it an unbearably long wait until Edward gets here, but I am running out of time." The irony in that that would not be lost on her mind. "I must—"

She spoke. "You?" Her eyes were like twin black pools. "You keep talking as though it is you, yourself, who must do this now. As though you would fight this raiding party yourself. You cannot mean it."

She always picked out some aspect of what he said that left him in sudden quicksand, something unexpected and beside the point. But yet it was not. It was not beside the point for them at all.

"It should be me. Sigrid, I cannot and I will not disguise from you what I am, what I do, what I have done most of my life since I was big enough to pick up a sword."

She was frowning, and then all of a sudden he

knew she had made some decision. Her eyes met his quite calmly before she took the breath to speak.

"What you are doing now must be right."

He could feel his aching muscles sag against the chair back. Only Sigrid. There was only Sigrid in the whole world who could floor him with no more effort than half a dozen words.

"Right?" he said, like some deaf half-wit who could not understand the most basic of ideas.

"Yes."

It did not seem possible after all that they had said. It did not seem possible that she could think he was right to go out and attempt to kill a party of her fellow Danes. But then loyalties could be more complicated than that. Perhaps it was because of what she felt for the prisoners, who seemed to mean more to her than people who faced the usual fate of defeated leaders.

Perhaps the bare fact that the shipmen and the army were Danish might not be enough to make up for what they had done to her town.

Loyalties were quite savagely and deeply personal.

But even so... "I can scarcely believe you said that. Even Alfwin thinks I am wrong. That was what the argument was about."

"I see."

Her voice held all expression back, but it was quite firm. Liefwin hesitated. He had not intended to bring that into his dealings with her, but she had walked in on the whole insoluble mess.

"Tell me," she said with the same firmness, and there no longer seemed any alternative. There was no hope and no point in concealing anything.

Yet it was so hard to find the words. In truth he

could not remember the last time he had tried to explain so much to anybody as he had to Sigrid. He did not speak of anything that was personal. Not now. But he just kept on talking, as though there could be some understanding in this where there was none anywhere else.

"Alfwin," he said, "believes I have betrayed our kinship by trying to save the prisoners. That our blood tie means nothing to me and is dishonored because I have not taken proper vengeance for his injuries. Or for my retainers and all of my men who are dead."

"The path of vengeance must always be followed? But...what do you think?"

He shrugged one painful shoulder. Everything, the words he was forced to say to Sigrid, all that he had done, all that he would have to do in the future, was more than it was possible to bear. "I no longer know what is right. I only know that it would have been impossible for me to have done otherwise."

She nodded and her eyes held acknowledgment. Those eyes knew that he was no longer talking of the dictates of military strategy, even though that was still in his thoughts, but of the deepest motivations that ruled his life.

He could no longer conceal anything.

With a sense of leaping into fathomless water, he came to the point.

"The reason I am telling you all this is because I want you to understand what you were doing yesterday when you nearly walked out of here with nothing except a deadweight of gold that somebody would have killed you for even in peacetime. You have to know what things are like beyond these four walls and how small are the chances that you would have survived.''

He paused, watching her face. The dark, smoke-gray eyes regarded him with grave attention. Did she, would she, understand? Would she believe him? Would she realize the importance of what he was saying?

''I tried to tell you that first night when we stopped by the walls and you were looking toward the gates. I said if you stayed with me you would be safe from all that. Despite…despite what happened between us, it is still so. I would not…such a thing will not happen again.''

''No,'' she said, her voice scarce more than a whisper. ''It could not, could it?''

Her gaze, locked on his, held all the pain he must have caused her. Her eyes were wide with it and yet he thought, from that look, that she believed him. But she just looked so hopeless and there was nothing he could do to redress that.

''Sigrid, you are as free in this place as it is possible to be. If you want to go into the town, you can go.'' Perhaps if she could face that much it might help her. ''It will be safe for you if you take Ceolfrith or someone with you. But you must not go beyond…''

Her shoulders stiffened. ''The town? What would there be for me there? Just ruins—''

''Not ruins. Not now.'' At least that much had been done. ''It is rebuilt. If you could see—''

''Rebuilt? Who would do that? No one would—*you?*'' The stress on that word held every nuance the irony in his soul could have desired.

''But why—oh, I see. Strategy. You want to keep

your men busy, and you need the fortifications so you
have rebuilt them and—''

''Not just the fortifications. The town.''

''The…the town.''

''Sigrid, there must be people there whom you
want to—''

''No! There is no one I care for and no one I want
to see. I have no reason to go there.'' The heart-
shaped face set. The eyes held bitterness that nothing
could relieve, least of all, anything he could say.

The only thing left to him was the will to save her
from the endless bloodshed that reigned outside.

''Then do not go, and certainly do not go beyond
the walls. Not now. Not yet.'' *Don't let your fate be…*
But he could not even think that. In case it happened.
He tried to block out of his mind all that had been,
tried to think of the future, her future. If he could
keep that safe, if she could, if this was the one and
only thing that they could achieve together…

''Sigrid you have to listen to me in this.'' But he
was forced to pause because of the constriction in his
chest. He did not know whether he could find the
right words. He could feel the moment slip beyond
him in the wideness of her eyes. He tried to hold her
gaze to communicate to her how important this was.
He tried to hold in his mind to whatever connection
there was to the mysterious thoughts inside her head.

He told himself she would listen. Sigrid was not a
restless spirit always driven onward to seek something
new. She would not endanger herself recklessly. She
would understand. She always understood things even
if she hated him. He would tell her.

''Sigrid, it is just that…'' *I could not bear anything*

to happen to you. I could not bear a repetition of the horrors of the past… But the power of the past froze the words in his throat, like blocks of ice forming across a river in winter.

"Outside these walls…"

She had stopped listening. The present brightness of her eyes had dulled into an impenetrable self-absorption. The sort that he had never known how to get through.

"*Sigrid.* Do you understand a word I have said?"

She started.

"Of course." But her eyes were wide and blank and the secrets seemed to fill them once more. "You have told me all you needed to say. All that…it was just that…"

She stopped. She produced a dutiful smile.

"Lord?"

That was what defeat looked like. It hid amongst the trappings of success, like a viper in spring grass. So familiar. But suppose this time it was impossible to bear?

"Lord?"

He surged to his feet, wanting only to get out into the air. Somewhere where no one could see him making such a fool of himself, at the mercy of the shadows of his past.

"I must go." Then the sudden sick rush of dizziness hit him. The legacy of his night on the mead bench. It was only a momentary lapse, just enough to make him clutch at the chair back. She would not notice. But she did. He felt her hand on his arm and there was alarm in the dutifully smiling face.

"It cannot go on like this," she said.

"I have told you, if there is a way to stop, I have not found it."

"There must be."

He heard the fear in her voice and he suddenly realized how he must appear to her, like some sort of savage. He had spent the night in his clothes, in a room that stank of ale and rank humanity. He could not remember shaving. Such thoughts had not occurred to him. He had just barged in when she was upset and had spoken of nothing but death and destruction.

He stepped away from her, away from the hand that could have no desire to touch him.

"Do not go yet. Please."

She sounded desperate. He could not understand it. All she must want was to see him gone. But then, however he had behaved, whatever he was, he was all she had in the hostile world he had just described to her in such detail.

"Please sit down again."

He did not want to stay. But still less did he want her to have to plead with him over anything. In a moment she would be calling him *lord* again.

"Please. Stay for a while…lord. I have some of the new ale. It is good. I will get you some."

Perfect. Just what he needed after last night.

"Fine."

She bustled about between him and the table. He did not want to disturb her. He got out of her way. The bed seemed nearest. He sat on it.

"There is a fresh pitcher. I shall not be long."

He leaned his aching head back, since there was no help for it, and swung his feet off the floor. He just watched her as she moved about. He did not try to stop her. She seemed to find such ordinary tasks as this almost comforting. Setting things right to her own satisfaction.

He watched her while he could. Before she was gone out of his life forever. It was so nearly over, the thing between them that did not have an existence, that had never had a chance to have an existence and never would. It was ending now.

He closed his burning eyes because he could no longer bear the sight of her.

The pain was waiting for him in the dark. Not just the pain of his abused body but something in his heart. He felt it so keenly that he would have welcomed the freezing touch of the coldness that had held him in its grip for so long.

But the coldness, at once shield and destroyer, was no longer there.

No weary spirit may stand against wyrd.

The words that came into his head were not from her favorite *Beowulf* but some other story, some other fragment of a poem that had lodged in the recesses of his mind. Something about a man who was completely alone, bereft of all kinship. He could remember hearing it without enough understanding, thinking such words could never apply to him.

He must go, as soon as she was finished, as soon as she was settled. There was tomorrow to see about. His hand gripped the side of the bed.

Chapter Twelve

Sigrid knew exactly what she must do. There was only one thing left. She took as long as it was possible to take over such a matter as preparing a single cup of ale. Her hands were quite steady, but her eyes kept glancing toward the decorated wooden chest in the corner. The one with the cross on the lid.

She did not dare look behind her at Liefwin until it seemed impossible to avoid it.

She let out her breath.

Then putting down the unnecessary ale cup she moved swiftly across the room.

She dropped to her knees among the clean, sweet-smelling rushes beside the bed. He slept.

She buried her face in the red-gold hair.

She could not stay like this forever. She had to move. She untangled her hand from the neck of Lief-win's tunic, but she could not raise her head. His hair felt soft against her skin. It was the only soft thing there was with him. She moved her face against its richness.

Moments like these made you greedy. But they did

not belong to her. Just as Liefwin did not. She untangled her hand again and made herself raise her head.

She looked at his sleeping face, pale, unshaven, with a smudge of grime across one eyebrow. The eyes were shadowed with exhaustion. The soft hair was a tangled mess. The fine clothes on the solid body were crumpled and smelled of ale and wood smoke. He did not look like the perfect thane.

She touched the face roughened by stubble very gently, hardly a touch at all. He did not wake. She did not want him to.

If she could stay like this. If things had been different…but there was no place for such dreaming.

She thought of everything he had said and the impossible gulf between them. She thought of Edward, the Saxon king, who would be here in two or three days. She thought of the horrors that had been lying all the time, unimagined by her, outside their door.

She studied the strained face, the small lines round his eyes that should not have been there in one who was not much older than her, the particular set line of the mouth that seemed to have been formed to smile.

She thought he slept deeply, in the dead and distant wastes of exhaustion. But if he were to wake before…she did not have much time.

Her hands moved to the leather belt at his waist, touched the heavy, gilded buckle, released it. Still he slept. She picked up the gold strap end decorated with the backward-looking beast with the enameled eyes and tongue, and threaded it through the loop of the buckle.

He did not move.

She grasped the tablet woven hem of his tunic, gently pulling the material upward, above his knees, across the solid expanse of his thighs. She stopped.

There was something indecent about pushing aside the skirts of a man's tunic, especially when the man was so...so very...she swallowed. She could feel the heat rising in her face even though there was no one to see her and no one knew what she did. Least of all Liefwin.

The heat was right through her. Fool that she was. She had burned her boats in that direction.

She tried to get a better grip on the fine wool in her clumsy fingers, rolled it back as carefully as she could. She tried not to look at the outward swelling mass of his thighs in the tight, dark trousers, the powerful, compact hips, the shadowed shape of his sex.

She could not stop looking.

She was so hot and yet she shivered as though she had the ague. She was moon-mad. There must be no one and nothing in the world like him. To make her feel so. In spite of everything.

She peeled away the smooth linen of his shirt, sliding the material across the warm, naked skin of his abdomen. Her gaze followed the smooth flatness of his belly, the strong curve of the rib cage; and then she saw it, the black disfigurement along his left side, stretching its ugly trail across his chest, up to his shoulder. She winced.

She forced herself not to think about how much it hurt or what he suffered from it, but to look assessingly. As though she had the skills of a leech, which she did not.

It looked...perhaps she had just forgotten how bad

it was. It was not worse, surely? Her gaze sought the patch of broken skin in the center of the damage, dreading what she might find. Such wounds from chain mail piercing the skin almost always turned bad. But it was clean. It really was.

She let out the pent-up sigh of relief held deep inside her. Her breath fanned across his mangled flesh.

She did not know whether anything was broken under all that mess. She was so ignorant. Most people were when it came down to it. Wounds healed or not, as fate disposed.

But you did need to give yourself a chance, as he would not.

She knew instinctively it was not something that could be reasoned with. There was something else that she did not understand. Even if he had taken to his bed like Alfwin, she did not know whether things would have been much different.

She straightened the shirt and the tunic, refastening the belt, even though it would be less comfortable for him. The last thing she wanted was for him to realize she had touched him.

She could not cover him with the bedclothes, because he was lying on top of them and he was far too heavy to move. Besides, she would only wake him and that was not part of her plan. She grabbed a rug off her own bed and spread it across him. She could do that much, surely.

She allowed herself the indulgence of two more minutes just to look at him. Then she picked up her cloak.

What burdened him was not something ordinary

and it was not something that anyone, either herself, or Ceolfrith, or the most skilled of leeches, would know how to mend.

It would take a miracle.

She would find one.

The man, Ceolfrith, was never where you wanted him. He was either under your feet at the most irritating of moments, or he was nowhere to be found.

The cold wind stung her face and she pulled the warmth of the cloak tighter round her shoulders. Clouds scudded across the pale blue autumn sky.

She did another circuit of the yard, trying to look as though she was just out in the fine, more or less fine, weather just to stretch her legs. She did not want to speak to any other of the Mercian soldiers. Not even to ask where Ceolfrith was.

She was on the track of her miracle and miracles were not to be explained.

"You...idiot."

That was an interesting Mercian word.

"You never do think. That is your trouble," roared Ceolfrith, who was never in the right place.

She put her head round doorway of Alfwin's bower and the afflicted saw her immediately.

"Sigrid! Lady. Will you not come in? Please? Have you seen Liefwin?" Because Alfwin looked so hangdog and desperate, she nodded and decided to go in. "Was he...is he...I suppose he is angry."

No, she thought, along with Ceolfrith, *you do not think, do you?*

"Not angry."

"Oh." Alfwin's face cleared with all the ingenuous

quickness of one who had scarce seventeen winters. "Then—"

"I think he just feels sad," she said.

She was aware of two pairs of eyes watching her: Ceolfrith's with assessment, Alfwin's with discomfort. There was silence. Sadness was a much trickier thing for boastful, overgrown, flat-footed warriors to deal with.

"It is my fault," said Alfwin finally. "Did he tell you what I said?"

Sigrid shrugged. "Only that you thought he had betrayed you by not letting Oslac kill six defenseless people."

Alfwin turned his head away and she did feel sorry for him then. He was so very young and he suffered much.

"Liefwin did understand, though, why you said it. He is not angry with you. He—"

"Lady, you are making it worse. I was selfish and I would not listen. I should never have said what I did to Liefwin. Not after what happened to him…"

"It is all right, I know about that," she said, thinking of the father murdered by Danes.

"He told you? About his wife? About Elswyth? Then you know how he feels, why he is like he is. She was so beautiful and he was mad over her and when she died—"

The hard earth-packed floor seemed to move under Sigrid's feet. *Beautiful. Then you know how he feels. Elswyth.* Who was…

"That will do, lackwit," said Ceolfrith. His large bulk moved up beside her. "The lady does not want to hear any more of your ramblings. Just shut up and try what I recommended before.''

''What?''

''*Thinking.*''

''Oh. *Oh.*''

Ceolfrith took her outside. They sat on a bench against the wall beside a leafless hawthorn tree. It was blessedly cold. Sigrid caught her breath.

''Not very bright, sometimes, Alfwin,'' observed Ceolfrith. ''Quite often, really.''

She tried to smile, to show him that she was all right.

She was, of course.

Looked at logically, she knew next to nothing about Liefwin. She had known him such a stupidly short time, after all. Just because it had been under rather desperate circumstances made it seem longer, deeper, to have more meaning than it really had. There was no reason why she should be even mildly surprised when she found out something about his past that she did not know.

She did not know anything about his past.

Not where he lived, what family he had, what had happened to him in twenty-four and a bit years.

I do not have a wife.

Elswyth. Beautiful.

''Ceolfrith…''

''Yes?''

A ready answer. Prompt. But she could tell his discomfort. In case Liefwin's bed warmer asked him about Liefwin's wife. Well, she would not.

There had been no reason for Liefwin to tell her. So there could be no reason for the uncomfortable

Ceolfrith to do so either. She thrust it out of her mind. She either wanted to do this for Liefwin, or she did not. She had known all along he was not mad over her and the fact that such madness had been reserved for his wife could make no difference.

"I want you to take me into the town. To the church."

The bulk beside her stiffened. "Do you now?"

The question held more than its face value and her first instinct was to give the foreign oaf the set-down he deserved. But she was too desperate for that. Miracles did not wait around. They picked their time and then you had to seek them or not.

She thought of Liefwin's pale face and the mangled skin hidden by the fine tunic and the way he would not give in.

"This is not finished yet," she said, in answer to the question unspoken. "I shall not go until it is."

"Really? Where is Liefwin?"

"Asleep. And I do not want him woken. Neither would you if you had seen him."

"I gather you know, then," said Ceolfrith, "that it is my fault he got hurt?"

"I did not mean—"

"I thought at first that he must blame me. But it was not so." Ceolfrith rubbed his nose absently. "He did not want to make me feel worse than I already did. Stupid lad."

Yes, thought Sigrid and her mind was filled with the memory of yelling accusations at Liefwin of being totally cold to one who loved him.

"But why?" she burst out. "Why, if you practically brought him up and he still cares about you and he rescued you to his own peril, why can he not talk to you?''

"If you know the answer to that," said Ceolfrith, "you know the answer to everything. So. Are you ready?"

If it had not been for Liefwin, she would not have been able to do it. The first step down the main street was the worst and then...it was as Liefwin had said. Rebuilt. But in quite a different way, so that she did not recognize it. It was no longer her home at all...and she did not miss it.

The church, standing alone in its patch of greenery, was untouched. It was the only stone building in the town. What she wanted lay outside the stone walls of the building itself, but still, she had never been inside and Ceolfrith would expect her to. She went in.

It was part of another world. You could feel it. She gazed round at the plastered walls, the friezes with haloed figures under arches, the delicate birds and beasts peering out coyly from a riot of vine leaves. And such colors. Red and green and bright blue. It was beautiful. She wanted to stay. She wanted to...there was no time. She glanced at Ceolfrith.

"I want to go to the holy spring, outside, to get some of the water. On my own."

Why could she just not say to Ceolfrith that she wanted the holy water for Liefwin? They had just been talking about Liefwin, for pity's sake.

Of course, Ceolfrith still might not believe her.

But that was not the real reason. She was afraid. Not so much afraid of the massive bulk of her English escort, but afraid that if she said such a thing out loud, something might break, either the miracle or, perhaps, her.

"I will come back. This is not over yet."

Ceolfrith grunted. "You know what? The older I get, the stupider I become. All right."

Maybe you could be stupid at her age, too, because for some reason she reached up to one meaty Mercian arm.

She moved before her English guard could react. Out of the corner of her eye she thought she saw a shadow cross the open doorway behind him. But she did not wait to see.

The ground was soft and muddy round the spring and she trod carefully, drawing out the leather flask from under her cloak, her whole concentration on what she was doing.

She hesitated, feeling as though she should do something respectful first, like say a prayer to the saint of the spring. But she did not know how. It was something—if the world had been different, if there had been such a thing as a future—she could have asked Liefwin about.

Liefwin. This was for him. It was something he understood and it belonged to his world. In that world the water from the spring could cure anything and it could not be wrong, surely, if she did this for someone else, for someone she loved.

Love. Her hand shook.

Love. That was the source of her fear. She had never loved anyone before. She did not want to admit that she did now. That she had done for days. Possibly ever since the first moment she had seen Liefwin in the firelit street and he had chosen to save her. Just as she had known he would.

She loved him, Liefwin the beautiful and cold, the kind heart, warm heart, full of equal measure of strength and sadness. She loved him, but she was no good at it. She was afraid she still did not understand what it meant. All she knew was that she would do whatever it took to help him.

The water was ice pure. She could see her hand turn white under its coldness.

She tried to keep the bottle steady. She thought she heard some disturbing rustle in the bushes behind her. Ceolfrith. The flask was nearly full. She tried to put the stopper in. Her hand had gone numb. She—

"You! It is you. You treacherous little bitch."

The voice spoke in Danish. She spun round. A pile of filthy clothes behind her unraveled itself into the weasellike shape of Harek, her husband's henchman.

"Harek?" She had thought him dead. Dead with Ragnar. "What are you doing here?" she gasped, the Danish words stiff on her tongue. "Why are you—"

"It is true, then. You are the Saxon's whore. *Any* Saxon's whore."

"What?"

"Do not try and deny it. I saw you feeling that man in the church, sliding your hand up his arm. And that was not even him, was it? The one you are supposed to be bedding."

There was hate in Harek's narrow eyes, but it did not disguise the jealousy, the familiar frightening greed with which he had used to watch her when he did not think Ragnar was looking. Not that he had ever dared to come near her. Not when Ragnar had been alive.

She stood up.

"Harek, this has nothing to do with you. I have nothing to do with you. Not anymore. The past is done with, over—"

"Over? Oh, no, it is not. It is not that easy, you slut. You are coming back where you belong."

"No!" It was almost a scream and the inescapable fear, the sick dread that had clung like a miasma around Ragnar, the terror that had ruled her mind, were back. As though they still had the strength to defeat her, could still hold her captive.

"No. Harek, let me go." She was on her feet, scrambling away for her life, but she could not get away from his hands clawing at her clothes. Her cloak came undone, Ragnar's amulet spilled out from the neck of her dress.

"You shameless bitch. You should not have that."

His hands loosened, fumbling for the leather strap. If she could get away…Ceolfrith…Ceolfrith was still in the church. He would…the strap broke, the knotted end stung her cheek. She lunged away.

"What on earth is going on here? Seize them both. The man and the girl."

English. An English voice. But not Ceolfrith. The drawn-out sounds were Saxon. She felt Harek's shock, used the moment to break his grip, twist away. She was free. She heard Harek scream something about vengeance. She tried to run. But there were other hands to catch her. English hands.

"Bring the woman, at least."

She could not move. She looked up. Recognition

was instant. The angry voice belonged to Oslac, the man who had allowed the town to be sacked. The man who would appreciate her charms if offered. Oslac the uncertain-tempered fool.

He realized who she was. She saw his face change, saw the sudden dawning of uncertainty, and then she knew someone else was behind her. Ceolfrith.

Liefwin's second in command took her back to the church and draped his oversize blue cloak round her shoulders. It was not enough to keep out the cold.

After some time, he said, ''I think we had best get back. It might be better if Liefwin hears what's happened from you.''

But she was too late.

Chapter Thirteen

She had a mark on her face. It was enough to drive Liefwin insane, the thought that someone had hurt her. He wanted to murder whoever was responsible.

But he could not. He could not do anything. Because the culprit had escaped. Because he did not know enough about what had happened. Because Sigrid's halting explanations were beyond his understanding.

She was terrified. She was sitting in a pathetic huddle beside the fire wrapped in Ceolfrith's cloak, and his, as well, and she was shaking.

He wanted to put his fist through the wall.

He began pacing up and down the floor before the murderous rage inside drove him mad. And the fear. It was the blackness of the worst nightmare he knew. The sort that would kill him.

She made a small wordless sound. He spun round and stared at the white face with the small red mark across the cheekbone. What he really wanted was to take the fear away from her. What he really wanted was for her to trust him.

"How could you have done it?" yelled Liefwin. "After everything I said to you this morning about going off on your own?"

She jumped and the shadowed gray eyes just seemed to get larger. But their gaze was not fixed on him. She had hardly glanced at him. Her eyes kept going back to the battered, muddy bottle which stood on the table between them. It contained, she had said, spring water. That, she had said, was what the whole disaster had been about.

She had wanted a bottle of spring water.

Something that any one of his men, or he himself, could have got for her without the slightest effort. But no, she had had to go into the town herself, give Ceol-frith, who had behaved like some witless five-year-old, the slip and nearly get herself abducted. Even now, the bare thought of that made him feel physically sick and the sweat start on his palms, but she simply sat and stared at the bottle.

"Sigrid!"

He was still yelling. He could not yet control his voice.

She did not look up.

He grabbed the bottle, just to break that unnerving stare, but his hands were slippery and the bottle was caked in slime and mud. It slid out of his grip, spilling water over his hand and the table, and landed on the floor.

She actually spoke.

"You spilled it," she said, and looked at him as though he had just murdered her firstborn with his bare hands, and the next thing he knew she had dropped to her knees among the rushes, shedding cloaks and seizing the nauseating leather flask with both hands.

"It is empty."

He looked at the bent head. It was so important to her, this inexplicable fancy, more important than anything he had said to her. He tried not to let memories take hold, the memory of someone else whose fancies he had never fathomed. Who had died because of it. He would not think of that. He would think only of what was now, not what had been. This was Sigrid, who was so completely herself, who thought about things in her own way.

He picked up the cloaks and dropped them over her shoulders, kneeling down with her amongst the rushes, holding the warmth of the thick wool around her. He could feel her body tremble, smell the fresh scent of her hair, catch the quickness of her shallow breath.

"You are so cold."

"It does not matter."

But he thought she leaned just slightly toward him and his arm tightened round her, whether she wanted it or not.

He felt her slender body go rigid, every small muscle stiff with tension.

But she did not actually pull away.

"How could you have done such a thing?" This time his voice was so low and hoarse it could scarcely be heard.

But she caught every word. There was a small shiver and then he felt it, the unobtrusive pull away from him. He resisted it without the slightest effort. It was not possible for him to let her go. He did not want to hurt her. He did not want to frighten her. He should not even care like this what she did or what happened to her, but he could not help himself.

He wanted her to tell him the truth.

"Why—"

"I did take Ceolfrith. I was not—"

"You left him. In a church of all places."

The pull against his arm increased. "It was only for a few minutes."

"What happened to you only took a few minutes." He would not, could not, let her move. "Who was that man? The Dane?"

"No one. Just a fugitive hiding out in the bushes who thought he could attack someone who was defenseless. It was just...nothing."

"Nothing? How could it be nothing? And you would not have been defenseless if you had taken Ceolfrith with you."

"I did not realize what would happen. I only wanted to go to the spring."

The spring. There they were, back at the ridiculous, improbable beginning of the whole story.

Liefwin had no way of knowing who the Danish man was. In the eyes of Oslac's men, the unknown Viking had assumed the prowess of Thor, god of thunder. Just because he had escaped them.

Ceolfrith had described Thor as a small weasel.

It was impossible to learn more, even though he had gleaned every detail he could of what had happened, from Oslac, from the men who had given chase, from Ceolfrith.

From Sigrid, who had wanted spring water: a desire without any reason that could make sense to him.

She had put herself in danger, gone into a town that she had said held nothing she wanted, for just that: nothing. A whim. Straight after he had tried to tell her how dangerous things were. After he had tried at the expense of so much bitterness to make her see. He had thought she had understood. She had not.

He was mad to think that what was so important to him could possibly mean anything to her. She had taken a blindly stupid risk for the sake of caprice, unless... Suppose she was lying to him?

The thought was like a knife through the guts.

Suppose she lied? Suppose she knew the Viking?

No one knew what had been said. No one could. Oslac and his men from Wessex did not speak Danish.

Yet she had struggled with the man, according to Ceolfrith.

She had a mark on her face.

He took a breath that required frightening care.

"He made good his escape, your Dane. Did you know that?"

The shudder that ran through her body at his words could have been his own. Her breath caught on a faint sound. Relief? Fear? He had no way to tell, and she did not speak. If the catch in her breath had been the start of a word for him, it was not given voice, and whatever she felt, or did not feel, was withheld from him.

He felt the coldness take his heart again. The coldness that stifled everything. Even his anger. He let her go and stood up.

"Sit by the fire again or you will get chilled."

She moved without looking round and the night-

mare that had begun so long ago staked its hold on
the present.

He did not even want to look at her, but his eyes
watched her move, the delicate little hands and feet
and the small bowed head the only things visible outside the folds of the cloaks. He watched the slender
fingers arrange the bulky wool more closely round her
body.

He could break down the wall of her resistance
with one hand. But the thought was pointless.

He turned away, crossing the room to get his spare
cloak out of the chest. He forced his mind to work.
There was tomorrow to be organized, and after tomorrow the King of Wessex would be here and it
would all be over.

What had happened today could make no difference to his future. His course was set. Nothing that
Sigrid did could possibly affect it.

Her life was hers, just as his was his.

He grasped the lid of the chest and for some reason
the familiar shape of the cross among the ornate carv-
ing on the lid caught his eye. His fingers, still damp
with spring water, traced its outline.

He was suddenly aware that the woman sitting
across the room from him, the familiar unfathomed
stranger, was staring at him. He could feel it without
even having to see her.

He looked round at the small figure and the heart-
shaped face that belonged to Sigrid. He saw her eyes.
And he knew that Dane or no Dane, whatever she had
done, if she had wanted him, he would have cast everything to the winds, the whole world, duty or rep-
utation or honor, to have her.

* * *

Sigrid woke to the sound of murder.

She lay rigid in the curtained bed, every sense stretched in the night blackness.

The noise came again, low pitched, desperate, spine-chilling in its hopelessness, as though all the nameless horrors of the world were concentrated in that one wordless sound.

She jammed her hand against her own mouth, as though that was where the sound came from and she could stop it. Or perhaps it was just an instinctive human reaction, that of a child confronted by adult terrors.

But it was not she who had made the sound.

Liefwin.

She leaped up, tearing back the bed hangings and plunging out into the firelit dark, toward the other bed.

She knew where the sword was kept, *liyt ræsc,* leaning against the wall by Liefwin's bed, ready for use.

It was still there.

Her hand grasped the gilded hilt, dragged it from the gold-chased scabbard. It was so awkward, too long, too unwieldy for her pathetic arm, and then it moved. Or that was how it seemed. She could feel the power of it flow up her arm, like fire, so fast, like its namesake.

It was alive.

You could do anything with a weapon like that, conquer the world. Except it was directionless. You had to hold it back.

Liefwin, she told it, like an idiot. *Save him. Must*

not harm… Her other hand was already hauling at the ghostly sea-green bed curtains.

Nothing. Except…the noise. The noise came again. She dropped to her knees.

"Liefwin."

The thin, terrified rasp of her voice was lost under the horrifying sound. He moved, like someone in the torments of hell. She stared at the thrashing body in terror.

"Liefwin!"

But he could not hear her.

She could not bear it, seeing Liefwin, anyone, like this. She caught at a flailing arm. Its strength was more than she had imagined, more than she could hold. But she dared not let go. She threw all her weight against the arm, flattening it and herself against his body.

He woke. She felt the shock of it run through him and he gasped. It was a ragged sound, but quite ordinary compared to the torment she had just seen. Only surprise, nothing more. She did not let go.

He spoke.

"Sigrid. What are you…" and then, "I was dreaming." The next breath was quite normal. No, not normal, controlled. "Did I wake you? It was nothing. I was just dreaming." The expressionless voice. Usual. Full of its habitual coldness. Dismissive.

But she was touching him and his skin was like ice and she could feel the wild pounding of his heart.

She held him, her own heart thudding like his.

"Did I give you a fright?" said the voice calmly, as though making an effort to be polite. "I am sorry. It was only a dream. It just happens sometimes." An almost imperceptible pause, skillfully glossed over. "It is just an annoyance. Nothing to worry you."

The voice was perfect. Almost. The arm she was not crushing moved round to touch her shoulder in reassurance, but a light touch, hardly there at all. He moved underneath her small weight and she knew he wanted her gone.

She tried to collect herself, to lever herself away, but her clumsy hand only brushed across naked flesh, everywhere. The bedclothes seemed nowhere at all. She was trembling. She did not know whether it was with the remains of her terror or what. *Liyt ræsc,* dangling forgotten out of her right hand, scraped against the side of the bed.

"What is that?"

He moved, straight through all her useless fumblings and she found she was sitting up but still hopelessly entangled with him and still clutching the gold-stamped hilt. A hand like a steel clamp descended on hers.

"It is *liyt ræsc,*" she said. "I am sorry. I know I should not have taken it, but I did not know what else to do. It sounded like…I thought someone was trying to kill you." She was babbling into the awful silence. She knew she was. "You must think I am foolish."

"Foolish?"

The hard gold hilt was eased out of her fingers. She let it go.

"What did you think you were going to do with it? Run my attacker through?"

"Chop his head off," she replied into the softer gold of the long, tangled hair under her cheek. "More effective.'' Her fingers twisted in one heavy coiling thread.

''It was so strange. I could hardly get the blade out of the scabbard but once the thing was in my hand, I felt as though I could have done murder, quite unaided. The sword would have done it. So that in the end I was afraid I would not be able to hold it back.''

''You felt that?''

''Yes,'' she said. ''It is a snake-blade and you have put runes on it.''

''Not me. They were put there long before I had the sword. I would have had *hægl,* the sudden destroyer.''

She shivered and her hands dug tighter into his flesh.

''But hagall, *hægl,*'' she corrected herself in Mercian, ''is also a transformation. Good can sometimes follow the worst. That is how life is.'' She paused and then said in a rush, ''I wanted to help you with the sword. Truly. And…it knew. I think I even spoke to it in my head.…'' She stopped and then added, ''I told you I was fool—''

She heard the sword hit the floor and the rest of the word was lost, along with her breath, and all power of thought and every sense that was not of him. His arms closed round her, pulling her on top of him, crushing her against his naked body so that her flesh pressed against his through the fine linen of her shift. Her breath matched the shallow quickness of his, her heart beat just as fast.

The strength in his arms did not hurt her, but he held her so closely. That must be as close as it was possible to hold another human being, and yet she could feel the frustrated tension in every muscle of his arms and his body, as though he wanted to hold her closer still.

Her hands reached round in response to that need for closeness, to touch him, to fasten on his naked flesh. Because the need was in her, too. She clung on to him and let her whole body rest where it would against his.

There was only silence and darkness and the small combined sound of their breathing. He did not try to kiss her, though the consciousness of it and their awareness of each other seemed to penetrate everything, every last sinew of her body, her breath, the fire-shadowed dark.

It was everything to her, this closeness to him. She did not know how she would ever be able to let it go. The thought filled her with a terrible longing that made her breath outstrip his. The end would come so soon and she no longer knew how she would be able to bear it. But stronger than that was the longing to make him well, to solve whatever it was that could blight something as strong and vital as he was.

"What were you dreaming about?" she asked.

Liefwin froze. He felt every muscle in his body tighten in instinctive resistance.

The answer to that particular question was *nothing* or *I do not remember* and if anyone persisted after that, he could always knock their head off their shoulders.

But he could hardly do that with a woman and one who was pathetically small even by female standards.

He said nothing. He tried moving away, but something pinched at his arm like a gnat that had grown unexpected teeth. It was her fingers.

"Please tell me."

He looked at the fingers.

She had earned the right to know. She had just tried to save his life with a sword she could hardly lift and would never have been able to control. He did not know why she should have done that, but she was braver than any of his men who had been trained to defend themselves since they could walk.

And the sword had spoken to her. Perhaps because of the runes. Transformation. The awareness of *wyrd* in the darkness made the small hairs rise at the nape of his neck. Fate and transformation.

But he did not see that good could follow evil this time, even though that pattern was eternal. Nothing could change for him. But perhaps for her. If she knew, she would be free of him, and then in a matter of days when she left here, her life would start again.

His hands moved her, very gently, and this time she did not resist. He sat up, placing her beside him, on the side of the bed that would allow her to move away unhindered when the time came for her to want to. He made sure they did not touch.

Liefwin leaned back in the shadows and took a breath. But the words he had never spoken would not come out of his mouth, and the sense of loss that choked him seemed not of the past but of the future.

He should say it. He must be able to. He had never been a coward in his life.

He took another breath and the words that killed everything took shape.

"I was dreaming of my wife—"

"Elswyth?" she said. "I heard—"

"You *know?*" The shock was like something physical. He could not imagine who would have—

"No. No, I do not know. I only heard someone say her name and that she was very…beautiful. Was she?"

He tried to get his thoughts into order. What a stupid, irrelevant question to start with. He could hardly believe Sigrid would have said it.

"Yes," he said, "she was."

And what of it? He nearly said the words aloud. What use was beauty? It might dazzle you for a start, and then what? It did not bring people any closer. It was an accident of birth, not a virtue.

He had been born with it himself in some measure, and for him it was one of the stock tools of the trade if you were forced into being a leader. It attracted people at first if you could look impressive. Like wearing gold and fine clothes. It was what people expected.

But an outward show like that was nothing compared to Sigrid's attraction. That seemed to come from the inside out. It did not lie in the wide shape of the gray eyes, but in their expression. It was not the pretty blond hair that caught you, it was the way she held her head and the way she moved. That expressed what she was.

"Did you love her very much?" said Sigrid, and perhaps it was the beginning after all.

"She was part of my life." He turned away from Sigrid's kind of beauty and looked at the dark.

"I killed her."

He heard a small rustling noise as she moved. He

had at least had the forethought to place her on the right side of the bed so she could escape unhindered. She would go and—

Something touched his hand.

It was all he could do not to jump out of his skin.

"Tell me," said Sigrid.

But it seemed impossible, again, for Liefwin to force himself to speak.

He cursed himself for weakness, for letting her touch him after he had said that. He should have known she would not just go. She was not a coward.

She deserved better than him.

He moved his hand from under her small, cold fingers. She was shivering. The fire was so low it was getting cold in the room. He should have thought of that.

She needed to be looked after.

He untangled some of the bedclothes to warm her. He watched the slender, naked arm reach out to take the cover from him. The dying glow of the fire caught her thin skin, the tiny gold hairs on her forearm. His gaze traveled down the arm, to the delicate curve of her shoulder, the shadowed softness of her breast scarcely concealed by the fine linen shift.

Just to look at her like that was enough to heat his blood. Madness. Her huge gray eyes watched him. He had to tell her. Everything. And then it would be over and she would be free.

He turned away from her and spoke into the blackness.

"Elswyth and I had known each other since we were children. Her family's lands bordered one of my family's estates. We saw each other often. It was always intended that we should marry. It seemed the right and natural outcome and so it was done. She was sixteen and I was an idiot of Alfwin's age.''

''Were you happy?'' said Sigrid, and there he was, at the edge of the abyss.

''I do not know,'' said Liefwin. ''I thought so. At first. At least, I was. But…'' How did he explain what he did not fully understand himself? The secret had died with Elswyth.

''It seems very young now, sixteen and seventeen. There is still a lot of growing up to do at that age and we did not grow together. We grew apart. They were not easy years…for anyone.''

Liefwin paused and risked a glance at the still figure beside him, wreathed in shadows. Always shadows between them. They were the shadows of death and destruction, stronger than anything. He spoke their shapes.

''They were years of such terrible uncertainty. Peace was always so fleeting. We did not have the defenses we have now. Not so many fortresses, no long-term campaigns like this. The raids were—''

''Ceolfrith told me about your father. You must have wanted to avenge his death.''

Why had Ceolfrith said that? How could he deny it? And perhaps it was all part of the story.

''Yes. What boy would not? It lived in my heart and then one day, when I was in my tenth winter, Ceolfrith and my uncles took me to the court and I saw the lady Ethelfleda, co-ruler of the Mercians as she then was, because her husband was still alive. I hardly noticed him. All I saw was her.''

Liefwin tried to remember how it had been in the

richly tapestried hall, with all the fighting men of Mercia gathered round and every eye drawn to the lady.

"I thought she was the bravest and the fairest sight I had ever seen. I thought that when I grew up I would save her kingdom for her and free it from the Vikings. It seemed so easy. I could not understand why none of her thanes had done this for her before. I thought all you had to do was to be strong enough and brave enough.

"I had no idea what such a thing meant."

There was no need to say more, not to Sigrid. He watched the slight figure pull the tangled bedclothes closer round itself and the sadness of that small gesture was unbearable. It seemed to reach right inside him until it was no longer alien, but part of his own pain, the pain of everyone who lived in this world. He tried to suppress it. The only things he needed to say to Sigrid were the things she could not know.

"I married Elswyth and I wanted her to be happy. But she was not. It was not just that I was not with her as much as I should have been, because of the fighting. It was more than that. It must have been something in me. I do not think I was the husband that she wished."

Intent gray eyes regarded him out of the shadows. They frowned. Perhaps she knew. Perhaps Sigrid, who seemed to know so much about people without being told, knew what the mysterious thing was that he had not been able to provide for his dead wife.

But she said nothing. Perhaps there were no words for it.

He looked away from the silent face and fixed his

attention on some obscure fold in the bedcover, as though it was the most important thing in the cosmos, and ploughed on into the silence.

"Perhaps if we had had children. But we did not. There was one, once, that she carried for three months and then…no more. I think that took something from her life. She had always been a restless soul, always seeking diversion and nothing I did was…I no longer knew what she wished."

He could see every individual thread of the fold in the bedcover in spite of the blackness of the shadows.

"Our last parting was bitter. She thought I should not have gone. But there seemed no choice. There were so few choices then. I had left her with the lady, because the court seemed the only thing left that gave her any happiness. She said she would stay there until…"

The fold in the bedcover vanished. There was nothing but the shadows, and the screaming in his ears. The screams he had heard and those he had not. Because he had been too far away.

"We were chasing a raiding party. Just the crew from a single rogue ship. Nothing important. Unless you happened to be in their path. They were making from the river to the monastery at the edge of the forest. We cut across their path and they turned back. As good as gone."

The shadows were so thick, now, blotting out the present and where he was.

"But I would not leave it at that. I had seen the village they had destroyed on the way. The corpses and the people left to die in their own blood. I had seen so many things like that before, but that day I was so angry and I..."

He stopped himself. They were not fit things to say to Sigrid, such loathing and rage, such terrible feelings that had led on to his own personal disaster.

"I am so sorry," she said, and her voice trembled. She had a soft heart. He did not know how she had kept it so. She deserved a different life than this.

"I wanted vengeance," he said, and the words seemed to strike through the black air between them, the harshest words that existed. But he was helpless to say anything else. She had to know the truth and she had to be free of whatever mistaken impulse had made her come to help him.

"I decided I would pursue the raiders. The men said we would never catch them, but I knew better. I knew I could do it."

Liefwin paused. "I have such luck, you see. That is why people fall over themselves to fight for me. I always achieve what I set out to do. I did this time."

The shadows wrapped themselves round him like familiar sprites.

"I had cut off their route to the river and I drove them inland. Their path crossed a road. Not a road, a local track. The sort that should be deserted except for a shepherd in the evening, or someone taking their horse to the smith."

The shadows were crushing him, taking his breath.

"But it had not been deserted. As we crested the hill, we saw them, a group of travelers. The shipmen had crossed their path and had killed them, for fresh horses and whatever else they could carry."

The darkness and the shadows were absolute.

"I think I knew, even from that distance. I do not remember getting there. Just walking though the bodies of my own men. All those sightless faces. All dead. And in the middle of the corpses was Elswyth."

The terrible words were said and there was no relief in the darkness. Liefwin could hear his voice still talking, as though it belonged to someone else.

"She must have left the court to go to her family. She had kin who lived farther east. The shipmen would have come on them like the wind. It must have been so quick. That is what I tell myself and it must have been so because they had not even had the time to take all of her jewelry. She was still wearing the rose crystal necklace I gave her. She looked as though she was asleep, as though she would wake up at any minute and tell me what a fool I was.

"But of course she could not. The back of her skull was crushed and her neck was broken." His voice stopped.

"What did you do?"

"I had my vengeance on the raiding party," he said into the dark. "Just as I wished. It was perfectly done. Not one of the men I had with me was killed."

"Yes." Her voice was like a small thread of sound, near stifled in the blackness. "But what did you do when…when you first found Elswyth? Did you weep? Did you yell and rage and curse and hit someone?"

"No," he said through the frozen lump inside him. "No, I did not. I could not, then. There were nearly forty men standing, surrounded by corpses and looking at me to tell them what to do. And somewhere just ahead were between thirty-six and forty Vikings looking for a way back to the river before night fell.''

"Yes. But perhaps when you...when it was over and—"

"But it was not over. There were the minor injuries to be dealt with, the captives we had freed, the dead bodies to be honored, the—"

"They had taken captives?"

"Yes. But if you think that puts my actions in a better light, I did not know. Not for sure. There had been no one left alive in the village to tell me. No. What I wanted was vengeance.''

"Yes.'' Her voice was back to a thread. He had said enough, surely, more than enough for her.

"Sigrid, you know all you need to, now, how things are. What I have done. Why I...'' But she did not seem to hear.

"But later,'' she said, "did you talk to Ceolfrith?''

Of course I damned well spoke to Ceolfrith. He carried out my orders. He swallowed it and sought for something else to say, but Sigrid forestalled him.

"I mean did you tell him how you felt?'' she said, and the abyss opened up and swallowed him.

"No,'' he said, and his voice sounded no louder than hers. Sigrid knew what his answer would be. "I did not speak to Ceolfrith. I could not stand anyone's pity after what I had done and...'' It was not just that. It was worse than that. Far worse.

"There was nothing to say. I could not say to Ceolfrith or anyone how I felt, because I did not feel anything. No, that is not true. It was there, underneath, like a pit of *hellebroga*. But I was somewhere else.

Quite apart from it. Not feeling anything. Like being dead, only not so.''

She would think he was mad. But she knew what he was. She had seen it and she had despised him for it.

"I still go on. I do everything that needs to be done. I do not shirk anything and I am still crowned with success. But inside I am…I do not need to tell you, do I? You know. You knew from the start that the fault was with me. You said so that night in the hailstorm. Do you not remember?''

"But I…I did not know when I said that what had—"

"It is what I am. The faults, all of them, lie in me. If I had been a better husband, if I had stayed with my wife when she wished, she would not have felt so desperate that she had to set out on such a reckless journey, just to find a family to be with.

"I was no husband worth the name to her. I did not protect her from harm, which is the most basic thing any man should do. If I had not—"

"Did you never think it was her fault? That she would not wait for you and decided to set off across dangerous country with what was presumably just a small escort? Did you never think it, in the middle of the night when you could not sleep, or when you woke up from one of your nightmares?''

No. No, I did not. He wanted to scream it at the top of his voice, but it was not true.

He had not thought it was possible to sink any lower. But it was.

"Yes. Yes, I have been quite capable of thinking that. Sometimes. At first. But it is not fair. You cannot say it was someone's fault for riding out on a summer's day to see her kin. You cannot blame her for the actions of a group of people full of greed who set out to plunder and destroy what belongs to others.''

"No," said Sigrid, "you cannot move the blame from them to someone else."

She did not say anything else. No meaningless words about how he could not have known and he had not meant it to happen and all the other things people had tried to say to him before he had shut them up. Just that. No more. And then silence for it to sink into his thick head.

But it only sank so far. He was beyond the reach of reason, even put like that. It only got as far as the top layers of his mind and then stuck there. It did nothing for the *helletrega.*

"It...I do not know what the English word for it is," she said. *"Wyrd?"*

"No. *Wyrd* can be changed. Nearly everything we do and everything that happens can be changed. We are still responsible until the moment of our final doom, until we are *fæg.*"

Liefwin shivered, although he was not cold. It was just the bleakness of the dark.

"I do not know why such things happen. Not just to me, or to Elswyth. To so many people. To you. They go on happening and they always will. There can be no end to such things in this world."

His eyes sought the carved wooden chest against the far wall that held his possessions, the one with the cross on the lid. There were too many shadows in the room and he could not see it. But that did not matter.

He could see it in his mind and he tried to hold it there. It was a sin to give up. He would not. No matter what was in his heart.

At the very least, Sigrid should be saved out of this mess.

He turned back to the small shape huddled in the bedclothes. He could just catch the lightness of her ice-blond hair, the pale shape of her face, the fancied gleam of the smoky-gray eyes.

"Go back to your bed, Sigrid. Go to sleep. I...I am grateful for what you did, but you know now how misplaced that was, what the truth is—"

He thought she might have spoken again, but his voice drowned it out.

"Sigrid, there are only two days left for us to get through. Then I will see that you get to your kindred. You will be safe. I will fulfil that promise—"

She tried to speak again. But he could no longer bear to look at her or to hear her voice, because it hurt too much. And the pain, which had been like a coiled serpent waiting for him, was no longer a separate force, but had become part of him at last.

He turned away.

"Just go. Now. There is nothing left that either of us can say."

He heard her move.

Chapter Fourteen

She did not know how to do it.

Sigrid sat scrunched up on the very edge of the bed and stared at the back and the brutal bare shoulders that had so terrified her that first morning she had woken up in the same room as Liefwin. They still terrified her.

She did not know where to start. She did not know whether anything she had said had reached him.

He had told her everything and he had spared nothing, least of all himself. He had said all it was possible for him to say, and then he had asked her to go. Perhaps she ought to respect that.

She could not.

She could not leave anyone who was in that much pain.

She could not leave Liefwin.

Not even if he wanted her to, and yet she did not know how she could possibly comfort such pain and such an unfair burden of guilt.

If she had been kinder to him throughout. If she had recognized the trap of pain he was caught in and what his coldness hid. If she had not said it was his fault. If she had not been so obsessed with the fact that he was English instead of seeing that he was worth more than anyone she had ever known. If she had followed her heart from the start...

If she had followed her heart.

It was the only guide in the wasteland that she had left. It would not let her abandon him. She touched the smooth white-cream skin that covered one huge shoulder.

She felt him start in shock.

He thought she had left him. He must have thought that he was alone again in the prison of isolation that had held him since Elswyth's death.

She was not Elswyth the Beautiful and she could never mean so much to him. But she would do anything in the world if it would comfort him. Her hand tightened against the naked flesh.

"Liefwin..."

But she only felt the thick muscles under her hand bunch in revolt.

"Liefwin, I—"

He moved. A lock of fire-gilded hair slid over her hand, then smooth flesh under her fingers as he turned. She tried to hold on to him, her hand sliding across his skin.

"What do you think you are doing?"

"Liefwin..." But all words now seemed to have deserted her. Whereas before she had been able to speak to him through the darkness, even if she did not know whether she used the right words, now she could say nothing. She was stuck repeating his name and trying to hold on to a body that wanted to pull free of her.

"Sigrid, I asked you to go. Will you go? Will you leave me? Will you just—"

"No."

At least it was a different word. But then her tongue clamped up on her. Probably because her mouth was so dry. He did not want her near him.

But now that she touched the hard planes of his chest she could feel the savage beating of his heart. Just as hard and fast as when he had woken from the nightmare. She had to try.

"Sigrid…"

And she was close enough to hear the catch in his voice, under the gruffness. It was unmistakable to her and it gave her the courage she needed.

"No," she said, "I do not want to go."

She tried to catch that thread of courage and hold on to it. She raised herself on one elbow and leaned over him.

His eyes, those freezing blue eyes, were glaring at her out of the dark. She made herself ignore them. She did not look at his face. She kept her gaze on the terrible shoulders, the thickly muscled torso, on the compact hips caught in the rumpled bedclothes and the elegant legs half covered, half exposed in the tangle.

The heart that was supposed to be guiding her thundered uselessly out of time.

She did not know where to start.

Seven years of marriage and she had no idea how to go about seducing someone.

She started with the shoulders because they were

so terrifying and if she touched them perhaps she could do more. She tried. Her fingers slid across his warm skin, far too fast because she was so nervous, skittered down across the shadowed dusting of hair that covered his chest.

She did not know whether her touch was too light or not light enough or…she avoided a bruise at the last moment, clumsily, so that her fingers splayed out across the other side of his chest, brushing the dark ridge of one nipple. She felt the jerk of unexpected reaction go right through him and her heart leaped.

"Liefwin," she whispered, "let—"

But he was not going to let her. He moved. Out from under her hand and she knew he was so furious that if he had been Ragnar he would have killed her stone dead.

He would pulverize her.

"Don't!" she shrieked, throwing her arm in front of her face with the speed of practice.

"Do not *what?*"

She was left looking over the top of her upraised arm at Liefwin, not Ragnar. And for some reason that went beyond her experience, she suddenly knew that he would not harm her, and that it had always been so from the start. It had only been she who had been incapable of believing it. The knowledge made some last piece of resistance break.

"Do not make me go," she said.

The words were barely discernible because her voice was shot through with incipient tears. Because she had ruined what she had set out to do and now there would be no hope at all.

But the truth in her voice, or perhaps it was his pity

for her tears, seemed to work where all her clumsy attempts at seduction had not. He reached out to her with all the skill at love craft that she did not have. She was lost, drawn into the strength of his arms, pressed close against the warmth of his body and her tearful breath expired against his lips.

She melted. There was no consciousness of anything else. Her arms closed round naked skin, felt it shiver, felt his kiss deepen, making her breath quicken and the tears slide out from beneath her closed eyelids. Her heart felt as though it would break just from his kiss. Because at the last moment he had not turned away but had given her her only chance with him. She held him fast and she thought her tenderness and the longing for him would choke her.

There was nothing she would not do to comfort him. Her desire for his closeness overcame the restraint that lived inside her. The difference in her must have been obvious to one with his knowledge and it must have been that that deepened his kiss into a passion that roused its echo in her.

She felt through his hot mouth and his tongue and his lips and through every muscle in his body how much he wanted her and she exulted in it. Because the consuming heat of that desire was what she had wanted to arouse in him, the white heat that would burn away everything for him, darkness and pain and misery. At least for this night. At least until tomorrow had to be faced.

She closed her mind against tomorrow and separation. Her arms enclosed his body and he sought her touch. It made her blood race and her hands move over his skin with adoration, smoothing across its contours with a glorious freedom, touching it as it was meant to be touched. For its own sake. Because it was Liefwin.

Her hands gloried in the denseness of his back, the muscular shape, the solid strength of it. It was right. It was just as it should be. She would not have changed so much as one tiny inch of it. Her hands slid upward across his beautiful shoulders.

She felt him cleave close to her and that movement brought a delight she had never expected. It was so strong and so intoxicating that she was brave enough to kiss him.

She made his mouth open and move against hers. She felt the dark warmth of his breath and the smooth, perfect touch of his lips and it was not just his touch, but hers. Because she kissed him. Not so well and so skillfully, she knew it. But still she kissed him and she felt his body thrill with it and that was what she wanted. To believe that he felt the same melting, sharp-edged pleasure that trembled inside her.

She wanted him to feel her love.

She could not speak it. She could not say what he would not want to hear. But if she could make him feel it… Just for this moment, this night. If she could make him feel how worthy he was to be loved.

She was burningly aware of the tightness of his body as he dragged away the rough tangle of the bed-covers crushed between them. So that there was nothing between his naked body and hers except the thinness of her shift. His hand slid up inside the flimsy material, lingering on the rounded curve of her thigh, touching the vulnerable softness of her abdomen, so that she shuddered in reaction and all her muscles tensed into a solid wall.

The hand moved higher, touching her breast, molding round its shape, pressing against the pliant flesh, finding the swollen peak, touching it as she had touched him. Her body jerked in just the same way. But he was not clumsy as she was. The deft fingers touched her and kept on touching her with a lightness that drove her out of her senses. Little stabs of dizziness were shooting through her, deep inside her belly, penetrating even lower, down between her legs, making *that* part of her tingle until she thought she would die of it.

Her body tensed and she did not know whether it was the dizziness or fear. She gasped against the heat of his mouth and the kiss broke and his hand slid down from her breast, across the clenched muscles of her abdomen, down between her legs…it was fear, such fear. Ugly and unstoppable. Growing.

She must not let the fear take her. Not now.

She felt his hand move across soft damp hair, find the opening to her body. She would not think of humiliating pain. There was nothing in his touch to hurt her. It was still so smooth and unforced. Liefwin's touch. Liefwin who was kind.

If only she could find the courage to do as she wished. She wanted no barrier between them. She wanted so much to be close to Liefwin. Because she loved him.

She opened her eyes. She wanted to look at his face, but it was lost in shadow. The solid width of his body above her blotted out what was left of the firelight. She was frighteningly aware of the tenseness in him, the ripened hardness of his manhood pressing against her.

Yet this was the man she loved. She would not make a fool of herself like last time. Men were men, even the best of them and... She shut her eyes.

She felt the firmness of his fingers, slippery against her moist flesh. She would let him. She would not betray by the slightest sound that—

The smooth fingers stopped. There was an instant's stillness and then the cold air of the dark room, shocking against her overheated skin.

"Liefwin..." She did not understand it. She had not made a sound before he stopped. She opened her eyes.

He was looking at her. His hand still rested lightly on the top of her thigh. His brilliant face, in the last glow of the fire, held all the heat that had been his touch. His hair slid forward in a wild tangle over his shoulders and the top of his chest. The shoulders moved with the force of his breath. But his eyes were wide and unreadable.

She realized she had let go of him and she was lying flat on her back with her fists clenched, rigid as something long dead, and her teeth bit her lower lip.

She had not known she had done that. She had not meant to. What must it look like to him?

She was such a miserable coward. She could see it all happening again. The same misunderstanding. He would leave her. He would go. He would be so angry that...it would not just be anger. She knew quite suddenly and with conviction how much she would hurt him.

She grabbed at him and her voice, no longer brave

with passion, but childishly desperate, said, "It is all right. You can do it to me."

"I can...do it to you?" said Liefwin.

He looked at the fragile, petrified figure of the woman and the huge eyes staring at him in desperation.

"Sigrid, I am not going to do anything to you that you do not wish. Is that what you think of me? That I..." His voice choked somewhere in the tightness of his throat. He tried to control the unevenness of his breathing, the wild pounding of his heart, but it was impossible.

He could not stop staring at the pale blur of her face and the huge eyes.

"What were you thinking? What were you doing when you...you stayed with me when it was the last thing I expected and then..."

The great shadowed eyes just watched him in silence. Cold fingers clawed at his pounding heart.

"Did you just feel sorry for me, even in spite of all that I have just said? Was that it?" He could just see her doing it. She could feel sorry for an insect somebody had trodden on.

"Did you think me such a pitiable thing that you felt you had to—"

"No! No, not like that. I wanted..."

But she stopped and then abruptly turned her head away and whatever she had wanted remained locked in her head, quite hidden from him. It hurt more than seemed possible.

"I do not understand," he said.

She did not even look at him and he did not think

she would speak at all. But she did, so softly he had to strain to catch the words.

"It is because I am no good."

"What?"

She flinched.

He took a steadying breath and tried to made his voice come out as gently as possible.

"What do you mean?"

She still did not turn her head.

"I am no good at this. Not like you. I do not know how."

The soft voice shook. But he did not think it was fear. It was bitterness. It was…and then he saw it, in a stray reflection of light from the dying fire, the thin white scar on the side of her face, running down from her eye. Her husband. The brave Viking.

He should have known. He should have seen what now seemed so obvious. If the *nithing* had been prepared to inflict that injury on her, how else might he not have mistreated her? Or at the very least destroyed her confidence, even though she had still seemed to feel some tie to him.

Liefwin watched the small, averted face and felt his hands clench into fists. How could anyone, even some barbaric marauding Dane, have…

She moved, turning farther away from him, the slender hands plucking at the tangled folds of her shift.

"I am not beautiful," she said quite clearly. "I know that."

The fingers dragged savagely at the flimsy material as though she had to hide herself from him.

"But Sigrid, you are. You are more than that. You—"

"Do not! Do not say things like that when they are not true. Not you. I could not bear it from you."

The growing coldness round his heart nearly choked him.

"Sigrid—"

"It is no good," she said. "Nothing is any good."

He saw her face. It was set, with no expression at all but…he recognized instantly what was in her eyes. It was as familiar to him as his own skin. It was the look that a prisoner has. Not one trapped by iron fetters but one imprisoned by their own thoughts.

Whatever her dead husband had done to her, whatever had been in her past, still lived in her mind.

He had tried to be so careful with her after what had happened last time. He had tried to restrain the wildness of the passion, the savage need for her that he felt and he had thought that she…

He had utterly miscalculated the depth of what she felt.

"I am sorry," she said. "I will go."

"No!"

He could not let her. Not like that. Not thinking what she did about herself. He caught at her arm and she stopped. But only because she had to. She still pulled against his hand with what strength she had so that he knew he would have to let go or he would hurt her.

"Do not go," he said, and into the split instant that remained to him to stop her, "I need you to stay."

They were not words he knew how to say. They seemed to leave some terrible gaping hole where his insides ought to have been, like a sword wound only worse because there was no defense for it. But she stopped. Really, this time, and lay quite still.

There was silence.

He let go of her arm carefully, in case his great thick hands had hurt her.

She did not move and he was not entirely sure he could still breathe.

"It is not true," she said. "You could not need me. Not really. I just…"

The woman wanted blood. He could not say any more. But her eyes fixed on him and he realized that the disbelief they held was not so much for him as for herself.

His overloaded heart filled with such rage that it would kill him. Not just rage against the unknown husband who must have abused her but that terrible helpless rage against the world they lived in, where such pain and misery was normal and would never change.

But set against that thought was the burning memory of the moment in this room when they had first confronted each other. And she had made him acknowledge the decision that had already been taken in his heart. That he had wanted her fate to be different.

"It is hopeless," she said.

"No," he said to the prisoner locked somewhere inside her. "It is not."

She turned her gaze from him and looked at the bed canopy.

"I cannot—"

"Do you remember," he said, interrupting her, cutting further back into the short span of their shared past, "that first night we were together in that filthy storage barn?"

"I—"

"We were just together, like this, in the dark. Nobody said anything because there was nothing that could be said. But we had each other."

"Yes. But—"

"We had each other," he said. "In spite of everything that parted us, neither of us was alone."

"No, but—"

"And you knew full well, and do not try to deny it, that I needed you just then as much as you needed me."

"But—"

"We helped each other," he persisted, and this time she did not deny it.

"I suppose so, but..." she said. Only four words, not even a complete sentence, and then she stopped again. But her voice had changed. He heard it. Because he understood, even if only in part, what she was struggling against. The small change in her voice gave him enough hope to go on. He slid down again, full-length beside her. But he did not dare to touch her.

"We helped each other just by being together," he said in the utterly confident voice that was the trick of his trade, "even though nobody did anything and nothing was expected. Was it?"

"No," she said, and this time there was no *but* attached at all.

"Although," he said, lightening his voice, risking

the next step into the dark, "I seem to remember you did take my hand. Quite boldly, I thought."

He moved his own hand suggestively toward where he thought hers must be. There was a silence during which he kept his own gaze riveted on the bed canopy and nothing happened.

He must have been too precipitate, too ill-timed. He had forgotten how to tease people. It was an art that had died in him long ago. He should not have tried...she touched him. He felt the small hesitant fingers take his. He wanted to grab hold of that slight, gentle hand and crush it so that it would never escape him again. He did not dare move.

"Aye," he sighed, "just like that. Or perhaps it was two hands. You were ever more forward than me."

"*Me?*"

"Aye." His fingers closed furtively over hers so that she could not move them. "You wanted to take advantage of some defenseless fellow who had nothing but a cloak between him and the prospect of ruin."

"I did not...it was you who abducted me—"

"Rescued."

"Rescued," she acknowledged. But Liefwin thought it was harder to rescue her from this than from an entire army. The hand under his trembled. But it did not try to pull away from him. The small fingers clung to him with the force that had once dug into his flesh and now dug into his heart.

"Rescued you at some peril to myself," he said.

"Oh. Yes. Three armed people who—"

"Not them. I am talking about afterward. I still have the scars."

"Oh! But I—"

"You have no mercy. If there was enough light in here, I could show you." He leaned threateningly over her and produced his other hand, open so that he would not frighten her. But there was no fear in the eyes that met his. There really was not.

"Idiot," she said, and the word that he would have killed anyone else for was more welcome than his own life.

"At least," she said, "I did not try and kiss someone while they were asleep."

Somehow Liefwin managed to swallow the surprise and the sudden dryness in his throat.

"You were awake? You were awake and you let me kiss you when we were strangers and…enemies?" But he was off balance and it was hard to keep his voice to the same lightness.

"You shameless and unprincipled wench," he tried by way of recovery.

"Yes," she said, and her voice was unsteadier than his. "I did not have any shame with you at all. Not even with the town being sacked outside the door. It did not make any difference. That is why I did not speak. I wanted you to kiss me."

"Like this?" said Liefwin through the tightness in his chest that had nothing to do with the damage to his ribs.

He touched her lips. They were warm and soft and too surprised to resist when he took them with his own mouth. He did not let them. Not at first and then when she had no breath left, he softened his touch, teasing her at the very edge of sensation so that she had to lean toward him if she wanted to prolong the kiss.

She did. Her mouth followed his and her hands found his shoulders, tangling in his hair, sliding underneath it, settling on his neck and pulling his head toward her.

She had actually done that of her own volition. She had wanted him. The knowledge burned inside him as though it would consume him, as though it would consume everything, all consciousness, all restraint. But he could not let it. It was like torture. He kissed her as gently, as tenderly, as deeply as he could. As long as she wanted it. As long as it was possible. Until he could feel her body move against his with an impatience she could no longer stop.

He slid his mouth away from hers and down across the fragile line of her neck, easing his pulsing overheated body away from hers. She tried to hold on to him, but he could not let her. If his body touched hers, if she moved against him the way she had, he would be lost.

"Liefwin…"

She had hold of one of his hands. He let her keep it.

He would use his mouth.

He touched her breast, just gently. It was so delicate, like the rest of her. She was so fine and small he was always half afraid of hurting her. But she was not a child. She was all woman, so softly rounded and so subtly full. She invited passion, inflamed it, and yet she demanded such care. It was the most erotic combination he could imagine.

He touched her with his tongue and, even through the barrier of the shift he had not dared to remove, he felt the soft peak of her breast harden in his mouth. He heard her moan and felt her move. He looked up, wanting to see her face. To his surprise, her head was raised, her shoulders braced against the bolster so she could watch him. Her eyes were wide and dark, her parted lips swollen from his kiss.

"Liefwin," she said, "kiss me. Just like that."

The hand that was not clutching his reached down. He bent his head under the touch of her hand, taking the small tight hardness of her with lips and tongue, without ceasing, so that the wetness of his mouth soaked the thin cloth and her body writhed with it.

He touched her until she trembled and until all her muscles tightened in anticipation and then he moved downward, brushing the thin material of her shift aside, still kissing the slender contours of her body, until he found what he wished.

The first taste of that dark moist flesh was almost enough to send him over the edge without her so much as touching him. He heard her gasp and felt the shock take her.

"Liefwin..."

The shock was in her voice, too. He gentled his touch, the way he had with the first kiss. But he did not stop.

Her hot flesh, blissfully, wonderfully swollen with the juices of her desire pushed against his mouth. He felt how she trembled. He could hear her ragged breathing. Every muscle in her body seemed tightened beyond endurance.

She would not stop him now, surely. Let her not.

Let her enjoy this of him if nothing else. Let her not be frightened.

His hand, stretched out above him, still clasped hers. He tried to convey reassurance through that simple touching of hands which had never failed them before. *Trust me,* he said to her in his mind. *Trust me.*

She did not move and he thought for moment that made his beating heart stop that she had frozen, just as before, locked in the prison of her misery and then the hand under his twisted, gripping his convulsively, the sharp little fingernails ripping his flesh, stinging. But he welcomed that. It was lost in a savage rush of joy and the pain was part of it, feeling her abandon herself at last to this moment. His mouth and his tongue moved across her exposed heated flesh until she screamed.

Chapter Fifteen

Sigrid gasped breath after breath. It was not human, the cry that came out of her throat. It belonged to some primitive animal rutting in the forest. It could not belong to her, and yet it was her own body that writhed under the dizzying waves of a pleasure that could not be borne. Her body turned molten and dissolved, and she was falling.

She reached out blindly for Liefwin and he was there. She felt his arms enclose her. She had no strength left and yet she clung to him, crushing his flesh so hard she heard his breath catch.

The bruises. She had forgotten. She let go instantly but he did not. He just held on to her as though he would never release her and she closed her mind to everything else and let him. He was stroking her hair and she could hear the thunderous beat of his heart.

It was a long time before he spoke and it seemed from a long distance away, even though he held her.

"So…was that well?"

"Yes." It was hard to force even that one word past her lips. Her head rested against swathes of soft red-gold hair and the smooth skin of his shoulder, warm, faintly damp and scented of man.

"I did not know," she whispered, and she could feel a different heat rising in her face. "I did not know that such things happened."

The large hand moved lightly across her hair.

"They should have happened for you. You should have known."

The awful sadness, the sadness that had twisted her heart in two, was back in his voice. She had forgotten that. She had forgotten everything in her own need for him when she had meant to give.

She caught the other hand from where it rested against her arm. She stopped. There was something dark and sticky on the back of it. A small trail of...

"That is blood."

Her gaze fixed on the sharp indentations that punctured his flesh. She swore. It came out in Danish.

"That was me," she said, "I—"

Since he could not hide what she had seen, he sighed deeply and said, "You were ever without mercy on me. A harridan."

But she could not smile this time. Her eyes misted over with useless tears, which he would not want. It was because she loved him so much and she knew how much he was hurt inside and she did not know how to help that.

"Or perhaps one of those Roman things," he suggested. "Or were they Greek? A harpy."

He was kind and she was not used to it. She would not cry all over him again. But she could not get any words out. Could not reassure him. Could not say how much she felt.

"No thanks for my endeavors," he observed. "Seduced and thrown aside…"

She took a huge breath. She would speak. She would requite the courage that was his.

"No thanks, you said?" She sat up. She leered at him, fiendishly, she hoped. Possibly like a Roman or a Greek harpy. Whatever that was and whoever they were.

"Seduced?" she inquired.

She slid a hand down the length of him, from shoulder to hip. She let it pause there. She relished the surprise in his eyes and more so the light behind it. It was a dangerous light. Breathtaking. But she was not afraid now. Liefwin had banished it.

She slid her hand round, just a little bit farther. She touched dark curling hair, rigid hardness, smooth skin. So smooth, so unbelievably smooth. Hot and—

He swore in English.

"Sigrid, I do not have nearly as much restraint as you think."

Somehow she kept her eyes on his.

"Good," she said.

His eyes glittered. She could sense the tension in every line of his strong warrior's body. Her damp palm rested against his swollen hardness, but he did not move.

"I made a promise to you that there would be nothing that you did not wish."

It was almost impossible then to hold his gaze. But she made herself do it. If there was one small corner of her where fear was not quite stamped out he would never know it. Never. She had to do something that—

She took off her shift. It was the last small, pathetic defense she had. She threw it away and let him see her.

The heat of his eyes was like a touch on her naked skin.

"I know what you promised," she said, "but I also know what I want."

It was the last thing she did say. The touch of his mouth on her swollen lips was like exquisite torture. But she wanted it. She wanted it as much as the touch of his hands, the feel of his body totally naked against hers. It was everything. Everything in her world. She would never feel such a thing again, never know anyone like him.

He touched her and touched her so that her skin tingled with it and to her shock she felt again that tight, aching need between her legs. Just from the smooth caress of his hands on her body. Just because she wanted him so much.

She would not have believed it could overwhelm her again. But it did. It was so strong—her need for him—that when she felt his hardness against the still-wet, newly aching flesh at the core of her she was already moving against him. Her legs widened to receive him, curling high round the solid mass of his thighs. She moved as though she was in a dream, just following him and what he did. Conscious only of how much he wanted her and the quickness of his breath and the tightness of him. So that when he entered her body there was no pain at all, only that smooth, other flesh sliding through the moist heat of her skin until it was complete.

But she gasped with all her breath as she felt him thrust inside her. She could not help it and her muscles tightened. He filled her so completely he must feel her tenseness. She thought she sensed hesitation, but she could not bear that. She could not bear him to think she did not want him utterly.

Her hands slid down across his hips, fastening on the thick muscle of his buttocks, pulling him hard against her. She heard the small sound he made, quite harsh and uncontrolled and it was the most deeply exciting sound in the world, and then she was lost in the powerful movement of his body and there was no restraint at all. And the release when it came was like setting free the bonds of hell.

She would never let him go and she did not have to. When it was done and his shoulders heaved with the unevenness of his breath and his heart still beat with too much force, she was allowed to hold him.

It was the first time such a thing had been allowed. She could not have said what the difference was between their touch before and what happened now, but she knew it was there. He was so wholly hers. She could not see his face and he did not speak. But she was permitted to stroke his hair and caress his shoulders and the vulnerable skin of his neck just as she wanted. Whatever she wished to do, however she wanted to touch him was permitted, nay accepted. There were no questions and no barriers.

They lay together for a long time in the silent dark. But at last her heart was so full that she had to speak his name.

He looked up, eyes dark with shadows, but not cold, not cold at all. She smiled at the eyes. Just some of the shadows lifted and he spoke.

"I thought…I thought I might have made you afraid again."

"No," she said with all the passion she had just lived through. "Not so. You are all that I wanted. All anyone could want."

But she saw by his face that he was not ready to hear such things spoken. Not yet, and her heart bled for it. She made herself swallow the choking feeling in her throat and achieve a passable sneer.

"I believe you flatter yourself, lord, as to your effect on me."

"I…oh, that is your opinion, is it?"

"Yes—" But the rest of it was lost in something close to a shriek as she was caught in an embrace that crushed and his mouth fastened on the thin skin of her throat.

She had expected a hard kiss and pressed herself back into the bed away from him. But it was not. It was light, tantalizing, rousing sensation and yet denying it. Leaving her wanting more, so that she twisted in the prison of his arms, no longer avoiding him but seeking his touch, rubbing her body shamelessly against his.

But he drew back from such greedy advances, scarcely touching her, just enough to rouse in her a molten core of need that left her burning in desperation.

Her hands grasped at his arms and his shoulders, hard, but she could not move him.

"Not enough effect, did you say?" His breath across her skin, more imagined than felt, was enough to make her shiver.

"Not…not yet perhaps."

The double meaning of their words was enough to bring the heat to her face. Because she was not used to such play between men and women.

"Then perhaps I could do something about it. If you wish." And he let her feel the renewed hardness of him against her flesh.

She lowered her gaze and the shivering in her body and the heat in her face got worse. Her hands tightened on the thickness of his shoulders, trying to draw him toward her.

He did not move.

She looked up, expecting more sport, but it was quite gone, leaving his eyes wide and dark.

"Then say it is what you want. Say you want me. Even if you have to lie to me to do it."

Sigrid's heart seemed to stop beating.

"It would not be a lie. It is you I want. I want you more than anything in the world..." But there was no time to see whether he believed her or what he meant. Or to guess why he had said that. Out of the pain in his heart or...she could no longer see his eyes, only feel his touch, only touch him in return and try through that blinded poignant sense to tell him.

Her body wrapped itself around his, opening as he thrust inside her, accepting that piercing hardness, matching her movements to his until she was obliterated in bliss.

Afterward she fell asleep, sated and exhausted, still touching his warmth. His hand rested on her shoulder, and there were no dreams at all.

She woke unable to move, her body heavy and torpid, aching with remembered pleasure. It was early. But outside her warm bed lay the cold light of morning.

It was gone, her short night with Liefwin. The only night she had known as a woman who could be wanted. He had made her believe that in the end, completely. He could have no idea of what that meant to her.

With the thin, clear light of morning came the knowledge that he had only needed her because of the depth of his heart's grief. She could not fool herself otherwise.

But just for that night she had been with him, not just in body but in spirit. It was her he had turned to and she had tried with all she had to help him. And he had not closed her out.

She rolled over in the warm bed and reached out her hand toward where he would be, the memory of last night's love and the tenderness of his touch still in some stubborn corner of her mind.

But even as she moved she realized what had woken her. The same thing that always woke her. The quiet sound of his movements in the room somewhere beyond the bed curtain as he made himself ready to go out.

Just as he did every morning. Every morning they had shared this room. As strangers. As enemies. As people who were nothing to each other at all.

What else had she expected?

In the night, people sometimes had to face their demons. In the morning, they knew their own mind.

She slid round. It was so cold. Perhaps the fire had gone out. Perhaps she ought to tend it. That would give her something to do. If only she was within reach of her cloak so she could hide herself. She yanked a layer of bedding free to cover her nakedness. She shivered. She did not have her shift because…well, that was last night. Last night was over.

She put her hand to the bed curtains. Obvious thing to do. But it took some courage.

"Liefwin?"

He had lit candles. He turned and her eyes dazzled against a gleaming, moving net of light.

"Sigrid—"

"No!"

She shrieked it. First word after the night. She watched the soft smile die out of his eyes. He finished fastening the last buckle that secured the glittering length of *liyt ræsc* against his hip.

But he did walk toward her.

He knelt beside the bed with that secret, spine-chilling rustle caused by thousands of tiny hand-crafted links of hard metal. It was one of the most frightening sounds in the world. In her world.

He held out one hand toward her. The chain mail on his arm, the chain mail on his shoulder sang their death song.

Her terror, irrational and beyond her control, would not let her move, would not let her meet his hand.

"No," she whispered.

The hand withdrew. The eyes watched her. They were no longer cold eyes, closed. You could see right down to their depths. Or perhaps they were now a mirror in which you saw your own despair.

"Sigrid, you knew. I told you about the raiding party and that I had to deal with it and why. That it had to be today. You know how things are. I tried to tell you.''

"Yes, but…I did not realize. Not like this. Not when…'' Her stumbling words dried up. The eyes just watched her. She could see the lines of exhaustion round them. She could see the paleness of the face that should be full of vivid color. In her mind she saw the ugliness of the wound spreading across his chest and down his side. That was one half of her terror and it was real.

The other half was not real. It was made of shadows that only she could see. They clustered round him, extinguishing the brightness of his chain mail, the glow of the candles behind him. The black death shadows caused by *draugar*.

"No. Not you. I do not want it to be you,'' she said and saw the last of the light in his eyes die.

"It is me. It is what I am. I cannot change that.''

"No! Liefwin…I did not mean—'' But she could not find the words under that gaze and everything she said seemed fated to go awry.

"We could not change anything, could we? There is far too much between us.''

He turned away in a fluid ripple of light. Gone. Gone and she would never—she lunged, grabbing at his arm. Her hand grasped chain mail, slid across hard, sharp metal, the links digging into her flesh so hard that she gasped. But she could not let go.

He stopped.

"Sigrid…''

He caught her hand, pulling it away from his arm, holding on to it so that she could not hide it. There were dents in her palm, plain to see, and what would later be bruises. But it did not seem to bleed.

"What did you think you were doing? You—"

She dragged the hand out of his grasp and balled it into a fist.

"The reason I do not want you to go is because I do not want to lose you."

"What?"

She had not wanted to put an obligation on him that he did not wish. She had not said it for that reason. He just had to know that there was nothing he could do that she would blame him for.

"I want you to come back," she said helplessly. "I am afraid."

He took the hand again. She would not open the palm. She could not read what was in his eyes. She thought he did not believe her.

She thought he did. She thought—

"Sigrid, there is nothing for you to be afraid of. I will be back. You know the strength of my luck. It is as good as a curse." He had found his teasing voice and his hand was so strong around hers, so alive.

But they were still there, the death shadows in the air, as though they listened. Perhaps they were only in her mind. Perhaps they were not for him. Perhaps he did not even feel them.

"But even if I do not..." He did feel the foreboding she felt. He must. "All will be well for you. Ceolfrith knows what I promised you. You will be provided for and as for the ransom—"

"The...Liefwin, there is no—"

"No ransom? You have deceived me?"

Do not laugh, she thought. *Do not let us make a*

joke of this, and yet if they did not, there would be no speech. Nothing possible to say.

"You knew I had no ransom?"

"I...I did begin to suspect...quite soon—"

"Oh! And you never said?"

"I, at least, have perfect manners," said Liefwin. And then, "It does not matter. I would not take it." The words came faster now, perhaps because they were more serious. "Ceolfrith knows my mind on this. He will see you have the means to do whatever you want."

"The means to...but...I do not want your money. I never—"

"You will when you know what it is. You will see it is apt. Besides, I know you have nothing. You never had anything besides that silver amulet you tried to impress me with on that first day. Now you are not even wearing that. You do still have it, do you not?"

"I—" But he was still speaking, not pausing for a reply, as though the next words possessed all his thought to the exclusion of all else.

"You must say yes. I must know that this is done. It...it would ease what is in my heart if I knew. Please do not refuse me in this."

That last was said so fast she had to pause and unscramble the words and then it was too late. He had released her hand and stood up.

He must have taken her silence as assent, because there was a small thread of relief through the tension in his eyes. But the black sense of foreboding in her only doubled. It pressed on her mind like some fell creature trying to burst out. If she could straighten her thoughts, fix her mind on anything but the thought of losing him…

"I must go. They are waiting for me and it is light."

That was all he said, but she could see that the foreboding was in him, too. It was in the way he looked at her, as though he felt that the next step he took might separate them forever.

She could not bear that.

"Liefwin—"

"It is all right. There is nothing we can say, is there?"

No. Nothing. Everything.

She scrambled out of the bed, careless of the covers, careless of everything except him. She caught him, like a glittering wraith of silver. Hard metal against her unprotected skin, cold and unyielding, except she found the warmth of his face, the soft mist of his hair.

"Be careful. Sigrid, you will—"

She found his mouth.

"Come back," she said against it. "Come back."

She took his lips.

It was impossible to stay inside the bower.

She tried it. But you could only pace the floor of a small room for so long.

She went out. It was fine, fine and crisp and cold. Beautiful. If you were not waiting in agony for your lover to come back from a battle. A lover who did not even belong to you. Not properly. Who never could.

She had never even said that she loved him.

She wished now that she had, whatever his reaction might have been. Even if he did not want her. At least he would have known, known how much there was in him to love.

She did not even know where he had gone. She looked round. She did not even know in which direction. She paused in the shadow of a doorway, feeling utterly lost.

"Lady! Lady, is that you?"

She started out of the pain of her thoughts.

"Lady—"

"Sit still you…wantwit. You will rupture something…"

She went inside.

"…probably your brain if you had one."

"Lady!"

Alfwin was sitting up, propped on an extraordinary number of pillows, but still sitting up. Ceolfrith hung over him like some gigantic fowl confronted by an egg that had hatched a day too soon.

"I am glad it is you," crowed Alfwin, "I wanted to tell you. Liefwin came to see me and…it was all right. I thought perhaps, you know…you might have spoken to him."

Sigrid smiled, the darkness of her mood suddenly shot through with a small streak of light.

"Not really. I did not need to. You mean too much to him."

"Yes, well," said Alfwin, suddenly fascinated by the wall somewhere to the right of her head. "You know it really was like you said. He was not angry, just sad. I wish he was not. I mean, I know because of Elswyth—"

"You did rupture your brains, did you not, boy?" cut in Ceolfrith. "I do not imagine Sigrid wishes to hear—"

"It is all right," said Sigrid. "I know."

"Well, I am entitled to my opinion," said Alfwin with feverish belligerence, "and I think Elswyth made him sad long before she died. I mean I know Liefwin was besotted with her and she looked like an angel, but she never did anything to make him happy."

Alfwin shot a challenging look at Ceolfrith.

"You can call it sour grapes if you like because she thought a...a stripling like me was beneath her notice. I never wished her the awful harm that befell her, but I still think it is true—"

"Hush," said Sigrid, before Ceolfrith could start bellowing.

But Ceolfrith did not bellow. To Sigrid's surprise he suddenly looked straight at her and said, "He was the wrong man for her. She was...light-minded and not, perhaps, one much given to caring. Liefwin was different. I mean...I know he used to be light of heart, too. He could laugh and turn people round the palm of his hand. But some things were always serious with him and I do not think Elswyth ever understood that." A pause. "Not the way I hope you do."

She could not have heard him correctly.

"I expect them back before sunset. If you were thinking of asking," added Ceolfrith, as though they had been discussing some mildly interesting change in the weather. "Now," said Ceolfrith, fixing his eye on Alfwin, "time you had a sleep, young lad."

"I just had one," said Alfwin, but without much hope.

"Well, now you are going to have another one, even if I have to knock out the last of your brains to achieve it."

Sigrid watched with a peculiar tightness in her chest as Ceolfrith disposed Liefwin's cousin against the pillows. Alfwin flashed her a grin over one meaty shoulder.

"Ceolfrith is just out of temper today. I could tell you why...ouch." The grin in her direction became conspiratorial and Sigrid had a sudden absurd sense of belonging, the way people ought to in a family.

"It is because Liefwin would not let him go with him to fight the wolfcoat. Ouch."

"A berserker?"

The world seemed to go dark and the warm, firelit bower was suddenly freezing.

"A berserker?" she said, again.

"The berserker," said Alfwin round a mouthful of bolster, "the one the shipmen sent to make the town fight against us. You know—"

"I think she does know."

Sigrid looked up to find that Ceolfrith was watching her. She did not know what was in her shocked face, but it was enough to make the suspicion dawn in his eyes and with it a sudden, savage anger.

"All set, then, lad?" he said to Alfwin. His voice held its usual heartiness, but his eyes held murder. "I think the lady and I will go outside."

She felt the cold autumn air on her face, but it was no colder than the shadows in Alfwin's room.

"It is not," she said wildly, while Ceolfrith's huge

ham hands dug into her shoulders. "It is not him. It cannot be. He is dead. Do you not understand me? He is *dead*."

"Oh, is he? And how would you know this particular berserker is dead?"

"They told me. That Ragnar was dead. Right from the start. Do you think I would not know if my own husband was dead? They gave me the amulet he always wore—"

"Your *husband*. And you…with Liefwin. You bitch. You lying bitch. You have betrayed him…"

The amulet. The amulet she no longer had. "Harek…" The word was a blackness in her mind. She scarce knew whether she had given it breath.

The huge hands dug deeper, numbing her shoulders.

"That was Ragnar's creature you met at the spring, was it not? You have just given me his name. And I thought it happened by chance. That is what I said when Liefwin asked me. I felt…sorry for you. I thought you were frightened out of your wits and trying to escape."

"I was. That is how it was. I had no idea. I went to the spring to get the holy water for Liefwin. I did not know."

"No. Just like you do not know Liefwin is going to be killed by your husband and you are both going to make your fortunes. Pity you could not keep your face straight just now—"

"Our *fortunes?*"

"Liefwin's share from this campaign. It is due to you if he dies. As if you did not know."

"I did not. He never…" But he had. *The means to*

do whatever you want… You will see it is apt… He had given her that. He had said it would ease his heart if she took it.

"Oh, you knew all right, you—"

"Vengeance," she said. "Vengeance."

"What?"

"That's what he said, when he ran. Harek, Ragnar's man. Vengeance. We have to do something. For Liefwin. We—"

"For *Liefwin!* Do not give me that—"

She stared up into Ceolfrith's face only inches from hers. She had to make him understand her. There was no other way. No time. She could see the pent-up wrath coming.

"He knows," she said. "Ragnar the Wolfcoat, where I am and what I am. Another man's mistress. He will kill Liefwin. And then he will come here and kill me. We have to go now, to Liefwin."

It was a toss-up whether he would release her or beat the last of her brains out. He did neither, but dragged her, running, toward where the horses were kept, shouting as he went.

People moved, in answer to that bellow. People seemed to know, through the yelling confusion, exactly what to do. But it still took forever.

"I am coming," she shouted at Ceolfrith. "I am coming with you."

"You? I would not let you do anything else. I hope you can ride," he added, throwing her up onto the back of a chestnut horse that was far too big for her.

She grabbed the reins, trying to keep the animal under some sort of control.

"Can you manage it?"

"Of course I can." But she was no horsewoman. She had never had the chance to be.

"It is just that I would not want to see a fine horse like that bolt in the opposite direction."

She swallowed any answer because she had no time to argue and no interest in it. All her mind, all her being was concentrated on Liefwin and how far it was until they caught up with him. And on the inhuman rage and the inhuman strength and the bestial savagery of her husband.

"All I want," she said, "is for us to be in time."

Chapter Sixteen

They were not in time.

The journey was a nightmare. Sigrid would never have managed if it had not been for the members of Liefwin's highly trained *éored*. They surrounded her, guiding the horse, steadying it amongst the others but never slackening their speed, and when the ground became too rough she was taken up with someone else, by the lightest, by those with the best mounts, passed around like some unnecessary sack of meal. No one spoke, but it was not from enmity of her. They did not know what Ceolfrith knew. It was simply that there was no time and no breath for speaking.

She broke the silence only once, shouting at the broad back of her escort of the moment.

"What is that?"

The leather-clad shoulders shrugged.

"The Viking raiders, lady. The shipmen. Yesterday."

That was all. Just those few words shouted through the wind and the blackened wreckage of the village, abandoned, still smoldering in parts flashed past and behind her.

She could see the fresh earth of graves.

They neared the forest. There was a stream up ahead. Too steep sided to cross? They would…her escort, a different escort, pulled the straining horse to a standstill.

''Why have we—''

''Lady, this is it.''

Her heart was so cold inside her, so cold she could not breathe. She would swoon.

She must not.

''Ceolfrith!''

She saw him, just ahead of her. She thought he heard her but he did not stop. He had dismounted. He was walking. He walked faster.

''Ceolfrith!''

She slid down, somehow from the back of the horse, not waiting for her escort.

There were figures on the banks of the stream. English. Mercian. You could tell even at this distance. They moved with that carefully ordered purpose that belonged only to Liefwin's men.

There were more bodies, on the ground, in the distance.

She started to run but the man held her back.

''Lady. Wait. The lord Liefwin will—''

''Liefwin!'' she shrieked. ''Where…''

''There by the riverbank, but wait.''

She could see two figures, isolated, at the very edge of the river. One knelt, the other was stretched out, full-length on the ground.

The one who knelt looked up, hair the color of molten gold, his face…

Ceolfrith ran ahead.

''No. Lady, not yet. Let Ceolfrith go…it is his nephew.''

She looked at the figure on the ground. He must be dead, because they had covered his face. She thought he was, had been, young. A little of his hair spilled out from under the concealing cloth, bright red, vaguely familiar.

She saw Liefwin stand up, slowly, as though he was hurt, as though he was old, twice as old as the dead man on the ground. She could not bear it. She pushed forward, dragging her protesting escort with her. But there she stopped of her own accord.

She was close enough to see Liefwin's expression. She could see what he felt, straight away. No mask of frozen coldness. It was as though the familiar face had been stripped bare and nothing was hidden because there was no longer any defense.

Ceolfrith stopped.

Liefwin spoke. She could not make out what he said, but she saw what she thought she would never see. Liefwin's hand reached out to touch Ceolfrith's shoulder, tentatively, almost as though he expected it would be repulsed and when it was not he embraced Ceolfrith, quickly and hard. It was returned. She heard the low rumbling murmur of Ceolfrith's voice and then they both turned, in accord, like people who had known each other forever, like one person, to look at the figure on the ground.

But only Ceolfrith knelt.

Liefwin began to walk toward her.

She was suddenly alone, in the middle of the *éored*. Her escort melted. There was no one near her. Only Liefwin. She wanted to run to meet him. She wanted to shout and cry out her distress and the wild selfish joy of her relief. She wanted to throw herself into his arms. She wanted to speak. She wanted to talk to him and never stop talking, never stop holding him. She wanted to know and feel that he was truly alive and whole and safe.

She just wanted to touch him, to have one word.

But he stopped before he reached her.

She could not move across the small space of ground that separated them. And he did not.

"Liefwin."

He did not take the step that would join them. He was like a stranger and yet he looked as she had first seen him, the bright chain mail streaked with dirt and blood, the handsome high-colored face set. But the eyes. The eyes were forever altered. Where their freezing opaqueness once had terrified her, now their hot depths did the same. But the difference was that she was no longer frightened for herself but for him, and what he felt.

"Liefwin."

"Get her away."

It was so much like a blow that she stepped backward. One of the *éored* dashed forward and caught her.

"Lord."

"Find her somewhere to sit and another cloak. Make sure she is warm enough and has something to drink."

He glanced at her face, just once, and her heart leaped.

"Just take her away. Now."

She could not say a word.

"Yes, lord."

Her shaking legs had failed her, but yet she must have moved. Because she was in a different place. At the very edge of the trees. There were people everywhere, bustling about her with their endless efficiency. Doing things. Mundane, practical things.

Everything their lord might require in his kindness to his mistress.

They did not know.

They had no idea.

She was sitting on a bed of bracken with her back against the smooth trunk of a beech tree. She was wrapped in three layers of wool and she was holding a flask of mead. They asked her to drink from it and it would have been churlish to refuse. They made English conversation, speaking slowly so that she would understand.

They were pleased when she answered them at random.

She waited.

She only knew when he came by the way her companions suddenly vanished, just as they had before.

He dropped down beside her on the bracken, wrapped in his cloak and free of the chain mail and, as far as she could tell, every trace of blood.

"He is dead, your husband," said Liefwin.

He sat with his knees drawn up, one hand supporting his head. She saw nothing but shadows and the full sweep of his hair. But that did not matter. She had already seen what was in his face.

"Yes." She did not know what to say. How to reach him…

"But then you know that. Because otherwise I would not still be alive."

Yes. It would not come out of her mouth this time. It did not need to.

She looked at the shadowed profile. If he knew who Ragnar was, he knew everything.

"Are you not surprised? Do you not want to know how it all happened? Why I am sitting here beside you and not Ragnar the Wolfcoat, your husband?"

"Tell me…t-tell—" Her voice stuttered to a halt.

"You wish me to tell you?"

"Yes."

It was like the torture of the blood eagle that Ragnar used to boast to her about. Where they carved you up and took out your lungs while you were still alive. The lungs still breathed. Just like hers.

"Please tell me."

"It did start well. For him. I mean we did not have the advantage of surprise that we expected. So the first few minutes were quite desperate for us. No one could get near your husband. But then I had told the men to leave him to me, which was very farsighted of me, was it not?"

"Liefwin—"

"So they did leave him to me. All of them, that is, except Cerdic."

Cerdic. The vague memory stirred by the sight of copper-red hair spilling around the covered head of the corpse resolved itself. She could see the figure of a bright, gap-toothed young man standing in the doorway of Alfwin's room, staring at her and then trying to apologize.

"C-Cerdic? Not—"

"Yes. He is, or was, Ceolfrith's nephew. He is now the corpse you saw as you arrived. But not one to look too closely on unless you have a strong stomach...why do you not try drinking the rest of that mead? We always have our best conversations when you are drunk."

She put the leather flask to her mouth. She was shaking so much it hit her teeth. She swallowed, turning away from him so that he would not see how clumsy she was.

"He knew, you see. Cerdic knew about my wound. Ceolfrith had told him. So I suppose Cerdic decided it would be better if he had a go at the wolfcoat himself and saved the day for all of us. What a wasted gesture that was. It was me your husband wanted. After all, he was entitled to his vengeance on me. Only I did not know that, then. And neither did Cerdic when he leaped to my defense."

"I am s-sorry." Such stupid, inadequate words.

"At least Cerdic has honor. That is more than we have, is it not? There is nothing more worthy of praise than to die in defense of your lord. Even one like me."

"You did not know."

"No. But it does not absolve me of much. All I did was the only thing left to me as Cerdic's lord. I fought with your husband, just as he wished."

Her eyes were shut, painfully tight, so that they ached with it. But that did not shut out the horror, the savage mind-numbing brutality that was Ragnar in the grip of the wolf's rage. The rage that fed on destruction and grew stronger from it.

"I killed him. You really are surprised at that, are you not?"

She was. And yet not so. She remembered the impenetrable determination in Liefwin the first moment she had seen him. When he had outfaced three men.

"Yes, I won. Not even the wolf's fury could stand against *liyt ræsc* and the runes of protection on the blade, and I meant to kill him. I knew full well it had to be quick or because of the wound I would be lost. I went straight out for his death from the start. But more than that, it was what I wanted."

Her fingers bit into the hardened neck of the mead flask.

"Yet you will know the last blow was his. To be able to explain to me exactly who he was and how his loyal wife had sent Harek to beg him for vengeance."

"No! That is not true. Liefwin…"

"Why should your husband lie to me when he was dying?"

"I do not know." But she could feel the black shadow like one of the *draugar* creeping over her heart, and Ragnar's body was lying somewhere close to them, exposed to the wide sky, unburied. "Perhaps if he could not have his vengeance on you with deeds he would have it with words. But they are not true words. I swear it."

She turned and looked at the unmoving figure of the man beside her. The golden head was tipped back, leaning against the side of the beech trunk. The hand at his neck shielded the lower part of his face and his eyes were in dark shadow. She could not see them.

''You must believe that...'' The desperation in her voice made it thin and high-pitched. False.

He would never believe her. She had nothing with which to convince him, nothing but the sorry muddle of her own stupidity and her own private fears to set against the horrors that he had faced this day.

She watched the small lights that filtered through the dying beech leaves play over the richness of his hair and his face wreathed in shadows. His wide hand, so still, flattened out against his face and the side of his neck held all the tension of a closed fist.

''Liefwin, I believed he was dead, right from the start. Before I ever saw you. The townspeople told me. They were falling over themselves to tell me that the one who had forced them into battle with you was dead. It was news that spread as fast as the fire between the buildings. I believed it just as they did. I had no reason not to and they had every reason to want it to be true. You can have no idea how people hated Ragnar.''

She took an unsteady breath.

''I said it to you straight away, as soon as I spoke to you. I had no reason to lie.''

''Unless you thought I was more likely to want a death payment than a ransom from Ragnar. You might have been right. Is that why you invented the ransom to fool me? What about your kindred at Shealdford? Were they a lie as well?''

Her hands twisted on the leather flask.

''Yes. Yes, they are but...but I only said all that because I was afraid and...''

She knew that was the wrong thing to say the instant the words left her mouth, just by the faint movement of his head. That was enough, quite enough to tell her she had hurt. That she had made things worse.

"I did not know. I did not know what to do. Everything was such a muddle in my mind and I had drunk too much mead and my tongue ran away with me."

"You mean like now."

"No!"

She flung the hardened leather flask away from her with all the force she had, so that it hit the trees with a crack and the mead splattered over the ground.

"Can you not believe me?"

"Yes," he said calmly, "I think I do. In some things. I do not think you were really sure about your husband until you met Harek at the spring, were you? How you ever managed to arrange that—"

"I did not. It was…"

"Chance?"

"No." Her mouth went dry.

There was a perfectly mannered silence.

"I think he came looking for me," she said, and her words dropped into that silence like stones down a bottomless well.

"Ah."

The irony of that small syllable was so polite, so…Mercian. It cut more than screams of rage.

"But it was not as you think. It was not of my choosing or my knowledge," she said doggedly into the well of silence. "It was because…I think it was because he had heard…it must have been because Ragnar had heard that…"

''That you were bedding a Saxon. How awkward. Is that why you decided to have a go at killing me?''

''What?''

''It was a pity I woke up at the wrong moment. It would have saved so much trouble. I suppose it was quite disconcerting to be found with a sword at your captor's throat. Was that why you thought you had to do something as desperate as bedding me in fact? Or were you hedging your bets in the unlikely event that the wrong person got killed today?''

She could have turned, then, and run into the forest, as far away as it was possible to run, and she would not have cared if she had never seen the light of day again. There was nothing here that she could say. There was no way to help the man beside her and there was no way to help herself. The blackness, the black shadow of Ragnar had blighted everything.

Vengeance really was his.

''I am sorry,'' she said. ''You can never forgive me.''

She did not expect him to speak. He had no need to and there was nothing left to say. She did not know whether he would let her leave unscathed. Perhaps he should not, out of duty to Cerdic. But she did not care if he killed her.

She had turned her head and gathered together her skirts when he spoke.

''I would have forgiven you anything but that last. Even the trick with the sword and meeting Harek.''

Her heart leaped so that it would choke her and she could not breathe. She dropped back down onto the sliding bracken, tangling herself in her skirts and nearly pitching headlong.

He caught her, deftly, with unthinking strength, just as always.

Without thinking.

But he had done that, off guard, and she would take the last opportunity she would ever have. She grabbed at the one hand that held her arm, covering it with her own hands.

"Liefwin, that was true coin, what was between us, not false. I did not go to meet Harek and he did not even tell me that Ragnar was alive. He did not have time. I did not understand what little he did say and I did not realize what it meant. Not until today, when it was too late. Not until Alfwin let it slip that the man you were pursuing was a berserker."

The hand under both of hers moved. It turned over. She saw what was clasped inside his palm, the smooth silver shapes. Odin's spear. Her gasp tore her throat.

"Would you like it back?"

"No! No, I never want to see it again."

"I thought you liked wearing it."

"No. No, I hated it. I never wanted it. They gave it to me to prove Ragnar was dead."

"But you gave it to Harek at the spring."

"I did not give it. Harek saw it, in the struggle when I tried to get away from him and he took it. He tore the leather strap. That is what marked my face. You saw that."

The hand under hers jerked and the silver talisman fell out. She let it fall. It was nothing. It no longer had any power. All that mattered was Liefwin. All that mattered was holding on to his hand.

"I did not go to the spring to meet Harek," she said again, the words tripping over each other with desperate speed into that small moment that was already sliding away. "It was you. I went there for you. I wanted a miracle."

The hand stopped moving.

"You wanted a what?"

"I wanted a miracle," she said, "for you."

"Perhaps you could explain that."

"It was…because of the wound."

"Because of—"

"Yes," she said, while she still had him. "I knew that it did not heal as it should. I did not understand why and I did not know what to do." It sounded moon-mad, stupid. Her words came out anyhow. In a jumble. She did not know why he still listened.

"So you thought you would take a trip out to the spring?"

"Yes. Because of the miracle," she said, and the air suddenly became charged the way it did before a storm.

"The…"

"The spring. It is magic. I mean holy," she corrected herself guiltily. "Oh, I know I am not a proper Christian and I do not understand such things, but you are and you do. So I thought, if it was for you, it would be all right and it would work. So I got some spring water and I brought it back. Only you spilled it.

"I know you did not mean to," she added, frightened by the tension she could see and now feel in him. "And it was all right because some of it landed on your hand and then you touched the cross, the one on the lid of the casket and it did work, though not how I expected, because you told me what it was that was wrong and now..." She thought of how he had embraced Ceolfrith, of Alfwin's grinning face. "Now you are no longer alone."

"That is mad," he said. "That is absolutely stupid."

Which meant that he might believe her, and though she knew it was impossible for him to forgive her, that did not stop the painful stirrings in her heart.

"I am stupid," she said. "I was stupid and cowardly not to tell you from the start who, what, Ragnar was. But I saw how much you despised him and what he had done. I suppose there never seemed the right moment to explain that the berserker who had killed and mutilated people, the one who had forced the town into battle with your men, had been my own husband."

Her gaze was fixed, even though there was no hope in it this time, on the hand trapped under hers.

"You can have no idea how much I hated being married to Ragnar, how much, in the end, I hated him."

"I do not understand. I thought at first...I assumed you must care for him, more from what you did not say than what you did. I thought your silence meant that your feelings meant too much to you to be displayed in front of an enemy like me. Even when you said he had hit you there was still something...some bond I could not understand that seemed to fix you to him. You always wore that strange amulet and I always wondered if it was his."

"It was. It was given to me as proof he was dead. It was found where they saw him fall. No one got to his body. But then…he was not really dead. He must have escaped into the trees.''

"Yes."

She shivered. "I loathed that amulet. I wanted to throw it away. But it was all that was left of Ragnar, all that was left of my life. Perhaps I felt guilty because I hated it, because I hated him, even after I thought he was dead. Or perhaps I was just afraid. Perhaps the amulet still had his power. It does not now.''

Her gaze picked out the faint sheen of metal in the gloom, so small, half-covered again in leaves, just as it must have been found.

"It must be buried. With him. If you will bury him.'' People did not do that for an enemy.

"Oh, I will bury him.''

"Then he is gone.'' The breath left her mouth. It shuddered. "The real truth is that if there was any bond between Ragnar and me it was shame, shame and horror. I nearly told you, when you asked me about the scar. I wish I had…'' Her voice choked over what the consequences had been. She made herself say it. "I did not have the courage.'' She took a breath.

"You see, I did not want you to hate me,'' she said with an irony that would not have disgraced a Mercian.

"So how…''

"How did I come to be married to an abomination? It was as I said. I would have given anything to escape my home. And I was dazzled by Ragnar. I did not know what he was then and I was young enough and silly enough to be proud of the way everyone scuttled around and deferred to him, whereas I had the privilege of being his wife. I thought it was all because he was so heroic. That lasted until the wedding night when he terrified me so much he had to hit me.''

She heard a sound that might have been a strangled curse and she remembered how much it had disgusted him last time when she had mentioned that, and how unaccountably angry he had been. Perhaps Mercian men did not hit people so often, or perhaps it was just Mercians like Liefwin, who had been cursed with a kind heart.

''It was not one of his berserk rages,'' she said. ''Not then. He was just drunk after the feast. Really, it was no worse than being at home. He brought me here, to the town. He was going to buy some land nearby with the…the plunder, although he never did. Life was quite ordinary. That was the problem.''

She paused. How did you explain something like Ragnar? It was like trying to explain the cruel force of the north wind.

''I think he was mellow with success when he saw me and he thought he would have a try at settling down and…burying what he was. Being like other people. But he did not like it, being just like anyone else, being treated as though he was ordinary. Or perhaps it was just not possible for him to be like others. I cannot know.''

She kept her gaze fixed on Liefwin's hand and hoped he would listen, that he would not be so disgusted that…she had to say it now before she lost whatever chance she had.

''But as time went on, he just became…angrier and

then one day someone argued with him, just our neighbor, over nothing it seemed. That was the first time I saw it, his rage. The noise…like a wolf howling, and the spit flying from his mouth and the look in his eyes. Like one possessed. Possessed with the wolf's spirit. He had such strength when he was like that. He did not seem to feel any pain himself, whatever anyone did to him, and there was nothing he could not do and nothing he would flinch from doing to someone else…''

Her voice failed, because of the memory of what Ragnar had done to their neighbor and then to the man who had tried to help him, and her hands shook over the one she held.

''But I have no need to tell you, do I,'' she said, and her voice shook as much as her hands. ''You know.''

But he did not answer that at all, did not say one word of what had just happened to him.

All she heard him say was, ''How could you live with that? How could someone like you bear it?''

''I did not, not really. He left after that and although he came back it was not often. I was occasionally convenient to him, more often a nuisance. So I scarce saw him and he roamed as he wished. With the army. Or harrying. Or seafaring. Or…I do not know all that he did. I did not want to know.''

''Yet today he would have killed me for you.''

''Would he? Can you really think so? No. He would have killed you because of the insult to his pride and because he cannot help it. He killed like that before he knew of me and he killed afterward.

He would never have stopped killing. That is what he was.''

She took a steadying breath and tried to still the shaking of her hands over Liefwin's.

''I did believe he was slain in the battle before I met you. I swear it. I never meant any of the harm that has happened today, to you or to Cerdic or…we rode past the remains of the village. I know he has killed others—''

''A lot.''

''Yes.''

''And any connection there might have been between us.''

''Yes.'' Her grip round his hand was painful. ''Except it was true, was it not? What happened between us. What we had for that short time. I loved you. Even though I did not really know how people went about loving each other. I loved you from the start. I tried to keep talking myself out of it. Only I could not. Like now. I still love you and nothing can stop it.''

It was becoming so hard to speak. Her throat wanted to close up with pain. She tried to swallow.

''I knew you could not love me…'' She gave up. Her voice stopped. And then she heard the sharpness of his breath.

''Did you? Is that what you thought? You do not know what my love was. My love really was the sort that would kill for you. I did not know, when I fought your husband, who he was. Not until it was too late. But if I had known, I would still have wanted to kill him. Not just for the sake of those poor people he has butchered. Not just for strategy. Not to placate Edward from taking his revenge on the wrong men. Not,

heaven forgive me, for Cerdic alone. But for what he
has done to you.''

The hand she had been clutching so hard was suddenly loosed. It touched her face, at the corner of her
left eye, just where the scar was.

''That is why I would have wanted to kill him. That
is what my love is and that is the death of it, is it
not? You cannot live with the man who has so willingly killed your husband.''

But her heart beat fast and her breath was as sharp
as his.

''Liefwin…''

Her hand reached out to touch him in a mirror image of his own gesture. It shook because she was so
afraid. But she wanted to touch his face. She had to
see it. To see what was in it now. To see if…she did
not think miracles were really possible.

Her fingers sought the hand at the side of his neck
that shadowed his face, hiding it from her gaze. The
hand was rigid, unmovable.

''Liefwin.''

Her fingers tightened, but the hand under hers was
wet and slippery. She realized, just as he let the hand
fall into her grasp, that it was slick with blood. He
moved into the sunlight.

''You could not live with that, could you?''

She screamed.

Chapter Seventeen

"**V**ile, would you say?" inquired Liefwin's cool Mercian voice over the dying sound of her scream.

Sigrid stared through a haze of sickness at the disfigured flesh and the sluggish blood on his neck.

She tried to breathe.

She knew what had happened. He did not need to tell her.

Wolves tried to tear people's throats out. It was what they did. Ragnar was, had been, the spirit of a wolf. She knew all about that. She had been made to learn it.

She told herself it was not unexpected. Not to her. She closed her mind against the fact that this was Liefwin's flesh and against the pain he must have felt and the sheer repulsive horror.

If she kept breathing, she would not swoon. It would be impossible.

She looked at Liefwin's eyes.

"Yes," she said, her voice every bit as cool, every bit as steady as his, "I would call that vile."

She saw the eyes flicker, just as she had hoped they

would and something indefinable, just for an instant, transcended horror. That was Liefwin's courage.

She could not imagine having courage like his.

She swallowed bile and lied.

"I have seen such things before."

She had not. She had heard it described, but she had not seen it.

Her neighbor and the other man had had quite different injuries, and on that occasion she actually had been sick.

She swallowed again.

"If you think to make me afraid," she said, "you will not."

"You really cannot lie, after all, can you?"

"No." She trembled, not just because of the blood but because he had as good as admitted that he believed everything she had said to him.

"Why did no one teach you to lie properly?"

"Because no one bothered to give me a thane's education. Can I get you another cloth?"

She twitched the bloodied remains out of his hand, but he caught her before she could move.

"Do not lie to me now, Sigrid. It is not worth it. I know when the end comes. I have always known. You do not have to pretend you can spend the rest of your life looking at the scars from this and thinking, *That was done by my husband just before this man killed him.*"

"Then we will buy you a gold neck ring out of the plunder, like Beowulf's."

"Sigrid, for pity's sake, will you stop doing this?"

She looked at his face and saw that all of a sudden

the defense of coolness and thanely irony was gone. His fast, warrior's hands caught her by the shoulders and he shook her. Which was better.

Providing he did not break her neck in the process.

He stopped. She gasped and felt her neck with caution.

"What are you trying to do? Give me some matching scars?" The bloodied hands round her shoulders softened in apology, because he was Liefwin and he would already fiercely regret that he might have hurt her.

"Sigrid, I—"

"I do not care," she said, while she knew she had him on the back foot. She tried to keep the desperation out of her voice and speak smoothly. "I do not care."

"What?"

"Whatever you are going to say and whatever you look like, I do not care."

"No? Perhaps not, not now, in the middle of a disaster. But you will, later, when you come to think."

"Liefwin..." She felt his hands tighten again involuntarily on her shoulders.

"Sigrid, I will not take your pity. Or your guilt for someone else's deeds, because you were married to a man no one could control."

She tried to hold on to the intensity of his eyes. She tried to make him keep looking at her because he had to understand what she felt and she was no good with words. Not like him.

"I cannot lie to you and say there is no guilt about

Ragnar and the things I did not tell you. There is,
but…Liefwin, you must listen to me. Please. There is
nothing that can be done about the past. You know
that. I do not have to explain it to you. But it is not
guilt that is making me speak and it is not pity. I told
you nothing could stop my love for you and that is
how it is. I cannot help it. And it must be like your
love because it does not stop for what is right or what
is wrong. You cannot say you have stopped loving
me.''

"I can."

Her heart nearly died out of fear. It hurt like a great
dark hole inside her, waiting to swallow her, waiting
to drag her back into the hopelessness that had always
been her life. She tried to speak past the fear.

"You cannot even lie properly after you have had
a thane's education," she sneered at Liefwin.

But she was shaking. Because he had only ever
spoken of his love as though it was in the past.

"Thanes do not lie. That is the first point in our
education.''

He was a thane. He was not the sort of man for
her. Never could be. She felt as though the dark hole
that was her heart would choke her. She felt as though
she would die of the pain and drop to the ground on
the spot. She could not breathe because of the choking, and the blackness was becoming real, taking her
vision as though she would faint.

Except she could not faint. She could not fall to
the ground because he was still holding her shoulders.
His bloodied hands dug into her flesh.

He was still holding her.

She dropped her gaze from the over-proud unreadable eyes to the mutilated flesh at his throat.

For the only time in his life he was not quite quick enough to stop her.

"No!"

It was a cry that could have been heard across the forest, or across the breadth of middle earth. It would bring the whole of the *éored* running, surely. It would bring the heavens down on her head.

But it was too late.

Her lips touched the hideously distorted flesh.

Her arms clung to him, defeating the convulsive movement of his body, moving with him so that he could not shake her off. She felt his back jar against the beech tree. Her arm was crushed against the rough wood.

He could not move her.

"Tell me," she said against the ugliness at his throat. "Tell me again that you do not love me and I will tell you the same and we will both be damned to eternity for liars."

He did not speak.

"No lies," she said. "No lies, ever again." She pressed against him with all the force she had and she would not let him go. But he must feel how she shook. He must hear the frightened tears in her voice.

There was an awful silence that lasted longer than eternity. Her whole mind was concentrated on one silent plea. That he would not turn her away. That the shadows of blackness had not killed love. *Please*. She tried only to hold it in her mind. Not to say it aloud.

But some hideous, distorted choking sound escaped her throat.

She felt his arms close round her with the care she had only ever known from him.

"Sigrid, you cannot—"

"I can," she said, through the choking in her throat. "I love you more than life or death or wrongs or vengeance." She focused her mind on the feel of his arms round her. "Tell me you do not love me just the same way. Liefwin...."

"I cannot. You know I cannot," his voice choked like hers. Not a trace of the Mercian thane. "You know that is how I love you and you know all the worst of me. Sigrid, if you could live with me, I would never want to be apart from you. But after what I have done, how could—"

"All I know is that I could not live without you and if you tried to make me, the shadows would have me, and I would die."

His arms tightened and he moved with her, into the sunlight that was stronger than any shadows in the world or in the mind.

"Sigrid, there are no shadows if you could love me. If you would stay with me..."

"I do. I would. I would never run away from you again. I tried to tell you last night that you were all that I wanted. I did not dare to say that I loved you then, but I did. I could not bear to be without you."

The arms around her tightened to the point of pain but she did not try to stop him, because she held him the same way.

"Then if you would come home with me as my

wife…do you really think you could marry a foreign liar?''

She tried to say yes, but it was lost under the power of his lips and the salt taste of blood and all the bitterness of the past was lost against the warmth of his mouth.

* * * * *

*Don't miss
FORBIDDEN,
Helen Kirkman's next
mesmerizing medieval,
available Spring 2004.*

...strong as an ox. A bargain... and finally to the more painfully against her, Rowena... to which she clung. It was important...

Chapter One

"...strong as an ox. A bargain..."

Rowena examined the arm left lying in her hands.

Such fine skin. Turned gold by the summer now almost at its end, but so fair and...this one was actually clean. It really must be the trader's showpiece. The slave's bronzed skin had been anointed with oil to flatten the body hair and show off the muscle. She twisted it experimentally and the tight muscles moved under the fine skin like corded rope.

St. Beren's bones! You could do more than plough two acres a day with that. You could do anything.

Anything...

The ghost of the most reckless, the most unlikely idea she had ever had began to shape itself in the back of her mind. Her body tensed with it. The idea trembled on the edge of existence.

Her gaze raked along the length of the arm. It was so solid, like a thing fashioned solely for strength. There was no shred of compromise in that seamless arrangement of bone and muscle, only power, a power without limit. It lay quite passively against her hand, but she knew what she held. It was dangerous.

Dangerous…and fascinating.

Historical Note
on the Year 917

King Edward "the Elder" of Wessex was the son of King Alfred the Great. His sister, the Lady Ethelfleda, and her husband, held the province of Mercia. Together they began to regain English territory lost to the Viking invaders.

In the autumn of 917, a great raiding army was gathered together in East Anglia, supplemented by *askr-men,* or those who came in warships.

The English had success against this army at Maldon, and various Danish divisions began to submit to Edward as he fortified his bases in the southeast.

The town in the story did not exist, but the story is imagined somewhere between the victory at Maldon and the final securing of Colchester.

The Anglo-Saxon Chronicles record that before Martinmas (November 11) King Edward went with a West Saxon army to Colchester where he restored the stronghold. Then all the people of the provinces of East Anglia and Essex that had been under Danish control turned to him. That turning was so great that the Viking raiding army of East Anglia swore oaths to him that they would henceforth keep his peace.

If you enjoyed this story and are interested to know about the colorful old English and Danish words used in the book, we would love to send you a glossary sheet that explains more.

Helen Kirkman can be contacted c/o Harlequin Historicals, 233 Broadway, New York, NY 10279.

ITCHIN' FOR SOME ROLLICKING ROMANCES SET ON THE AMERICAN FRONTIER? THEN TAKE A GANDER AT THESE TANTALIZING TALES FROM HARLEQUIN HISTORICALS

On sale September 2003

WINTER WOMAN by Jenna Kernan
(Colorado, 1835)

After braving the winter alone in the Rockies, a defiant woman is entrusted to the care of a gruff trapper!

THE MATCHMAKER by Lisa Plumley
(Arizona territory, 1882)

Will a confirmed bachelor be bitten by the love bug when he woos a young woman in order to flush out the mysterious Morrow Creek matchmaker?

On sale October 2003

WYOMING WILDCAT by Elizabeth Lane
(Wyoming, 1866)

A blizzard ignites hot-blooded passions between a white medicine woman and an amnesiac man, but an ominous secret looms on the horizon....

THE OTHER GROOM by Lisa Bingham
(Boston and New York, 1870)

When a penniless woman masquerades as the daughter of a powerful marquis, her intended groom risks it all to protect her from harm!

Visit us at www.eHarlequin.com

HARLEQUIN HISTORICALS®

Sometimes, there *are* second chances.

SUSAN WIGGS

ENCHANTED AFTERNOON

Beautiful, charming and respected as the wife of an
ambitious senator, Helena Cabot Barnes is the leading
lady of Saratoga Springs. But beneath the facade lies a
terrible deception. Helena has discovered — too late — that
her husband is a dangerous man.

Unable to outrun her past, Helena turns to Michael Rowan,
a man she once loved, a man who broke her heart. For
Helena, the road to trusting Michael again is long and
hard. But Michael has just discovered a shattering truth…
and a reason to stay and fight for the woman he once lost.

**With a deft hand and a unique voice, acclaimed author
Susan Wiggs creates an enchanting story that will take
your breath away as it reaffirms the power of love and
the magic of forgiveness.**

"With its lively prose, well-developed conflict
and passionate characters, this enjoyable,
poignant tale is certain to enchant."
—*Publishers Weekly* on *Halfway to Heaven*
(starred review)

MIRA®

On sale September 2002 wherever paperbacks are sold!

MSWBWIBC02

Savor the
breathtaking romances
and thrilling adventures
of Harlequin Historicals®

On sale November 2003

MY LADY'S PRISONER by Ann Elizabeth Cree

To uncover the truth behind her husband's death,
a daring noblewoman kidnaps a handsome viscount!

THE VIRTUOUS KNIGHT by Margo Maguire

While fleeing a nunnery, a feisty noblewoman
becomes embroiled with a handsome knight in a
wild, romantic chase to protect an ancient relic!

On sale December 2003

THE IMPOSTOR'S KISS by Tanya Anne Crosby

On a quest to discover his past, a prince masquerades
as his twin brother and finds the life and the love
he'd always dreamed of....

THE EARL'S PRIZE by Nicola Cornick

An impoverished woman believes an earl is
an unredeemable rake—but when she wins
the lottery will she become the rake's prize?

Visit us at www.eHarlequin.com

HARLEQUIN HISTORICALS®

HHMED33